Praise for Leslie O'Kane
and her Molly Masters mysteries

RUFF WAY TO GO

TO GO

Leslie O'Kane

FAWCETT BOOKS • NEW YORK

A Fawcett Book
Published by The Ballantine Publishing Group
Copyright © 2000 by Leslie O'Kane

www.randomhouse.com/BB/

ISBN 0-7394-0901-8

Manufactured in the United States of America

In memory of my father, Stephan P. Mitoff,
1924–1998

The author wishes to acknowledge the considerable efforts and contributions of the following wonderful individuals: First and foremost always, Mike, Carol, and Andrew O'Kane; Robin L. Lovelock, D.V.M.; Meredith Hutmacher; the members of Lee Karr's critique group and especially Christine Jorgensen; and last but never least, the Boulder critique group, especially Claudia Mills, Phyllis Perry, and Ina Robbins. Thanks, guys!

Chapter 1

"Look, Allie, we got puppies!" my neighbor shouted across the street to me. The words sounded more like " 'Ook, Owie, 'ee 'ot 'uppies!" because she's only five and has a tendency to drop opening consonants.

Melanie was gesturing emphatically with her little hands for me to cross the road. If she knew me better, she would realize that I'd jump through flaming hoops to pet a dog, let alone cross our quiet street in Berthoud, Colorado, to see puppies. What made me especially curious now was that I'd gotten the distinct impression that Melanie's mother would jump through those exact same hoops to *avoid* seeing a dog. Perhaps I'd misinterpreted and was about to be introduced to guppies.

I deserted my task of fetching the mail, which was almost always for my mother anyway—my having temporarily moved back home less than a month earlier—and trotted across the street, saying, "You got puppies? Where?"

"At my house! Come on!" Melanie was jumping up and down, her dark hair bobbing with the motion. She grabbed my hand, her fingers warm and sticky. It was a bit depressing that she didn't have to reach all that high in the process. With my free hand, I fluffed up my sandy-colored hair a bit, grasping for the extra quarter inch of height that drew me closer to the five-foot mark.

"Up there!" She pointed at the Randons' front porch, where Cassandra, Melanie's mother, sat on their redwood porch swing, enjoying this warm late May afternoon. My eyes were immediately drawn to what looked to be a purebred Siberian husky. Even from this distance, she appeared to be under-weight and was nursing what looked like an indistinguishable mass of dark fur balls.

We trotted up the driveway, the gravel crunching beneath our feet. The husky and I locked eyes. Hers were the palest of blue, and she watched me warily from her vulnerable posi-tion. If this dog and her owners had been my clients, I would have immediately launched into a lecture about the impor-tance of establishing a quiet, warm, sheltered place for the dog to nurse. As it was, I would have to be tactful. Not my strong suit. At least the dogs were on a throw rug, as opposed to the hard porch floor.

"Hello, Allida." Cassandra Randon gave me a big smile, which was unusual. In her mid-thirties, she was only a couple of years older than I, but she'd given me the impression that she'd decided the two of us couldn't possibly relate to each other. She seemed to think my being single and working with dogs for a living made me a female Mowgli, if not a Tarzan-ette. "Melanie couldn't wait to tell you about our temporary acquisition."

"Temporary?"

"Yes, we're fostering a female dog and her litter for a couple of weeks, until the puppies are old enough to be weaned."

"That's nice of you," I said slowly, trying not to make it obvious how surprising it was to me that she, of all people, would volunteer to house homeless dogs.

"It was Paul's idea. He's a real dog lover. He wanted me to see what having a dog would be like, kind of wend our way gradually into pet ownership, you know? He swears he'll do all the work."

This was the most she'd ever said to me at one time. Her having a dog must have made her feel that we had something in common. "That's really a good—"

While I was speaking, Melanie released my hand and reached down for one of the puppies. I grabbed her around the shoulders and pulled her back just as the husky started to growl at her. Cassandra, meanwhile, gasped and leapt to her feet.

"Never try to pick up a puppy while he's nursing, Melanie!" I scolded, putting myself squarely between the girl and the dogs. "The mother dog will—"

"I knew she'd be vicious!" Cassandra interrupted.

"Are you referring to me or the dog?" I asked.

"Come here, baby," she said, holding out her arms. This time the intended target for her words was obvious, and Melanie, both hands pressed fearfully to her mouth, raced to her mother and all but disappeared into her mother's broomstick-style skirt.

"There, there," Cassandra said, patting her daughter's back. Then Cassandra clicked her tongue and focused her pretty blue eyes on me. "I meant the dog, of course. Her owner is a convicted felon. I should have known I couldn't safely bring the dog here with my small child."

"Was this through the Humane Society?"

"No, through that new privately funded animal shelter up in Loveland." Her attention once again focused on her child, she cooed, "Are you all right, sweetie?"

No good could come of making such a fuss out of the child's having received one very justifiable warning from a dog. Melanie was either going to develop a trepidation around dogs matching her mother's or learn to play the dog's every action for Mom's attention.

"Weren't you able to attend the training sessions for their dog-foster program?" I asked.

"Well, sure, we went, but I was hardly expecting to get a dog that was raised by a criminal."

"Setting that aside for a moment, Cassandra, let me ask you something. If you were nursing baby Melanie and someone rushed up and yanked her out of your arms, wouldn't *you* growl?"

She pushed her short strawberry-blond hair back from her forehead as she straightened, making her several inches taller than I; but then, so was everyone. "I see your point, Allida. Apparently, we should have been paying more attention in class." She looked down and, in a babyish voice, added, "Shouldn't we have, Melanie? Didn't they tell us about how mommy dogs are protective of their baby dogs?"

Melanie, her head still half buried in the folds of her mother's skirt, nodded.

Beside me, the puppies had finished nursing, and the husky got to her feet with some effort. Four of the puppies had drifted off to sleep, but the fifth was making its wobbly way around on the small oval-shaped rug. His size and ability to walk indicated the puppies' ages to be four or five weeks. They would be able to begin weaning soon.

I leaned down for a closer look. The pups had the soft fluffy fur of almost any dog, but their collielike ears, square jaws, and curled-over tails indicated to me that they were half rottweiler, or perhaps American Staffordshire terrier—commonly known as a pit bull.

The husky cautiously approached us, testing my reaction and that of the Randons, who, fortunately for the sake of the already stressed dog, did not step back. The dog's appearance was so clearly one of gentleness—her ears up, eyes alert, getting our scent. I walked to one side of her until I was even with her shoulders, then turned to face in the same direction as she—this being the least confrontational approach in a dog's perception—and stroked her thick, smooth fur.

"What's her name?"

"Suds," Cassandra answered, clicking her tongue. "As I understand it, her owner is a big beer drinker."

"Guess that's better than naming her 'Foam,' " I muttered.

"Such a good dog Suds is," I said enthusiastically while giving her an ear rub. Cassandra raised an eyebrow in response to the odd speech pattern, but by my accounts, we were even. If I could put up with her baby talk to her daughter—not to mention her daughter's unusual enunciation—she could put up with my speech idiosyncrasies when talking to dogs.

My initial impression was that this was a really sweet dog and that the Randons, as dog-owner beginners, were very fortunate not to have gotten the typical high-energy husky.

Suds was soon trying to lick my ear—which I don't tolerate under any circumstances, and I don't care what species of tongue we're talking about. I rose and said, "Cassandra, I have some free time here. How about if I give you and Melanie a quick brush-up course on care and feeding of a nursing dog?"

"That would be nice. Thank you."

"We can start with my helping you set up an appropriate location in your house for Suds to nurse her puppies." I gave her a big smile, mostly because I was so proud of myself for having tactfully worked that into the conversation, but she didn't seem impressed.

"I thought huskies were outside dogs. That's why I thought it would be fine if we just . . . closed off a section of the porch."

"The front porch is out of the question. You can't supervise your visitors out here." The woman must have slept through all of the animal shelter's classes; my guess was that she was being passive-aggressive in response to her husband's efforts to get a dog. Then again, I was painfully aware that my skills at psychoanalysis began and ended with canines. "Let's see what else we can come up with. Do you have a mudroom, by any chance?"

She did, and we soon had a corner sectioned off with some cardboard sheets the shelter had provided, and made a reasonably comfortable surface with the throw rug from the front porch covered by newspaper. Cassandra decided that, during warm days, she could just prop open the outer door to this room and close the inner door.

Once having given mother and daughter the basics on how and when to handle puppies, we were soon seated at her patio table with the puppies napping nearby, while Melanie and Suds played peacefully—that is, if one ignored Suds's happy barks, which I could but which caused Cassandra to massage her temples and shoot withering looks at Suds.

This was a true dog neophyte, and I found myself imagining what a wonderful challenge Cassandra would make for me, if given the opportunity to convert her. I so wanted to say, *You've got the dogs, you've got the happy, appreciative child, and you even inherited the nice fenced-in yard from the previous owners. Let me show you the joy of a family bonding with a dog. Let me teach you how to communicate with dogs and experience the richness of it all.* But I decided my pronouncement wouldn't go over well now. Best to wait another day or two until she'd begun to adjust to the concept of dog ownership on her own.

Having let the conversation lag for too long, I asked Cassandra, "You said earlier that Suds's owner is a criminal?"

"Armed robbery, as I understand it. I got this secondhand from Paul, when he was checking into all of this dog stuff in the first place. All I know for sure is that the owner's in jail and won't be released until sometime in July. At which time he wants Suds back, but none of the puppies. I guess the father—Suds's mate, I mean—was a stray or something. In any case, he's out of the picture. Typical male, I guess," she added with a laugh. "Knock her up and then skip town."

"If the owner's serving time for armed robbery, he couldn't have been around when Suds got impregnated. Who was watching the dog at the time?"

"I guess his wife, who left town and deserted the dogs."

I automatically bristled at the thought of abandoning one's pregnant dog, but resisted the temptation to point out the irony in Cassandra's not noticing how irresponsible that was of the woman, while having joked moments earlier about the wanton dog's "typical male" behavior.

Cassandra watched her daughter's joyful play, a wary, almost fearful expression on her own pretty, well-tanned features. "I hope I haven't made a big mistake in taking on so much. All I agreed to was to foster a dog for a little while, to see what having one was like. I mean, Paul and Melanie are just so avid about having a dog and all, but what if Suds's former owner gets out early? I know he wants his dog back. I don't want to take the chance of his coming back for his dog and, you know, casing our house in the process."

"I've heard only good things about the Loveland animal shelter. They would never put you at risk. I've been thinking of volunteering there myself, in fact. I volunteer at the Boulder Humane Society whenever I can, to do some initial training on the dogs."

She furrowed her brow. "I thought you were a dog trainer. Isn't that competing with yourself?"

"I'm not a dog *trainer* per se. I work with owners and their dogs to help them alleviate their pets' undesirable behavior patterns. I get more work through shelter referrals as someone to help newly adopted dogs acclimate than I lose by giving those same dogs at least rudimentary training."

Suddenly Suds pricked up her ears and dashed inside the house, barking. The puppies, too young to bark themselves, followed their mother. Cassandra gave me a questioning look.

"Maybe somebody rang the doorbell."

She rose and followed the dogs into the mudroom. I got up, too, figuring it was time for me to leave anyway. "It's the doorbell, all right," she called over her shoulder. "Guess it's true that dogs' hearing is better than humans'."

"Let me answer!" Melanie cried, brushing past me to gallop through the door.

Melanie dashed on ahead, but Cassandra was struggling in her attempt to push puppies and Suds back with her foot. "Allida, can you help me keep the dogs in this back room?"

"Sure. Suds, come."

Suds obeyed, and enough of the puppies followed suit to allow Cassandra to leave the room. With the help of a subsequent "sit" command, I managed to escape myself, unaccompanied by any furry four-pawers.

"Edith. This is a surprise," Cassandra was saying to the visitor on her front porch as I entered the living room. Both her voice and her posture were stiff. The name meant nothing to me, and I had no view out the front door from my angle. Cassandra made a small motion with her head as if, I thought, to indicate my presence.

"There's a rumor that you've got puppies here," the woman said pleasantly.

"We got puppies!" Melanie shouted, hopping once again.

All the enthusiasm with which she'd greeted me earlier today had apparently been due to the subject matter alone and not to me. That was not surprising. Children don't tend to take to me as naturally as dogs do.

"Yes, Edith, but I can assure you I won't let them get into your yard or make too much commotion, so you needn't worry."

"Oh, heavens, Cassie. I'm not worried about that. I merely meant that I'd like to see them."

"Well, but we just . . . got them settled down and I'm afraid if I open the door, they'll be rushing all piggly-wiggly through the house, peeing as they go."

Spoken like a true dog lover, I thought.

In spite of Cassandra's demurral, Edith stepped into the house. She was attractive, with chin-length hennaed auburn hair and patrician features. Seeing the two women side by side, I wondered if this could be Cassandra's older sister. Cassandra had mentioned keeping the puppies out of Edith's yard, although Edith was more dressed up and made-up than I'd expected a Berthoud homeowner to be. In her white pants and shoes and captain's-style navy blue jacket, an ascot carefully arranged on her thin neck, she looked too cosmopolitan for our little town out in the sticks.

"This is Allida Babcock, from across the street," Cassandra said. "Marilyn's daughter."

I held out my hand and said, "Nice to meet you," just as Edith was saying, "We've met." I hastily added the word, "again," but Edith was already furrowing her brow at my gaffe.

"You do recognize me, don't you? I live next door to the Randons."

"Oh, yes. Of course. You're Shogun's owner. The adorable silky terrier."

"At least my *dog* made an impression on you."

"It's just that I work with dogs, and they seem to naturally capture most of my attention. Plus you must have gotten a haircut since the last time I saw you. It looks great, by the way."

"Thanks, but my hair is quite unchanged. Actually, I got a nose job."

"That looks great, too," I muttered stupidly. I should just accept the fact that strangers' dogs do mean more to me than their respective owners, but I was determined to salvage the conversation. "How is *Trevor* doing these days?" I'd intentionally accentuated "Trevor," proud at having remembered her husband's name. I even remembered meeting him; when I'd first moved back in with Mom, he and I had gotten each other's mail and he'd come over to make the switch.

"Trevor and I are getting a divorce."

With our conversation doomed since minute one, I should have seen that one coming. "I'm sorry to hear that. If you'll excuse me, I think I'll go home now."

"Thanks for your help with the puppies, Allida," Cassandra said, her hand trembling slightly as she fidgeted with an errant lock of her reddish blond hair.

She seemed truly uneasy, perhaps at the concept of being left in charge of child and dogs. "Don't mention it. Please don't hesitate to ask if you have any questions. This is what I do, after all, and"—I stopped myself from saying that I was really quite good at it and amended my statement to—"I really love it." Both sentiments were true, but the latter was less egotistical.

I went home and let our three dogs inside: Pavlov, my beautiful female German shepherd, followed by Doppler, my equally beautiful—though considerably smaller—buff-and-white-colored cocker spaniel, and lastly our newest acquisition to the family, Mom's recently adopted sable collie, Sage. Though I also thought of Sage as beautiful, he had a bumpy Roman nose and one ear that stayed up and the other down.

I silently nagged myself that I needed to make more of an effort at courting clients for my fledgling business. There was no good reason for me not to have advertised my services to Cassandra. She and Paul seemed to be very well off financially and could have used my help.

Mom still wasn't home, so I made and ate my lunch alone. She owns a small plane and gives flying lessons at the airport in Longmont. My father had also been a pilot, but died in a car accident when I was young. My brother's a pilot as well, and Mom is always holding out hope that someday I'll be spontaneously cured of my fear of heights so that I can uphold my end of the family tradition.

The doorbell rang. I leaned back in my chair in the kitchen to see who was there. On this warm day, I'd left the front door open and could see Edith through the screen. The dogs, though trained not to bark at the doorbell, started to come en masse with me to the door. I instructed them to sit by the entrance to the kitchen, then invited Edith inside, curious as to why she was here.

I really should have made up for my earlier transgressions, but try as I might, I barely said hello before turning my attention to the silky terrier that, unleashed, sat by her feet. It was a pretty, thin little dog, smaller than most housecats. He had long black fur with reddish brown highlights, a long sharp nose and pointed upright ears. He trotted in with complete confidence until he spotted the two big dogs at the far side of the living room. His hackles rose, but he made no sound. Pavlov—and Doppler, for that matter—were far too well trained to pay Shogun any mind, but Sage rose and trotted in our direction. He merely gave Shogun a dismissive sniff, then walked away and lay back down by the other dogs, deliberately turning his back on us in the process.

"Hi, there, Shogun. That's a good dog," I said, and promptly sat down on the floor.

"He's shy with strangers," Edith said, but her dog leapt onto my lap before she could complete her sentence. She raised her eyebrows, but continued, "While I was chatting with Cassandra Randon, she told me that you're a dog psychologist. I want to hire you."

That was an unexpected day-brightener. Here I'd been, less than twenty minutes ago, thinking about cultivating more clients. Maybe next time I should concentrate on wanting a million dollars. "Oh? What seems to be the problem?"

"Trevor wants sole custody of Shogun. I'd like to hire you to testify on my behalf."

"At the divorce hearing?"

"When it comes time to settle the estate, yes." Edith took a seat on the couch, smoothing the fabric of her white slacks to maintain perfect pleats. She had completely ignored my dogs thus far, indicating to me that while she may or may not be deserving of Shogun's custody, she was not an indiscriminate lover of all dogs. "You see, Trevor bought Shogun for me, to act as a guard dog when I was home alone. He was traveling a lot at the time, you see."

I nodded, but I could also "see" that most men, when selecting a "guard dog" for their wives, would opt for one that weighed more than ten pounds.

"Trevor got close to Shogun, too. Nevertheless, he's my dog, not Trevor's. And yet Trevor is insisting that I'm not good enough to Shogun and that he wants and deserves total custody."

"So you want me to determine which of you should have the dog?"

"No, I want you to testify that I should have the dog. Period."

While his owner was speaking, Shogun lay down and rested his chin on my knee. There is a feeling I get sometimes when I spend time with a dog, a certain eagerness to please, that strikes me as beyond the normal bounds of canine behavior. Shogun had this in his quickness to accept me. This was probably due to his feeling disoriented from the divorce, not unlike a child who felt the rift between his parents that he couldn't comprehend, and so assumed it was his own fault.

"I can't do that unless that's what I decide is truly best for Shogun."

"I see. Well, then, what do you need to do to make the decision?"

"To be honest, I've never done this before, but I would imagine all I'd need to do is witness the dog's behavior when he's here with you, do the same when he's with your husband, and give my opinion."

"Fine. Let's do it right away. I want this matter resolved *pronto*." She rose and quickly checked the alignment of her

ascot and the hang of her jacket. "I have to get back to my
store, but I'll be back home after five. Let's set up an appointment at my house for five-thirty. I'm sure Trevor could meet
with you tomorrow."

"You've already spoken with him about this?" I asked,
surprised.

"Of course not," she answered in patronizing tones. "I
haven't had the opportunity to do so. I'll call him as soon as I
can, though, and have him get back with you to set up his
appointment. I'm sure Trevor will be more than reasonable.
Up until you decide to award custody to me, that is. See you
at five-thirty." She headed toward the door. Shogun made no
move to follow.

Edith was behaving as if Trevor and I were the sheep and
she the border collie. I was sorely tempted to tell her honestly
that this was my day off; the nature of my business was such
that I had to work weekends. Truth be told, I was still too
aware of the precarious status of my newly formed business
to give myself even these Tuesdays—as well as Mondays—
off, but rather, tried to keep my appointments on those days
to a minimum.

During our conversation, her little dog had shut his eyes
and completely settled himself on my lap, and I enjoyed the
warm sensation of his slight weight. "I need to tell you,
Edith, that dogs really get quite traumatized by divorces. Has
Shogun been keeping up his regular daily patterns?"

"Yes, he's . . . exactly the same. He doesn't miss Trevor at
all."

"That would be unusual." Especially since the little dog
had been trembling as he slept. "Where is Trevor living
now?"

"Northern Longmont. At a duplex that is totally unsuitable
for Shogun, I might add." She looked at her dog—who gave
every appearance of wanting to stay in my lap—gave me a
sheepish smile, and said, "I really must be going. Shogun,
come."

* * *

Three hours later, in my currently empty downtown Boulder office—my officemate currently away for the afternoon—I had completed my one appointment for the day and was now trying to decide how much money to invest in advertising. I decided to call my lone media connection—an irascible talk-show host who was between jobs—and see what she would advise. Before I could do so, Trevor Cunningham burst unannounced into my office.

He was a small, thin man, but had a booming voice as he shouted, "What's this about you deciding who gets to keep my dog?" With his cascade of hair—center-parted and short on the neck but long on top—and his long, sharp nose, he looked like a human version of his dog, even though that was a cliché I didn't put much stock in. Temperaments were much more likely to be shared between dog and owner than appearances.

"I take it you're referring to Shogun?"

"Yes. I love Shogun. *She* doesn't. *She* wouldn't even have known what a silky terrier was if it hadn't been for me. My sister breeds them. That's where we got Shogun."

"Your sister sold him to you?"

"That's right. Edie only wants Shogun to keep him from me. She never showed any interest in that dog till I left her and took Shogun with me."

"But she has custody of Shogun now, doesn't she?"

"For the time being. I swear, though, I'll get my dog back if it's the last thing I do." He paced as he spoke, wearing a path in the linoleum in front of my desk.

"She told me that Shogun was a gift to *her*."

"From *me*, yes. But she never appreciated him. I took care of Shogun from the very first day."

"If that's true, Trevor, you have nothing to worry about. Edith has promised she'll abide by my decision." That was stretching the truth a bit, but I instantly decided that if Edith refused to give me such a promise during our appointment later that day, I wouldn't proceed. "If you're the main caregiver, the dog will likely want to stay with you, and I'll see that in his behavior."

He stopped pacing and met my eyes. "I hope so. Shogun hasn't been himself in months now. He's turning into the stereotypical nervous lapdog."

I nodded, so far finding myself empathizing with him rather than with my actual neighbor, which spelled neighborhood discord for Mom and me. It seems to be harder for divorcing couples to work up an amicable settlement for which one gets the dog than which one gets custody of the children. Judges seem to treat dogs as they would any other kind of property, and that is neither realistic nor fair.

His temper totally evaporated now, Trevor sighed, flopped his hands at his sides, and said, "See what you can do, Allida. I'll go along with your decision, whatever it is."

"I'll be meeting with Edith and Shogun in a couple of hours. Can you arrange to have him at your place for a visit tomorrow?"

He said he thought he could, and we set a tentative appointment for the following evening.

Late that afternoon, I arrived as scheduled at Edith Cunningham's house, having parked in my garage and walked over. The house was silent. I rang the doorbell, then saw a magenta sticky-pad note sheet affixed to the door. Its shaky lettering, written with a felt-tip pen, read:

> Shogun and I are in the backyard.
> I won't be able to hear the bell.
> Please come around the house.

That explained the house being so quiet. A gust of wind nearly knocked me off balance as I left the porch.

I cast a glance at the clouds that seemed ready to let loose a torrent any moment now. With the weather as it was, this was not necessarily going to be a representative meeting. Dogs are often disconcerted by thunderstorms. Some are so fearful that they can actually endanger themselves and jump through glass windows to escape the sound.

The Cunninghams owned quite a large piece of property.

The family that owned this place during my childhood had kept horses in the back pasture. Trevor had removed the electric fence for the horses and allowed the pasture to grow wild with native grasses and vegetation. Their remaining fence was dog-appropriate, enclosing a moderate-sized backyard.

What was not dog-appropriate was that the gate was wide open. I swung the cedar gate shut behind me, the latch fastening with a noisy thud.

"Edith? Shogun?"

No answer.

I tried to assure myself that they must be in the old barn or shed behind the fence and couldn't hear me from there. It's just that the dog *should* have heard me. Shogun was less than five years old and shouldn't have had any hearing problems.

A drop of water splatted in front of me, then another hit my head. Where was the dog? Why hadn't he heard me or picked up on my scent by now?

I quickened my step, trotting in my sneakers around the large Australian pines alongside her house. "Edith? Shogun?"

Still no answer.

I gasped at the sight that greeted me.

Cassandra Randon was lying motionless on her stomach on Edith's wooden deck. Her legs within her jeans were twisted at an awkward angle. Her wide-open and unseeing eyes were fixed in my direction, her expression permanently contorted in horror.

Chapter 2

There was blood everywhere, matting and darkening Cassandra's hair. A jagged piece of flagstone—two inches thick and ten inches or so wide and deep—lay near her head. The stone had once been a decorative rock in the garden beside the redwood deck, but was now covered in blood.

"Help! Somebody call the police!" I yelled as I rushed up to her. My words seemed to be swallowed in the air.

She'd been bludgeoned. I felt Cassandra's carotid artery, having to divert my eyes from the sight of her fractured skull. No pulse.

I needed to contact the police. I stared in the direction of Cassandra's house—no puppies in the backyard, no sign of her daughter or her husband, who was probably still at work. Oh, my God. Poor Melanie! A little girl, left without a mother.

Who was going to tell her and her father about Cassandra's death? Suddenly I couldn't remember Mr. Randon's first name, and that struck me as a horrible failing. I'd found his wife's body, and I couldn't even think of the man's name.

What was she doing out here on Edith's deck? Edith and Shogun were supposed to be back here, not Cassandra. Furthermore, who was watching Melanie?

My vision fell on an odd pattern in the blood, little markings that extended from the deck on down the steps to the landscaping rocks.

Paw prints.

My head and stomach spinning, I headed toward Edith's sliding back door, intending to call the police. As soon as my hands touched the glass, a terrifying realization hit me. Cassandra's killer could be inside!

Edith's phone was in plain sight on the kitchen counter. With my palms pressed against the glass and my heart pounding, I tried to decide what to do. My instincts were screaming at me to run home, to call from there.

What if Melanie was waiting at home, right next door, for her mom to return? She could come outside to their shared fence to check on her at any moment. I couldn't let the little girl find her mother this way.

"Move!" I demanded of my recalcitrant body.

The door was unlatched and slid open easily.

"Edith? Shogun?" My voice was so shaky it sounded foreign to my own ear.

There were no sounds, no vibrations through the floorboards that might indicate someone was here and coming toward me.

A second frightening realization hit me: Could Edith be here inside the house, a second victim? My stomach lurched at the thought. I didn't want to search for her, didn't want to acknowledge this possibility.

My vision fell on Shogun's combination food-and-water dish on a plastic placemat in the kitchen corner. That was bad planning. The food dish should always be separate. The owner needs to leave the water dish out, but have total control over the food dish, which maintains owner authority. Part of me was horrified at myself for thinking such mundane, irrelevant thoughts at such a time, but another part recognized that my struggle to grasp at the familiar was the one source of comfort I could find.

I scanned my surroundings for any signs of Edith's still being inside her house, perhaps even struggling with the killer. Or could a crazed Edith herself be waiting in the next room to bludgeon a second victim?

A pair of gardening gloves were beside the phone. Otherwise, everything was neat and nothing looked amiss. No disconcerting odors.

It was as if Edith had received a phone call and then left

home, taking Shogun with her, but leaving her houseguest outside on the deck. Had Cassandra been visiting and then remained alone, perhaps to give me a message on Edith's behalf?

That scenario left me with the chilling possibility that Cassandra might not have been here when the killer arrived had it not been for me and my appointment with Edith.

The phone was a portable. I snatched it out of its base. My hands were shaking horribly. I felt so disoriented I couldn't get the dial tone, couldn't figure out I needed to press the talk button first. I dialed 911. When the dispatcher answered, I cried, "There's been a murder. Cassandra Randon."

"Are you Cassandra?"

"No! She's dead! She's the victim." I took a breath to calm myself, but it did nothing for me. I stared out the glass door. The rain had started to come down for real now. "My name is Allida Babcock. I live across the street. I'm at her next-door neighbor's house, where it happened."

"Are you alone on the premises, ma'am?"

"God, I hope so." Surely the violence right outside could not have touched the inside of the house. But what if Cassandra had brought Melanie with her? Could she be hiding inside? Mostly out of concern for Melanie, I decided to make a quick check of the house.

Like so many other houses in Berthoud, it was a quaint two-story home. Phone in hand, I stepped out of the kitchen and onto the soft wall-to-wall carpet of the front rooms. In the immediately visible rooms, everything was neat, no signs of a struggle. All inner doors were closed.

"What's the address there, ma'am?"

Distracted by my fears about my youngest neighbor's safety, I stammered, "I . . . don't remember the address. It's just across the street from—"

There was a flash of lightning, followed all but immediately by a terrific crack of thunder. The line went dead.

"Shit!" I hadn't given the address! "It's okay," I assured myself aloud. Our emergency dispatch undoubtedly had caller-identification capability. The dispatcher must have simply

asked me the address for verification. The police would arrive shortly.

Even so, I had to make a quick check of the house; I
couldn't simply wait for the police while a terrorized five-
year-old child might be in some other room.

I hung up the phone and grabbed one of Edith's gardening
gloves. Holding the glove like a pot holder to prevent my
leaving fingerprints, I opened the first door off of the kitchen,
which had a locking knob. This was the garage. No cars.
"Melanie? Are you in here?" I cried, though I doubted she
could easily hide from view. The area was neat, remarkably
so for a garage. I listened for a moment, but heard and saw
nothing to indicate a child's hiding place.

I went back inside and raced from room to room, upstairs
and down, trying not to leave fingerprints but throwing each
door open and leaving it that way, calling, "Melanie?" I
checked the closets as well, which were neat but full of
Edith's things, no space left vacant by Trevor's having
cleared out his own possessions. If the little girl was here, she
was well hidden and wasn't coming out for me.

Meanwhile, the rainstorm hit full force. The drops were
hitting on the roof so hard, it sounded as though I were inside
a kettledrum.

The paw prints! They could be an important clue, but the
rain would wash them away!

I dashed back through the kitchen and out onto the deck.
The rain was falling in torrents. Cassandra's body was getting drenched, and my inability to do anything preventative
struck me as obscene. I took off my jacket and draped it over
her, thinking as I did so how similar she looked from this
back view to Edith. Their hairstyles were nearly identical,
though under normal conditions, Cassandra's hair was a
lighter shade.

The dim realization hit me that I was crying. This all
seemed so senseless. The cruel and ultimate violation of
the way things should be. The taking of a life. A young
girl suddenly motherless. I prayed for Melanie's safety and

well-being, that she was alive and physically untouched by the horror here.

Cassandra and I might well have become friends someday, brought together by her puppies. Now I regretted not having made more of an effort.

The prints were already gone, the blood mixing with the water. Had the paw prints been Shogun's? Another dog's? Either way, the dog would have to have been here after or during Cassandra's murder.

Trying to visualize the paw prints, I knelt, chilly rain running off of my hair and down my back. The prints had been roughly the size of the circle I could make with the tip of my thumb against the tip of my index finger. They might have been too big for Shogun's paws, but it was impossible to say for certain. My proof had washed away like so much water.

Maybe they'd come from one of the puppies next door, or even from a medium-sized dog, such as a cocker spaniel. Cassandra could have brought one or more of the puppies over here with her. A loose or stray dog could have come through the open gate as I did when I'd first arrived, Shogun being small enough that another dog might not hesitate to violate his territorial boundaries.

Shielding my eyes from the rain, I looked in the direction of Cassandra's property, still deathly afraid that I might spot a petrified Melanie standing there. The length of fence was deserted.

Through the drumming of the rain, a pair of sirens wailed and drew louder. I told myself that it didn't matter that the paw prints were gone. The police wouldn't need this evidence. For all I knew, Edith had become so enraged at something Cassandra had said, she had killed her and run off with Shogun. Or one of the puppies could have been here with Cassandra, then raced off in a panic and was now back next door with the others.

Except . . . where *were* the puppies? Inside the Randons' house? They weren't in the yard when I arrived at Edith's. So, if a puppy had been here with Cassandra, how could he have gotten back inside with the others? Whoever let the puppy in would have to have noticed either his absence or his bloody paws.

In the rapidly darkening conditions, someone wearing a policeman's uniform under a black rain poncho came through the gate. Maybe this was the local sergeant. Mom knew him fairly well, on a personal level. It wasn't as though we had a lot of crime in Berthoud. The town was all of five or six blocks in either direction.

"You Allida Babcock?" the man called over the sound of the pounding rain as he approached. His right arm was bent at the elbow, as if he were set to pull his gun on me if I gave the wrong answer.

"Yes." I stood frozen in place and found myself staring at his cap, visible beneath the poncho. He had a clear plastic cover on it that resembled the cheap shower caps from motel-room giveaways. "Cassandra Randon lives next door. I'm worried about her five-year-old daughter. I also don't know where the owner of this house is."

"Come with me, ma'am. You need to get out of the rain." He was using condescending tones, thinking I was too stupid to come in out of the rain on my own. It was just that I didn't want to leave her out here in the rain, I wanted to explain, but suddenly couldn't find the words.

I looked at him in confusion, wondering why I should come back that way, around the outside of the house, instead of inside. "But . . ." I waggled my thumb in the direction of Edith's house.

"We need to secure the scene, miss. Let's go to my car. You can get into some warm clothes and give your statement at my office."

He ushered me back out through the gate. There were two white-with-blue-markings Colorado police cruisers out front, which likely comprised the entire department of our little bedroom community. Edith's front door was now wide open, her note to me no longer visible. Other officers must have been inside, "securing the scene."

I yearned for the safety and familiarity of my own home. I was shivering with the cold rain, though its intensity was starting to abate. "Can't we just go to my house? I can give you my statement there and make sure my dogs and my mom are okay."

Before the officer could answer, Edith Cunningham drove up in her black Lexus. She tried to pull into her driveway, which was blocked by one of the officers' cruisers.

She parked her vehicle at a cockeyed angle and got out as if propelled. "What's going on?" she cried to no one in particular, her face pale and her eyes wide. "This is my house! What's going on!" She spotted me then and ran toward me, a second officer stepping forward to intervene.

"Ma'am, there's been an incident at your home," the officer said solemnly.

"What do you mean, 'an incident'?" She stepped sideways to speak to me over his shoulder. "Allida. Is it Shogun? Has something happened to him?"

"No. I thought he was with you."

"He isn't. Did somebody kidnap him? Is that why the police are here?"

I didn't know how to answer that, and my head was filled with my own questions. Could someone have been so intent on stealing the dog that they killed Cassandra when she happened onto the scene?

I noticed then that Edith hadn't changed clothes since I'd last seen her. Nobody would have worn white pants while gardening. So who had worn the gardening gloves in Edith's kitchen?

Frustrated with not getting an answer from me, Edith focused again on the officer. "You need to ask Cassandra Randon, next door, if she saw Shogun. She called me at the store an hour or two ago and asked if she could borrow some gardening supplies. She has a copy of my house keys. I told her to help herself. Maybe she took Shogun home with her."

At Edith's mention of Cassandra, it now hit me that Cassandra had changed into jeans and a sweatshirt. Earlier she'd been wearing a skirt and blouse.

"I'm afraid Ms. Randon had an accident, ma'am," the officer said.

"Accident?"

More worried about the welfare of Cassandra's daughter than anything else, I asked Edith, "Do you know where Melanie is?"

"No. I've been away at my shop. She must be home. With her dad. Someplace." She was totally flustered and gesturing wildly as she spoke. Her face was starting to turn as red as her hair. "I don't understand anything you people are telling me! What kind of an accident are you talking about? Why aren't you letting me into my own house?"

The officer put a hand on her elbow and tried to lead her toward his cruiser. "Come with me, ma'am, and I'll—"

She whipped her arm free and her eyes flew wide. "Trevor! That bastard! I'll bet he stole my dog," she muttered incongruously.

The officer with me gestured at the second officer, who ushered Edith back into the passenger seat of her own car. He sat behind the wheel and talked with her. Edith started crying almost immediately and tried to use a cellular phone, which the officer pulled from her grasp.

Yet another officer was on the front porch of the ranch-style brick home on the other side of Edith's. This housed a couple in their late fifties or early sixties who were the only remaining people from my childhood in the neighborhood. Harvey and Betsy Haywood. They had always been so grumpy toward me and my family that I'd called them Mr. and Mrs. Hatesdogs. Not exactly the cruelest of names, but it had struck me as such at age six. Their two daughters had been teenagers then. My mom had hired the eldest as a baby-sitter, and the four of us minors had a mutual lack-of-admiration society going. The Haywoods' daughters should be in their early forties now. I wondered if we'd all still dislike one another.

Harvey and Betsy had stepped out onto the sheltered area of their porch to speak to the officer. Harvey, wearing the old-man uniform of knee-length shorts, black socks, and a sleeveless undershirt, rocked on his heels. Betsy was wearing what looked to be the same housecoat she'd worn virtually every day twenty years earlier. In a gesture that seemed uncharacteristic of the garrulous woman I remembered, she brought her hands to her lips as the officer spoke.

Wait a minute! They lived right next to Edith's property, on the opposite side of the Cunninghams'. Why hadn't they heard me calling for help?

My mother approached in her white and blue King Cab pickup truck. No one could ever mistake us for anything other than mother and daughter, though at five-six she's considerably taller than I am. She often wore her long brown hair—which she'd only recently begun to dye—in a braid. I watched her expression change in an instant from curiosity to concern to fear as she spotted me with the officers. Just as her face registered panic, she threw open the car door and was out of her car running toward me.

"Allida! Are you all right?"

"I'm fine," I said as calmly as I could, though the sight of my mother when I was already this traumatized made me have to battle tears. "It's Cassandra Randon. She was killed."

"Oh, my God. Where's Melanie?"

"Nobody seems to know."

The officer beside me cleared his throat and stepped between us. "Ma'am? Why'n't you get some dry clothes for your daughter? She has to come with us."

Mom gasped and looked at me.

"I have to go make a statement, Mom. I found Cassandra when I went over to see Edith Cunningham."

The rain was starting to pick up again, but Mom turned and stood glaring at the policeman as if she intended to pick a fight on my behalf. Never one to back away from a confrontation, Mom would not have surprised me if she clobbered him.

Just then, a middle-aged man in uniform left Edith's house, walking with a confidence in his step that gave off the aura of authority. "Andy," Mom called to him. She gestured at me. "This is my daughter."

"I know, Marilyn. But right now she's also the primary

witness in a suspicious death. 'Fraid we've got to take her in for questioning."

"Then I'm coming with you."

"Did your mom see you earlier this afternoon? Or was anyone with you at your office?" Sergeant Millay asked me. We were seated in a tiny room within the small brick building in downtown Berthoud that housed the police department. The walls were plain white, a fluorescent ceiling fixture the only light source, a table and four chairs the only furnishings. My mother, I knew, was seated on the bench just outside this room, when she wasn't pacing in front of the door and its little window.

This line of questioning instantly got my heart going. I tried to reassure myself that, because I'd found the body, I had to account for my whereabouts during Cassandra's death. But the concept of the police acting as though I were a possible suspect in a murder case frightened me to the bone.

"Yes, there was my client, as I already described, followed by Trevor Cunningham, Edith's . . ."—I hesitated at adding the word "estranged," knowing the police would already suspect him and not wanting to make it obvious that I did as well—"husband. He left at about three-thirty."

"How long did it take you to drive between your office and the house?"

"Forty minutes."

I could see by his expression that he was doing the mental calculations.

"Did you see or speak to anyone else in between those times?"

"No."

"And you say you went to the Cunninghams' residence to interview Mrs. Cunningham's dog?"

I opened my mouth to make a snide remark about how difficult it was for dogs to fill out my questionnaire, but decided that was the wrong tack. "In a manner of speaking."

"Could these paw prints you say you saw have been from a cat?"

"No, there are very noticeable differences between the two types of prints. A dog's digit pads are much bigger than a cat's. Plus cats have retractable claws, yet I remember seeing some toenail prints."

"And you also don't think the prints were from Shogun?"

"Right, although I can't say for sure. With a silky terrier, we're talking about a very small dog. My impression, though, was that the paw prints were left by a somewhat larger dog."

Sergeant Millay held my gaze with his hooded eyes for a long moment, as if appraising my credibility. He finally looked down at his notes. "Okay. You last spoke to Cassandra Randon at . . . what time did you say?"

"Roughly quarter after twelve, when I left her place and went home."

"And you found her body at what time?"

"Five-thirty. I got to Edith's house right on time for my appointment." I didn't know why he was asking me about the times again; Edith had to have spoken to Cassandra hours after I had. Why wasn't he asking *her* about the times?

"Do you have a lot of stray dogs in the neighborhood? Or folks that don't keep their dogs on a leash or in their yards?"

"Not that I've noticed, but I'm not really familiar with the neighborhood anymore. I've been living in a different state for about a dozen years, and I've only been living in my mom's house for a couple of weeks now. You'd have to talk to my mother."

"Sounds as though we got us a stray dog *now*, though, with Mrs. Cunningham's dog being missing."

"It looks that way, yet if that's the case, it really surprises me. This happened in Shogun's yard, his territory, which dogs typically try to defend from intruders. It would be far more typical for Shogun to stay and bark incessantly. He wouldn't have understood what was going on with Cassandra's struggle, but it would have upset him. For Shogun to run away and leave his territory unprotected, he'd almost *have* to have been chased off. And in that case, typical canine behavior would have been for him to not go far, then return after the intruder had left the property and start barking . . . at Cassandra's body."

"I see," he answered, though I got the distinct impression that he was mentally lumping me into the same category as psychics and tarot-card readers.

"You're not a dog owner, are you, Sergeant?"

"Me? No. Got a couple of cats, though."

"Cats are independent, territorial animals. Dogs are pack animals. Very different personalities. Dogs see no reason to ever separate from the pack, and they consider their owners their pack. As puppies or young dogs, they like to go out and explore. But by the time *most* dogs are Shogun's age, they've lost their wanderlust. They tend to consider their role to be to guard the pack's territory while they wait for their pack to return, no matter what happens in the interim."

He gave me a smile that hinted, at best, of grudging tolerance of my having voiced my opinion, then consulted his notes. "The gate on the west side of the house was open, you say. Did it strike you as unusual for Mrs. Cunningham to have left a gate open like that?"

"That's unusual for any attentive dog owner. It rather defeats the purpose of having a fence." Uh-oh. I was losing patience and getting snippy in spite of myself. The last thing on my agenda was to make enemies in law enforcement. "It's possible that Edith knew the dog would stick right beside her while she was in the yard and so never paid attention to the gate, but it's more likely that whoever killed Cassandra left the gate open."

Sergeant Millay rested his elbows on the small rectangular table between us and drew his face closer to mine. "Yet you just got through saying how Shogun wouldn't have run off anyway."

"True, but that's not to say he wouldn't ever run into the street, for example."

"Thing is, Officer Sweitzer said the gate was closed when he arrived. You must've closed the gate behind you when you came into the yard. Why?"

My pulse started to race at Sergeant Millay's insinuation

that he considered my closing Edith's gate suspicious. I already regretted my action. At the very least, I'd probably overlaid any fingerprints on the gate latch with my own.

"It was just . . . force of habit. I'd read the note that Edith left, telling me she and the dog were in the back, and since I was there to observe the dog, it was only natural for me to have shut the gate so the dog wouldn't run off in the process."

"That's another thing." He paused and slowly read over his notes, dropping his chin in the process. I could see a bald spot on the top of his head. "You said before that you left the note exactly where it was, in plain sight on the front door. Didn't as much as touch it."

"That's right."

He stared at me, his expression blank. "When we arrived at the Cunningham residence, Miss Babcock, there was no note."

This was a shock. "There wasn't?" I had to stop myself from demanding whether or not he was sure about this. "It must have . . . blown off the door in a wind gust," I said, growing tense and detecting a desperate tone creeping into my voice.

"I considered that possibility myself, Miss Babcock." The gray irises beneath the hooded eyes seemed to be looking straight through me.

He leaned even closer, and I could smell onions on his breath. "So I called Officer Sweitzer a couple minutes ago and had him ask Mrs. Cunningham. She says she never wrote you a note."

Chapter 3

I gave myself a moment for Sergeant Millay's chilling words to set in, my mind reeling at the incomprehensibility of this. The thought that the sergeant didn't believe me, might even suspect me of being the murderer, put me into a panic.

What could this mean? Could Edith have killed Cassandra, then, by lying about the note, sought to set me up somehow? No, because she arrived after the police did, so she couldn't have retrieved the note.

"But Edith *had* to have written the note. Unless . . . unless whoever killed her wrote that note to lure me into the backyard, then took it down after I read it. Maybe to keep you from being able to analyze the handwriting or get fingerprints off of the notepaper."

Sergeant Millay said nothing, his face as motionless as the rest of him as he sat and watched me. I, however, seemed incapable of controlling my nervous gestures as I combed the fingers of both hands through my short hair, only succeeding in making it stand on end with static electricity.

"Wait," I said, realizing that I might have made an incorrect assumption about the note. I couldn't remember the exact wording and tried to picture the note in my mind's eye. "The note wasn't signed and wasn't addressed specifically to me." My thoughts raced ahead of my words. The note might never have been intended for me. Trevor could well have full access to his former residence. He might have called Cassandra and asked her to come over. "Maybe the killer wrote that note to Cassandra, in order to coax her into the backyard, where she was ambushed."

"Unfortunately, we can't check with Cassandra to ask about that possibility."

I gritted my teeth to keep from objecting to his cutting remark. I was already all but jumping out of my skin. I didn't need him sniping at me, as well.

"The thing is, Miss Babcock, you told me earlier it was less than fifteen minutes from the time you got there and read the note till we arrived. True?"

I nodded.

"So, again, what happened to the note?"

"I don't know. It blew away? The killer took it?" Despite the now-unbearable heat in the stuffy room, I hugged myself, my turmoil causing my midsection to do an internal tap dance.

This time I was the one to lean forward and force him to meet *my* eyes. "Sergeant Millay, all I know is, there was a note on a magenta-colored sticky-pad sheet fastened to the front door when I got there. And, no matter how this might look, I didn't kill her."

He met my gaze unflinchingly and gave me no external clues as to what he was thinking. "Okay. Well." He rose and hitched up his pants, which had slid slightly below waist level on his pudgy frame. "Thank you. Let us know if you think of anything more that might help us."

He gave me a little smile, which I didn't return. I had a feeling I would be seeing his placid face in my nightmares.

When I stepped out of the interrogation room, it felt as though I'd taken my first breath of air since this ordeal began. Mom was already standing by the door. She was taking great care to align her Day-Timer in her purse to her satisfaction. Straightening whatever objects happened to be on hand was something she habitually did when she wanted to appear busy and unconcerned. She'd likely done nothing but worry the entire time I'd been giving my statement.

We said little during the drive home. It was now after seven P.M., and the sky at dusk was beginning to darken. My mom, though, seems to have an ability to emit soothing vibrations at times like these. That's part of what makes her

such a good flight instructor. What hit me as most extraordi-
nary, though, was that Mom had to be bursting with anxious
questions about what had happened right across the street
from her home, yet she managed to refrain from asking.

Finally, once we'd pulled into the garage, she said, "I get
the feeling your session with Andy didn't go well."

"You mean Sergeant Millay?" I asked, wanting to gently
establish the fact that I did not enjoy the same kinship with
the man that she did.

She nodded.

"No. In fact, it was awful." I let out a sigh as I got out of the
car and waited for her. I held the door for her, and we went
inside the house together. The garage door opened to the
kitchen, where our dogs were lined up to greet us. Pavlov, my
German shepherd, was first in line, with Doppler, my cocker
spaniel, in the middle. Mom's collie, Sage, wagged his tail
while I petted each dog in the proper sequence according to
their self-determined hierarchy. "I've never been so scared
in my life. I even feel *guilty*, though I did nothing wrong. It's
as if every mean-spirited thing I've ever done in my life
that's gone unpunished is now . . . sitting on my shoulders,
mocking me."

Mom, showing a bit of favoritism, gave Pavlov and Doppler a quick, cursory greeting, but was now stroking her collie, Sage. "What have you ever done that went unpunished?"

"Oh, there was"—though a few things had immediately
popped into my head, I realized that there was no way I
wanted to tell my mother, even though many years had
passed—"not a single thing, now that you mention it."

"Thought so," Mom said with a smile.

Though she'd managed to help me turn down my anxiety
by a notch or two—aided greatly by my being back home
with my dogs—I now felt inordinately tired. I dropped into
one of the captain's-style wooden chairs at the table.

Mom pulled out a chair beside me and took a seat. "Don't
worry about Andy." In response to my furrowed brow at her
use of his first name, she said, "Sergeant Millay, rather. He

can't possibly suspect you. You had no reason to kill Cassandra Randon."

"True, but I'm not going to sleep well till he catches whoever did this."

"Neither will I. Nor will anyone else in the neighborhood."

Except, perhaps, the killer. "Which is what bothers me the most."

"What's that?"

I met Mom's brown eyes, so similar in appearance to mine, though hers were now surrounded by crow's feet, which she preferred to call "extended laugh lines."

"I didn't notice any unusual cars parked on the street. And there was a note for me on Edith's door that disappeared by the time the police arrived. That means it had to be somebody in the immediate vicinity." Somebody who was still there, watching me, when I'd first arrived, I silently added, giving myself the shivers.

"Who could possibly have wanted to kill Cassandra?" I asked. "As far as I could see, she was a stay-at-home mother, leading a quiet life out here . . . far from the madding crowd."

"That was my impression, too."

Remembering the horrific scene on Edith's deck, a theory occurred to me that could explain both the murder and Shogun's disappearance. "Maybe I was way off on paw sizes, and the prints I saw in the blood were from the husky, which could conceivably have attacked and killed Shogun. If so, maybe Edith went nuts and killed Cassandra accidentally. Cassandra might have bent down to grab the dog just as Edith was in midswing with the . . . rock that killed her."

Mom shuddered a little at the image. I hated the theory myself, mostly because it meant an innocent dog had been killed, in addition to Cassandra. "That's not at all likely, Allie."

"Did you know Edith well? Are you sure she wouldn't have done it?"

Mom shook her head and fidgeted with a crumb that had wedged itself into the seam between the main section and one flap of the table. "I've never felt especially comfortable around her. She's always struck me as being too preoccupied with appearances. I just meant that I couldn't picture her going into a rage over another dog injuring hers. Edith has never impressed me as being all that devoted to Shogun. Besides, she's so meticulous, I can't imagine her doing anything as messy as committing murder, especially not on her own property."

Plus there were those perfectly clean white pants of hers, which couldn't have stayed that way if she was the killer. I sorted through images of Edith I'd collected throughout the day—sitting on our couch, so prim and proper; stepping into Cassandra's house and calling her "Cassie," although Cassandra had seemed tense. "I detected some . . . odd undercurrent going on between Cassandra and Edith when I was at Cassandra's house earlier. What do you know about their relationship?"

In a gesture akin to a shrug, Mom tilted one hand, which now rested on the table. "They seem to be the best of friends. They're always dropping in on each other. The families moved into the neighborhood within a year of each other, four or five years ago. Even though the Cunninghams are a few years older and didn't have children, the couples seemed to socialize frequently."

"That reminds me. Did you know the Cunninghams are getting a divorce?"

"I'd heard rumors, and it certainly doesn't surprise me that they're true. Trevor once told me that Boulder was far enough out in the boonies for him, but that Edith had insisted on moving out here to run her dress shop where there wasn't the stiff competition. As a matter of fact, a month or two ago, Cassandra mentioned to me that Edith was trying to convince her to become a business partner, but that she'd decided not to accept the offer. She was hoping to get pregnant again soon and wanted to keep being a stay-at-home mom."

"Was there anyone in the neighborhood who had a big grudge against her, or anything?"

Mom tilted her head and thought for a moment. "While you were being interviewed at the police station, an officer spoke with me, too, and asked me that same question. But there really wasn't. She was a sweet, quiet person."

Pavlov was standing by the sliding glass door, waiting to be let out, and Mom did the honors. Her face looked weary, almost haggard, when she returned and faced me. "Allie, as much as I hate to say it, this might have been some random act of violence, right here in our quiet little neighborhood. Some maniac driving by, perhaps, who happened to spot her."

I shook my head. "No, I can't believe that, Mom. For one thing, there has to be some explanation for that note."

Pointless as it was for me to try to mentally solve this murder, I couldn't help it. I couldn't shake the fear that I'd stepped into the murderer's trap somehow. In any case, there was no way to feel the least bit in control of my own safety and well-being until I could begin to understand what was happening. And why.

"What about Edith's other immediate neighbors, Mom? Have you seen much of the Haywoods lately?"

"No. They're exactly the same as they always were—keep mostly to themselves, don't seem to go out much, especially now that Harvey's finally closed his hobby shop and retired."

"They should have heard me call for help. It's hard to understand how they could have not heard me."

"Maybe they just—as the cliché goes—didn't want to get involved."

"That'd be just like them, all right. But what's going on these days with their daughters?"

"One lives right here in Larimer County, I think. The other is married and off in the Midwest someplace."

The doorbell rang. I told Mom to stay put and let me get it, while Sage and Doppler joined me for my short walk to the front door. Though some work still had to be done with Sage, Doppler and Pavlov were trained to do a down-stay when I snapped my fingers and pointed at the floor if I decided I didn't want them underfoot. This was one trick they were unlikely to be called upon to use anytime soon. Until the killer was in custody, the more dogs surrounding me, the better.

I flipped on our porch light, though it really wasn't all that dark outside, and swung the door open without checking through the peephole. I had to hide my strong visceral reaction at the sight of Cassandra's husband. The moment I saw him, I remembered his name. Paul.

He looked every inch the stricken man who'd just learned of the loss of his wife. His shoulders were now so stooped and his posture was so caved in that he seemed to be no taller than me. He was normally a sturdy-looking man of average height. He had a pale complexion, with thinning, curly dark hair. My heart ached for the man. I didn't know him well and, in fact, had only crossed paths with him a couple of times.

I didn't know what to do. Even though I barely knew him, I opened the screen door and put a hand on his upper arm, gave it a squeeze and said, "Paul, I'm so terribly, terribly sorry."

He looked at me as though he were in a total daze. He wore no coat and was shivering noticeably in the chilly evening breeze. "Allida. I came back from taking Melanie and the puppies to the park, and they were here. The . . . police, I mean. The sergeant told me she . . . that somebody had . . ." He shook his head. "It had to have been a hideous mistake. Nobody would want to kill Cassandra. Someone must have assumed it was Edith. Maybe a hired thug, whatever they're called, who wouldn't have known she was the wrong woman."

"Maybe so, Paul. I have no idea how or why this happened. How is Melanie?"

He didn't answer, blinking as he watched my face, as if he didn't realize I'd asked him a question.

"You found Cassandra, right? That's what . . ." He let his voice fade as if his sentence took too much effort to complete. "Was she already . . . Did she say anything to you?"

As sincere as Paul's heartbreak seemed to be, I'd skated on thin ice enough times as a child to recognize those same tremors below my feet that I now felt. Cassandra would have trusted her husband if he'd told her to meet him at the neighbor's house; she might have read that note and stepped into his ambush. Just in case, I wasn't going to mention the dog tracks I'd seen, nor anything else that might be construed as my knowing anything important about the murder. "No, she didn't. It was too late by the time I got there. I'm so sorry."

He gave me a sad nod. "I . . . don't mean to . . . I told the sergeant I was just going to get a couple of things out of the house. He doesn't want us staying at our house now. Even though they searched it already. Our house, I mean. They probably thought . . . ." He let his voice trail away, and I wondered if he meant that they thought he might have been responsible for his wife's death.

"At least you and your daughter have each other."

"Yeah, but without Cassie—" His voice caught. "Then there's . . . the dogs. They're all back at the animal shelter now. We can't have them at the hotel with us. And I don't know if we'll ever want to live in this neighborhood again. Not after this. Besides, he was a criminal. Their former owner was, I mean. Maybe he had something to do with my wife's death."

"I'm sure that can't be the case. Cassandra told me today that he was in jail."

"Yes, but what if . . ." He stopped and shook his head. "None of this makes any sense. There's no point. I just . . . I want my wife back. I can't do this alone. I can't raise Melanie by myself. I'm not a good enough parent."

"Cassandra told me you were a wonderful father, and I'm sure that's true." I was beginning to yearn for my mother to step in for me. She was so much better with this sort of thing than I was, and she knew Paul. But I could tell from the sound of running water through the pipes that she was currently otherwise occupied and probably couldn't overhear.

"It was only because of her."

I wasn't sure what he meant; probably that he was only a good father because of his wife's support, but I let it pass.

It struck me then that a person's death has a dreadful ripple effect, a passing along of emotional pain in an ever-growing circle. As much as I detested myself for feeling this way, I wanted to close the door, not to have to witness Paul's agony at his tragic loss. At the same time, I wished I'd been more open and available to friendship with Cassandra. I would never get the chance now.

"Did Edith tell you what my wife was doing at her house? When I left with Melanie, Cassie told me she was going to be making dinner. But she hadn't even gotten anything started."

"What time was that?"

"I don't remember exactly. Sometime after four-thirty, though, because that's when I got home. Early. I even came home early today. To see the dogs. If only . . ."

Finally I heard my mother's footfalls coming from behind me. I stepped aside, but Paul, to my surprise, backed away from the door at the sight of my mother. He made a small pushing gesture at her and said, "Marilyn. I've got to go. I can't survive this."

"Paul. I'm so sorry."

Mom ignored his initial attempts to walk away and reached out for him. Then she held him as he sobbed in her arms. I had to look away. At least Paul, in his shock and grief, wasn't treating me as a suspect. That might change, though, once he'd had a chance to let this all sink in.

My vision happened to fall across the street. Trevor Cunningham was parked in front of his former residence, watching the three of us, as if waiting for our conversation to finish.

Mom released Paul from the hug, and Paul pulled himself together enough that it seemed he would at least be able to drive. As we watched him get into his car, Mom called out, "Please let us know if there's anything we can do."

Meanwhile, Trevor started to approach Paul, but then froze as Paul held up a hand, said something under his breath, and drove off. Paul's words seemed to shake Trevor. He dropped his chin, his overly long, center-parted hair immediately falling into his eyes, and his long, pointy nose again giving me that unmistakable impression of a human silky terrier. The muscles in his jaw were still working as he headed up our walkway.

He looked up when he reached our porch, his gaze locking on my mother. "Hello, Marilyn. This is all so . . . overwhelming. Tragic. Cassie Randon, of all people. Someone who would never hurt a fly. You gotta wonder what's coming to the world."

Mom nodded. "I can't believe it. If you can't be safe in Berthoud, you're not safe anyplace."

"True." Trevor Cunningham sent a glance my way, then gave Mom a shake of the head, followed by a second look at me.

"I suspect you're here to speak to my daughter about your dog."

Trevor winced and nodded, the long top strands of his hair once again falling forward into his eyes. He dragged his hair back into place as he spoke. "I . . . feel guilty for worrying about Shogun at a time like this, but yes, I am. He hasn't shown up yet, has he?"

"No, he hasn't. I'm sorry. We'll keep an eye out for him, though," Mom said as she went back into the house, shooting me a look that meant: *Holler for me if you need support.*

I felt a bit awkward standing outside with a guest on what still felt to me like Mom's porch and not my own. "Did you want to come in?" I asked Trevor, half hoping he'd say no.

He shook his head. "I've only got a minute or two, Allida. I don't want to be here long enough to have to cross paths with Edith. The police seem to think I had something to do with Cassandra's murder. I didn't. I swear to you. I went straight to my office after I left yours and didn't leave until I came here."

At least the police were spreading their innuendos around. "How did you find out?"

"Edith called me," he said through an instantly tightened jaw. "She insists that I came here early this afternoon and kidnapped Shogun, which is just plain nuts."

I nodded. "If it's any consolation, the sergeant acted as though they were suspicious of me, as well. Maybe that's just their way."

Trevor started to smile as if reassured, then glanced back at his former house cum murder scene. His eyes had widened with alarm when he faced me again. "You . . . found the body, didn't you?" He took a step away from me, as if suddenly realizing that I was a possible suspect. Of course, *I* knew better, and his sudden dose of discomfort around me didn't mean he was off *my* list, either.

"Yes. And Shogun wasn't there when I arrived."

"Are you positive that Shogun wasn't with Edith when she got back home? Maybe in her car someplace?"

"No, he couldn't have been with her. The officers would have interviewed her, and she couldn't have kept the dog hidden away that long."

He swept both hands back through his hair that, once again, was trying to fall into his eyes. "As I see it, there're only two possibilities. Either Edith did this and is hiding the dog now for some reason, or somebody killed Cassandra and kidnapped my little dog."

"There's a third possibility. The gate was left open. Under all the traumatic circumstances, Shogun might have just run off and hid someplace. If so, he'll come back."

Trevor was already shaking his head. "He's not the sort to do that. He always stays within hearing range of our voices. If you left the gate open while we were gone, he might go out, but he'd just sit on the front porch."

"Maybe with you and Edith separating, though, he wasn't acting himself."

Trevor searched my eyes. "He's a great little dog, but he's not a champion show dog or anything. He's not worth that much to anybody but me. Why would someone take him?" he asked as if my previous statement hadn't registered. "Do you think they're maybe going to try to ask me to pay ransom money?"

"No. I just can't believe anyone would do that, Trevor. Not when the person might be linked to the murder. It'd be too risky."

He nodded, his shoulders sagging. This was someone who struck me as totally devoted to his dog. Could I have gotten the scenario correct before, but with the wrong principal player? Trevor could have come looking for Shogun, found him badly injured or dead in a fight with Suds, and accidentally killed Cassandra when he meant to strike down Suds. That was far-fetched, but the very act of murder was so beyond my comprehension that any explanation would seem "far-fetched" to me.

For obvious reasons, this was not the theory to volunteer at the moment. "How often has Shogun been to your new residence, Trevor? If he really did feel closer to you than to Edith, maybe he's on his way there now."

He brightened a little at that prospect. "He's been at my condo at least half a dozen times. Do you think he could find his way all the way there?"

"Maybe." In truth, it was only a remote possibility, but certainly not out of the question. I'd heard of instances where dogs managed to travel hundreds of miles to reunite with their owners.

Just then, an avocado-colored Volvo pulled up that I recognized as belonging to Russell Greene, my officemate. Suddenly our house was turning into Grand Central Station.

A couple of months earlier, when I first moved back to Colorado, Russell had rented the front room of his two-office suite to me. He also had a crush on me, which I was recently beginning to reciprocate. We'd been out on a couple of dates and enjoyed each other's company. We seemed to have considerably different interests, but he was such a decent, caring person that I couldn't help but be attracted to him.

He got out of the car, smoothing his dark mustache. As always, he was nicely dressed, wearing dark slacks, a royal blue silk tie, and a striped shirt. He was short, which made us nicely matched, and had a well-proportioned, compact build. In a land of midgets, he and I could rule the world, but as it was, people kept flashing us annoying what-a-cute-couple grins when they saw us together.

He gave me a nervous smile as he jogged up our steps, and I suddenly remembered that he wasn't simply dropping by unannounced. Damn it all! We had a date tonight!

He held a hand out to Trevor, who'd paused before making his departure as if to learn the identity of my visitor. "Hi. Russell Greene."

"Trevor Cunningham." He hesitated. When neither of us spoke, he forced a smile. "Guess I've taken up enough of your time, Allida. I just . . ." He ran his hand through his unruly hair. "If you hear anything, if he comes back, please let me know."

"I will."

"Have a good evening."

"Call me if he's at your place when you get back."

Trevor nodded, then got into his car and drove away.

We watched him go. "Missing dog?" Russell correctly surmised.

"Yes, under excruciating circumstances. My neighbor was murdered a few hours ago in Trevor's backyard, and the dog apparently ran off."

"Your neighbor was *murdered*? Oh, my God. I'm sorry, Allida." He turned to face the Cunninghams' house. "I wondered what all of the police-scene tape was for." He searched my face, his own expression downhearted. "I guess we should take a rain check on our date, huh?"

His willingness to postpone our date made me less eager to desert the idea myself. I suspected that curious friends and acquaintances would be calling constantly tonight, as soon as word got out that there was a murder in Berthoud. Staying home and fielding those calls was infinitely less appealing than being wined and dined by Russell. "No, but I'll need some time to get ready."

"You look . . . great the way you are. Don't feel you need to change on my account."

This was truly generous of him, as I was wearing the khakis and simple blue cotton blouse that my mother had brought to me at the police station.

"Russell, hello," Mom exclaimed from behind me. She was smiling broadly and rushed up to greet him. She and I hadn't discussed the topic, but Mom seemed to have a closer affinity for Russell than for any other man I'd dated. I suspected that was largely because he was the antithesis of my former fiancé in so many ways. That one factor scored huge bonus points with Mom, as well as with me. "I didn't realize you two had a date tonight."

"How are you, Mrs. Babcock?"

"For heaven's sake. You don't need to be so formal. Please. Call me Marilyn."

At least she hadn't suggested he call her "Mom." Come to think of it, this date wasn't well timed for Mom's sake.

"Oh, Mom. I just realized you shouldn't be home alone after what just happened. Maybe I should—"

"Don't be silly. The police will be all over the neighborhood. This'll be the safest block in the country tonight. You two go and have fun."

We went back and forth on the issue for a short time, but I actually agreed with her assessment of her safety. I fetched my purse, said good-bye to the dogs, then joined Russell and Mom on the front porch.

"I'll have her back home safe and sound in a couple of hours, Marilyn."

She gave him a frighteningly warm smile, her dark eyes positively sparkling with motherly joy. "Keep her out as long as you like, Russ."

I felt my cheeks warming and headed down the walkway ahead of Russell in an attempt to end this conversation as quickly as possible. Ever the gentleman, Russell outraced me and opened the door for me. I could feel Mom watching me as I fastened my seat belt.

This entire incident served as a timely reminder not to dally too long before looking for a new place to live. Despite the disaster my first Boulder rental had been—I'd accidentally rented a room from a lunatic—the bottom line was that I was too old to be getting a parental send-off for dates. Russell gave her a cheerful wave, which I was disinclined to second, and we left.

We'd barely turned the corner before Russell asked, "Do the police have any prime suspects?"

"At least one." Not wanting to risk slipping into a morass of self-pity, I didn't let on that I was referring to myself.

"Do you think it could have been one of your neighbors? Such as that guy you were just talking to?"

"It's possible, I guess." Actually, it was more than a mere "possible"—more on the order of "likely"—but Russell's face paled visibly even at that. His obvious fear for my safety made me reach for other theories. "It could somehow be tied in with Cassandra's adopted dog. The owner of the mother dog wants her back once he's out of jail. Maybe this was a career criminal who hired a buddy to go get his dog back, and the guy accidentally hit her too hard."

"You think somebody might have killed a person over a *dog*?"

I couldn't help it; I tensed and glared at Russell for saying the word "dog" as I might say "cockroach."

He cleared his throat, then asked quickly, "Was she a friend of yours?"

"No, I'm not as . . . extroverted as I wish I were. Maybe if I'd been more aware of everyone's comings and goings . . . Oh, I don't know. There's no way I'm going to figure this thing out. I'll just have to trust that it's an isolated incident, because otherwise, Mom and I are right across the street, like a pair of proverbial sitting ducks."

We formed an unspoken agreement to change subjects at that point and made small talk instead. We reached the northern side of Main Street in Longmont and stopped for a red light. A small dog caught my eye just as we were crossing the intersection. He was running alone down the shadowy sidewalk, heading away from us.

"Turn right! Follow that dog!"

My cry had come too late for us to make the turn safely. Russell hit the brakes, which set off a cacophony of honking horns behind us.

"What dog? I don't see a dog!" Russell blurted over the noise of his squealing tires from his sudden hard right turn. We managed to squeeze into the street that the dog had run down without causing a fender bender, but I was already too focused on catching sight of the dog again to feel as grateful, or as contrite, as I probably should have.

"I thought I saw Shogun. The dog that's missing."

"Way out here in Longmont?"

"This isn't too far for a dog to have gotten on foot in several hours. He could have come looking for Trevor, his owner."

I strained my eyes and made a constant sweep of vision as we slowly drove ahead. It was getting hard to see in the rapidly darkening evening. There was no sign of the dog and our search was probably futile.

Just then I saw the dog darting around the corner ahead of us. "There he goes! Down that alley!"

"It's one-way the other direction," Russell pointed out as he drove past the alley. I craned my neck to get a better look at the dog and was certain it was some breed of long-haired terrier.

"I've got to get him. Even if it's not Shogun, he could get hit by a car. Let me out of the car."

Russell signaled and pulled out of traffic. "I can't park here. I'll go find a space and come help," he said while I scrambled out of the car.

I ran down the alley. Though it was, thankfully, reasonably well lit by the outdoor lights on the back of the buildings, the dog was already out of sight once again.

I'd gotten halfway down the narrow alley when someone suddenly stepped out from behind a dumpster. I gasped and automatically jumped back.

The man grabbed my wrist.

Chapter 4

I choked back a scream.

The man who grabbed my arm was not much taller than Russell—roughly five-foot-six. Unlike Russell, this man had been looking up at life from the bottom of the drain for quite a while now. His clothes were filthy and in tatters, his dark hair matted, and his leathery skin smeared with dirt.

"Hey, little girly," he said, leering at my chest. "You got any money?"

I twisted my arm around so fast that I wrenched it free from his grasp. "No, and I don't have time for this right now," I said with deliberate attitude. If there was anything I'd learned from being a petite woman who often works with large, aggressive dogs, it was that you can't gain dominance by letting yourself show fear. "I'm trying to find a dog I saw run this direction."

I took a step deeper into the alley, but he stepped sideways, blocking my path. This time, at least, he didn't touch me. "You mean the little mutt? Charlie?"

As he spoke, I got a disgusting whiff of alcohol on the man's breath. I had to get out of here. The dog was probably not Shogun in the first place.

Feigning a casualness I didn't feel, I asked, "You know the dog I'm talking about?"

The man tried to muster some dignity and self-confidence by squaring his shoulders and meeting my eyes. His were bloodshot and red-rimmed. "Yeah. The one that jus' run by me, right? He's just a stray, but I got to callin' him Charlie."

"I doubt we're talking about the same dog. This one

looked to me to be a full-bred terrier." In truth, I hadn't been close enough to conclude any such thing, but had gotten the impression that this dog was too healthy to have been a stray.

"Naw. He's jus' a mutt. Tell ya what, though. Seein' as you want him so bad, how's 'bout I sell him to you for twenty bucks?" He took a step in that direction and had a glint in his eye that worried me.

"Um, okay. I'll go get some money."

"Meet you back here in jus' a minute, then," the man said, then took off down the alley.

I turned and headed the other direction. I wasn't about to wait around and find out what his intentions were. Bravura's one thing, but out-and-out stupidity is quite another. For all I knew, he'd come back with another man or two.

Russell met me before I'd gotten all the way out of the alley. I breathed a little easier at the sight of him.

In a tribute to his superior planning skills, he'd brought a flashlight. "Couldn't find the dog?" he asked.

"No, and what's worse, I ran into someone who apparently makes this alley his home. He says he'll sell me the dog for twenty dollars."

"Hmm. Well, if it turns out the dog is Shogun, I'll give him the money."

"That's generous of you, except we might get knifed in the process." I gestured at our surroundings, deserted except for the cars that were streaming past on the adjoining street. "This isn't exactly a safe house for business dealings."

"True." He held out his keys to me. "The car is parked a block and a half from here, just off of Fifth Avenue. Why don't you go and wait for me there? I'll bring the dog, if the guy comes back with him."

This was an extremely magnanimous suggestion on his part, as Russell has a substantial fear of dogs.

"No, Russell. We either both wait or we both leave. I'm not going to get you into a potentially dangerous situation and then wait demurely in your car to see if you come through it safely."

"Then we'll wait here. Otherwise we'll probably never know for sure if this is the dog you're looking for or not."

My heartbeat had returned to normal, and I felt safe with Russell, even in this setting. "Okay." I turned on Russell's flashlight and trained the beam along the general area the dog had been running. "I suspect he'll come back with some stray dog instead. Still, it's worth twenty dollars to me to get a stray off the street and safe at the animal shelter." I grinned and joked, "Especially since it's *your* money."

There was a puddle nearby, and fortunately, the dog had run directly through it. I circled a wet paw print with my fingers. As far as I could recall, it was approximately the size of the prints on Edith's deck. This verified to me that a small terrier could have left those prints, as could one of the puppies.

Russell watched me with a furrowed brow, but made no comment.

We both straightened at the sound of footfalls approaching up ahead. I felt Russell stiffen at the frightening appearance of the man who'd grabbed me. He'd returned, empty-handed. He sneered at Russell, then focused on me. "Okay. I got the dog in a box for you, right around the corner. Got my twenty bucks?"

"Give us the dog and we'll give you the money," Russell said logically.

The man shook his head. "Naw. I ain't gonna let you see the dog till I get paid for him. If it ain't him, you still owe me, and I got no guarantee your girlfriend here will live up to her end of the deal. Give me the money up front or else no dog."

Russell got out his wallet. "Here's a five. You'll get the rest when you bring the dog."

He frowned, stared at the bill in his hand, then shoved it into a pocket. "Okay. Be right back. Wait here."

The man took a couple of casual steps, then broke into a run.

Russell sighed, then looked at me. "Thought so. He hasn't got the dog, and we just got scammed. I just played along in the hopes that he'll use the money to get himself a decent meal."

More likely he'd use it to buy booze, but I didn't want to dampen Russell's optimism. I focused the beam at the wet tracks, growing fainter as they were farther away from the puddle.

Russell said, "Let's try to track the dog and see if it's Shogun."

"Thanks. I'm sure you'd rather we head to the restaurant, but I really do want to see if I can locate this dog."

He grinned and took my hand. "Actually, it doesn't matter to me what we're doing, so long as I'm with you."

My cheeks warmed, but not merely from embarrassment at Russell's kind words. I'd had more of a reaction to Russell's simply holding my hand than I would have liked. Certainly more than I would have admitted to him. I was still very unsure of whether or not it made much sense for me to pursue a relationship with someone who seemed to have so little in common with me. This vague sensation that my hand somehow felt right in his wasn't going to count for much a few years down the line.

The last time, I reminded myself, I'd made the mistake of letting my heart run roughshod over my brain, I'd been all but destroyed. My fiancé ran off with my maid of honor. Nothing of the sort was ever going to happen to me again.

We kept up a brisk pace, worried that the wet prints would evaporate, but there seemed to be enough puddles that the dog had run through to keep us on target. The man and Russell's money, on the other hand, seemed to be long gone. We managed to track the dog across three blocks, till we reached an impasse at a loose board in a gate on someone's property, which the dog had squeezed through.

"Guess that's that," Russell said. "We can't go traipsing through someone's backyard."

"No, but . . . we can knock on their door and ask if they've seen a terrier."

Russell grimaced slightly and peered over the fence at the house, which I could see through the slats was small with white clapboard siding. "All right. But for the sake of the owner, we have to go around and ring the front door rather than trespass through their backyard."

"Well, all right, but this is awfully conventional. I was really looking forward to scaling the fence and banging on a bedroom window," I said with a forced sigh.

"They're probably just sitting down to dinner now, and if we—"

"I'm kidding, Russell. Of *course* I meant that we should go knock on their front door, not the back." Actually, that was a lie, but I was certain that the thought of using the front door would have occurred to me before I'd even gotten myself halfway hoisted over the fence.

I masked my impatience when Russell made the sensible suggestion that we get the car and drive to the front of the house on our way to the restaurant. My appetite hadn't returned, and I suspected that my thoughts were really much too centered around Cassandra Randon's murder and Shogun's related disappearance to be much of a "date" anyway. But I do *try* to be fair, and I had already promised Russell I'd go out with him tonight.

It took us several minutes to get around to the house. I convinced Russell to let me go alone to speak to the inhabitants. A Hispanic woman who wasn't even as tall as me opened the door and said, "Hello?" More compelling than the fact that I'd found another short person in Colorado was the yipping sound of a small dog barking from within the house.

"Hello. My name is Allida Babcock. I'm looking for a lost dog that may have come into or through your backyard. It was a little silky terrier, about yay high." I spread my hands about a foot apart to demonstrate.

She shook her head at me. *"No entiendo, señorita. Un minuto, por favor."*

A moment later, a boy who looked to be about ten emerged with the woman and said in an accent, "My mother doesn't speak English. Can I help you?"

"Hi, there. Yes, I'm—"

I stopped as a dog dashed into the room. He was a terrier mix—similar to, but definitely not, Shogun.

"I was looking for a lost dog, and I think I made a mistake and thought I recognized your dog. What's your dog's name?"

"Rojas."

I knelt, ostensibly to pet him, but also to gage if this was indeed the same dog I'd mistaken for Shogun. The long fur of the two dogs was very similar, and seen from the back, it would have been impossible to tell the dogs apart. "Did I just see your dog running down an alley?"

"He gets out of the yard a lot."

"You should fix the loose board in your fence. Rojas could get hit by a car or something."

"I will," he said, too quickly for me to believe him.

I thanked him and his mother and left. By the time I left, Russell was standing by his car, watching me with a look on his face as if I were considerably prettier than I really was.

"Wrong dog," I said simply.

He held open the door for me. We made our way back onto Main Street.

"Thanks for helping me find the dog and putting up with the delay."

"Glad I could help. I'm just sorry it didn't make any difference."

"I don't know if the missing dog is related to the murder or not, but I'd sure like to know if those were his paw prints in . . . the blood."

"You saw bloody paw prints?" Russell asked, his voice rife with alarm.

"I guess I didn't tell you. I found her body."

"God. No, you didn't tell me. That must have been terrifying."

"Yes."

Russell said nothing, but the color was starting to rise on his cheeks, which seemed to happen to him whenever he was nervous about something. "Maybe it'd help if you could get away and get your mind off of what happened for a while. I was wondering if you'd like to join me on a trip with my friends this weekend."

"A trip?" Uh-oh. What would this involve? An over-nighter? I liked Russell quite a bit, but dearly hoped that he wasn't about to put a damper on our relationship by trying to rush things.

"Yeah. We're going rock climbing."

"Rock climbing?" I repeated, making no effort to disguise my distaste for the sport. Sadly, Russell would have had a better chance trying to rush things.

"Nothing intense, I promise. In fact, one of the guys is bringing his girlfriend and this is going to be her first climb. Have you ever gone before?"

I shook my head, thinking of how unlikely it was that a dog lover with a pathological fear of heights was going to meet a rock-climbing enthusiast with a pathological fear of dogs.

"If you're at all interested in giving it a try, I could give you some pointers tomorrow morning before we head out. We could meet first thing at Boulder Rock Climbing Club. It's right across from the Y. They have an interior wall."

"I can't, Russell. I have a pretty intense fear of heights."

He paused, then chuckled. "That balances things out nicely. Me with my fear of big dogs and now you with this. Maybe we can be chased up a cliff by a pack of wild dogs someday and go loony together."

I laughed and Russell turned and then pulled into a parking lot. "We're here." Our eyes met. Neither of us moved for a long moment.

I'm not sure which one of us initiated the kiss; probably it was mutual. At the soft sensation of his lips on mine, my heartbeat quickened. I felt a surge of unexpected warmth that made me want to respond too intensely. Uncertain about my feelings and his, I drew away.

Our gazes locked for a moment. In the blink of an eye, his face changed to that of the one man I'd been physically inti-mate with and who'd broken my heart. Though the image left me as quickly as it came, I was shaken.

I turned my face away and said, "I can't do this. I'm so sorry, but my going out on a date tonight is . . . really bad timing."

Russell sighed and ran a hand through his hair as he settled back behind the driver's wheel. "Of course it is. This was stupid of me. I'm sorry."

"Don't apologize. I'm the one who should have known better than to try to go out on a date tonight."

"Let me get you some dinner anyway."

"No. I'm not—"

He started the engine. "Taco Bell drive-through okay? Even if you're not hungry, you could order something for your mom. In case *she* hasn't eaten."

I was touched by his kindness, but only gave him a feeble nod when he looked in my direction.

Less than an hour later, the three of us, counting Mom, were washing down Taco Supremes with Coors Lights, laughing our heads off at Mom's embellished stories of intrepid flight students. The dogs had been banished to the back deck, where they were lined up, noses to the glass door.

Russell and I avoided each other's gaze, and he'd avoided his fear of being around my dogs by positioning his seat so that his back was to them. And yet, I was beginning to feel strangely on edge in his presence.

The next morning I, as usual, had no clients scheduled; because most people don't take time off from work for appointments with a dog behaviorist, my work schedule generally began when theirs ended. I decided to pay a visit to the Haywoods, the grouchy couple who lived on the other side of Edith's house. I rang the doorbell three times before anyone responded, although I'd seen a curtain flutter while I was walking up their steps.

Mrs. Haywood opened the door, but left the chain in place. She peered around the edge of the door and said in a voice gravelly from years of smoking, "What do you want, Allida?"

"Good morning. I came to ask you if I could check your bushes. You see, there was this note on—"

She shut the door. I waited a moment to see if she was simply removing the chain, but when she didn't open it, I rang again. This time she flung the door fully open, looked me up and down, and, before I could say anything, called over her shoulder, "Harvey, it's the Babcock girl! She says she wants to take a look at our bushes!"

"What's she want to do that for?" Harvey's deep but phlegmy voice rumbled from some interior room.

Betsy threw up her hands and shuffled away from the door. "Beats me. Should I tell her she can go ahead?"

A minute later, I was still standing on the porch, listening to them bicker about which of them should deal with "that Babcock girl." It was Harvey who finally drew the short straw. He was wearing slippers, dark pants, and a sleeveless undershirt.

I forced a smile, which was greeted with, "Did you go 'n' lose a baseball in our yard again?"

"Uh, no, Mr. Haywood. I haven't played baseball in this neighborhood for almost twenty years now. I wanted to check your property to see if a note had blown over here in yesterday's storm."

"Di'n't you get the chance to read it?"

"No, I . . . I mean, yes, I read it, but I need to find it to prove my story. This is about Cassandra Randon's murder yesterday."

"Oh yeah. Yeah. Terrible thing." He crossed his thin arms, the flesh of his former biceps sagging.

"See, someone left me a note that may have been blown onto your property yesterday." In spite of myself, I could hear my voice rising and my enunciation becoming more careful, as if Mr. Haywood were hard of hearing, though he'd given me no indication of that. "Did you find any pieces of paper on your property last night or earlier this morning?"

"No. We don't take care of the outsides of the place. Susan does that."

"Susan?"

"Yeah. Susan. My eldest daughter. Your baby-sitter. She comes over here three, four times a week."

"Was she here yesterday afternoon? Or anytime after the storm?"

"Beats me. Betsy!" he called without bothering to turn. "Was Susan here yesterday? The Babcock girl wants to know when she was here last!"

"*I* don't know, Harvey! Tell her to ask *Susan*!"

Betsy's words were accentuated by the clanging of pots. By the sound of things, she was dropping pots on top of one another from a considerable height.

"You'll have to ask Susan," Harvey said to me. "Lives over in Lyons. Last name is Nelson now."

"Could you give me her phone number? Or her address?"

"Yeah, yeah, well, all right. I'll do that." He started to shut the door.

"So, is it okay with you if I look around outside for the note?"

He gave me a dismissive wave. "Yeah, yeah. Go ahead. You should be more careful with your things, Allida. I know it's hard on your mama, raisin' you two all by herself like she is. You should watch yourself. Make it easier on her." He shut the door.

At least he didn't call me a "young'n," I thought as I headed down the steps. It was strange to think that the Haywoods were probably only ten years older than my mother, if that. They seemed to have come from a different world. One in which couples shut out the outside world and yelled at it when it intruded.

Their property, unlike the Cunninghams' next door, was unfenced. That struck me as incongruous with their unfriendly demeanor. The Haywoods had a thick row of unkempt juniper bushes along the side of the house that faced the Cunninghams' home. That seemed a likely place to begin my search.

This was a matter of literally beating bushes. I had to keep parting the prickly branches, and I was wearing a T-shirt. The skin on my arms was getting scratched, the little wounds from the sharp needles and rough bark itchy and painful.

After thoroughly examining the outer side of the hedges, I tried to look between the house and the dense shrubbery. There was not much room, so I crouched down, wondering if there was any point to this. The deputies had probably already done this yesterday.

The soil here was a fine sand, sheltered from the elements by the eaves on one side and the juniper bushes on the other. I saw at once that there were no shoe prints back here, but rather something more immediately intriguing to me: paw prints.

They were roughly the same size as the ones I'd seen yesterday. It stood to reason that if the dog who left the prints could be identified, that dog's owner might be the killer. I decided at once that I would rather keep those prints intact than mess them up while searching.

Energized, I raced up the front steps, intending to ask whichever Haywood answered whether or not a small dog was on their property yesterday. Nobody answered my first ring. I gritted my teeth and pressed the doorbell a second time.

Finally, Betsy Haywood flung the door open. "Here." She thrust a piece of paper into my hand. "Our daughter's address and phone number."

Though the handwriting was decidedly different, she had written the note with a black felt-tip pen on a magenta sticky-pad sheet.

The paper and its writing implement were identical to the note I'd seen on Edith's door.

Chapter 5

I pondered the notion of ringing the doorbell again to ask about the notepaper. If the Haywoods had left that note on Edith's door, though, this would only alert them to the fact that they'd incriminated themselves just now.

Who else could I ask? I had a client appointment in Boulder over the noon hour and could visit the Haywoods' daughter, Susan Nelson, on my way to my client's home. Resolved, I pocketed the note and was soon heading west toward Lyons.

This drive used to be on a single-lane country road through sparsely populated areas northeast of Boulder. Now urban sprawl had filled in the wide expanses of fields on the south side of the road, though cornfields still spread to my right, the Rocky Mountains a purplish blue in the distant background. We'd had a particularly wet May to date, and I found myself appreciating the greenery, almost lush for the semi-arid front range.

After mentally replaying yesterday's scene from the moment that I'd parked my car in Mom's garage until I'd entered the Cunninghams' backyard, I realized that, while it was true there were no unfamiliar cars parked on the road, I hadn't seen whether or not a car was in the Haywoods' driveway. That meant that Susan Nelson could have been visiting next door and I wouldn't have noticed.

It was possible that she had an intense problem with Cassandra, one that had developed into a murderous rage. The teenager I recalled from my childhood struck me as having been capable of murder. She'd certainly threatened me with death enough times, at any rate. My memories of her were so unpleasant—a wide mouth full of braces, framed with frizzy hair, perpetually screaming at me—that I found myself easing the pressure on the gas pedal and had to force myself to go the speed limit.

During the drive, I tried to piece together the odd little snippets of information I'd learned during my visit to Betsy and Harvey's house. The paw prints in the dirt alongside the Haywoods' house could have been there for several days, if not weeks. With no fence, any dog off the leash could have investigated that particular area. In fact, during a visit to Mom a couple of years ago, I'd seen Betsy Haywood swing a broom to chase off a dog who'd ventured onto their front lawn.

And yet, now that my course was taking me farther and farther away, it struck me that there was something significant about those particular prints, some peculiarity, perhaps, that proved them to be identical to the bloody ones I'd seen the day before. I wanted to turn around and take a second look at those paw prints. At the same time, my sudden urge to reverse directions might only be an unconscious excuse to avoid seeing Susan again. I assured myself that there was no rush; the prints would still be there when I returned to Berthoud.

Upon further reflection, I wasn't sure about the significance of the notepaper. While it would be a huge coincidence if the notes had come from separate pads, it was also a stretch to think that the Haywoods would be so careless as to use the same paper twice. Or could the killer have first lured Cassandra, or me as a scapegoat, into the backyard with the note, then planted the notepad in the Haywoods' house to frame the Haywoods? It seemed strange that the grouchy Haywoods would have a bright magenta-colored notepad. But then, trying to match people's stationery to their personality was probably every bit as foolish as matching styles of collars to dogs.

Even so, the address on its familiar sheet of paper was all but burning a hole in my pocket. At a wide shoulder of hard-packed dirt and gravel, I pulled over and did a pencil rubbing of the paper, tilting the pencil to give light, wide strokes from

the side of the lead so that the impression from the note that
had been atop this one could be seen. This was a trick that any
self-respecting, budding secret agent learns as a child. Unfortunately, Susan's address obscured the faint markings from
the preceding sheet.

Fifteen minutes later, I reached the outskirts of town.
Lyons is a nice little place, not unlike Berthoud. It's some-
thing of a bedroom community for Boulder and is a conve-
nient stopping place for those traveling to or from Estes
Park—a tourist town just southwest of Rocky Mountain
National Park. I wasn't especially familiar with the streets,
but reasoned that the town was small enough for me to find
Susan Nelson's street without too much trouble.

Eventually I found the address her parents had given me
and parked on the street. Although the yard and gardens were
lovely, the house itself was unimpressive, to put it kindly. Its
white paint was peeling, and the screens on the two front windows hung in tatters from their misshapen frames. I rang the
doorbell and was glad to hear someone working the latch after
just one ring, unlike my experience with Susan's parents.

As a teenager, Susan had been rail-thin with frizzy brown
hair. The woman who opened the door was considerably
heavier, stood at least five-foot-nine, and was quite attractive. She wore a red tank top and a denim skirt. As usual,
though, my eyes were drawn away from the person and to the
little dog barking by her sandaled feet.

The dog—a toy breed just a bit taller and bulkier than a
silky terrier—had a thick coal-black coat, with a foxy face
and upright ears. As he circled his owner's ankles, I saw that
he had no tail. A schipperke! That's a Belgian dog, originally
bred to chase rats and guard canal barges. The schipperke
wasn't a rare breed of dog, yet I had never met or worked
with one. For all of the dog training I'd done in Chicago, I'd
never happened to run across one.

"Can I help you? Or are you just here to stare at my dog?"
the woman asked in a voice dripping with sarcasm.

Reluctantly, I returned my gaze to the woman before me.
"Are you Susan Nelson?"

"Yeah. What's it to you?"

How nostalgic. Though her looks had improved considerably, her grating voice hadn't, which sounded to me like a car
engine cranking over. Plus there were those unforgettable—
and loathsome—ice-cold mannerisms of hers. "I'm Allida
Babcock. We used to live in the same neighborhood."

"Allida Babcock?"

"Yes."

"Well, I'll be." She gave me a sly smile. "Come on in here
and let me take a look at you."

I had an involuntary shudder at her odd phrasing, which
sounded to me like something out of *The Beverly Hillbillies*,
but I stepped inside. The air reeked of cigarette smoke. We
occupied the small square of warped green linoleum that
served as the entranceway to the living room, where everything was as unkempt and shoddy as the outside of her house.

"You're the scrawny little kid I used to baby-sit for?" She
eyed me at length, then laughed heartily and said, "You
haven't changed a bit."

"Nor have you."

The smile faded. "So, what all brings you to my humble
abode?"

I glanced again at the schipperke. Her dog's paws would
be just about the right size for the prints at Edith's. The
schipperke had become distracted by a prism's rainbow on
the wall, which came from a crystal hung from the window.
The dog was leaping at the rainbow, trying to catch it. There
were scratch marks on the wall, so this wasn't a new activity.

I decided to work my way gradually up to a discussion of
paw prints at the murder scene and said the first thing that
popped into my head. "My mother mentioned you were still
in the area, and I thought I'd come by and say hello and
apologize for that time I Super-Glued your shoes to the
porch."

"That was you? Damn. I always blamed your brother for
that one."

"I figured you would. That was the major reason I did it."

"Yeah, well, I know what it's like to grow up with a

sibling, believe you me. Mom and Dad are still pretty ticked, though. You'd be surprised how much work that all took to scrape the chunks of glue and repaint the floor."

Half kidding, I said, "I guess I should tell them how sorry I am. I'm somewhat overdue for giving them an apology."

She shrugged. "Couldn't hurt. I'm telling you, they remember it well." She held my gaze as if completely serious. That was what came from her parents' leading too sheltered an existence—still being bent out of shape twenty years later over a childish prank.

"We had a major upheaval yesterday in the neighborhood. Did your parents tell you about it?"

She nodded. "Yeah. Mom called me and filled me in on all the sordid details. Was that you who found the body?" She acted mildly curious, nothing more. Perhaps she'd never even met Cassandra.

"I'm afraid so. Did you know Cassandra Randon?"

She shrugged. "No. Only in passing." She gestured at the couch, which ran the length of one wall. Its once-purple velvet fabric was soiled, and a missing leg had been replaced by a cinder block. "You want to have a seat?"

"No, thanks. I can only stay a minute." All I wanted to do, really, was glean information about her parents' relationship with Cassandra without tipping my hand.

Feigning a casual attitude, I said, "I thought I saw your car in your parents' driveway yesterday." I was lying through my teeth, of course, and it would have taken no effort for Susan to stop and wonder how I could possibly know what type of car she drove. If she asked, I'd be in hot water, as I had no idea. But I had nothing invested in this relationship, anyway.

"Yeah, I was there. Visiting. I come over and mow the lawn, water the flowers, drop off groceries. That sort of thing."

"I thought so," I bluffed. "You *were* there when I was calling for help next door."

"I . . ." For the first time, she conveyed some emotional reaction, her round cheeks reddening. "I never heard you call for help, or I'd've done something. I must have been gone by the time you got there. Nothing much was happening when I left my parents' place. But they told me the police arrived five minutes after I'd gone."

A two- or three-year-old had galloped into the room and was now playing "catch the rainbow" along with the dog. She was angling the light into one palm and trying to cup the other hand over the top as if the colors were a butterfly. The dog's snaps at the colored light were barely missing the little girl's fingers. Their actions made me too nervous to concentrate on Susan's words.

"Susan, I don't mean to butt in, but if your daughter 'catches' that rainbow on her hand, your schipperke might bite her hand."

Susan gasped and grabbed the child's hand, leading her out of the room. "Chelsea! Let's go back to our coloring books, shall we?"

I glanced over at the crystal to see if I could take it down. It was fastened to the top of the window frame, too high for me to reach without standing on a chair.

While Susan got her daughter resituated, I took the opportunity to coax her dog over to me. "What a good dog you are," I said, crouching down. The small black dog took a wide stance, held his—as best I could tell from my angle—ground, and started barking at me. This was classic behavior for the loyal-to-owners-but-wary-around-strangers personality traits I'd heard were so indigenous to the breed. Although I personally don't put quite as much weight on breed personality profiling as some other canine experts do, it was useful in predicting behaviors, to a point.

Susan came back into the room and immediately removed the crystal from the window, reaching it with no trouble. The show-off. She laid it on the dirty sill and turned toward me with a furrowed brow. "So this explains why there's all the scratch marks on the wall. I never realized that's what Boris was doing." Susan gave me a visual once-over, her hands on her hips. "How did you know that he's a schipperke?"

"I'm familiar with most breeds. I'm a dog behaviorist."

"A behaviorist?" She snorted. "Is that some glorified term that lets you charge more for working as a dog trainer?"

I waited a moment to keep from blasting her for her snide remark, then explained calmly, "Dog trainers do just that—basic obedience training. I specialize in dog behavior problems, which sometimes includes their inability to follow instructions."

"Huh. Well, I gotta say, I could sure use your services, if only I could afford them. Boris isn't trained yet. We only got him a couple weeks ago. He barks like mad at everybody who comes to the house and seems to think he owns the place. We have to keep him out in the yard a lot, but then he barks and bugs the neighbors."

"Come on, Boris!" a little voice called. The girl raced through the living room, giggling as the much faster Boris did his best to stay behind her and interpret the rules to this game.

"You know, I've got to say right off the bat that rambunctious, untrained dogs and toddlers don't mix well."

"Ah, I'm not worried." She flicked her wrist in the direction the girl had run. "She ain't my kid. I'm just doing day care for a neighbor. See, I lost my job and I'm trying to scrape together some money to help ends meet." She chuckled, but the sound was bitter. "I wasn't kidding when I told you that I couldn't afford to hire you."

"Does your husband work?"

"Oh, sure." The color rose in her cheeks. "He's a real hard worker. He's a contractor, you know, for carpentry, that sort of thing. It's just that that's a hot-or-cold kind of business."

"So is any self-run business." My clients also tended to come in clusters.

My mind raced as to how I could work the conversation around to paw prints. "Funny that I never noticed you over there in the past few weeks, but I guess you can't really see much of your parents' property from my mom's place. Do you bring your dog along when you go over there?"

"Sometimes. Why? Did you see him running around on your property?"

"No, I'd have noticed him, for sure," I said with sincere admiration as he deserted the girl and returned to the living room to bark at me. Boris was a bright-eyed, healthy-looking dog. "What about yesterday?"

"What do you mean?"

"Was Boris at your parents' place with you yesterday?"

She shrugged, but was now watching me with a wariness that matched her dog's. "Why do you ask?"

"There were some paw prints that I was curious about, that's all."

"Paw prints? You mean, in the blood or something?" Her eyes lit up, and I got the impression that she was calculating how she could gain personally from this information.

Her assumption that the paw prints had been made by the blood was not such a big leap as to implicate her, I decided. "No, nothing as dramatic as all of that. The . . . Cunninghams' dog is missing and I'm trying to help them locate him."

Having tired, finally, of keeping an eye on me, Boris searched the wall for another rainbow and, not finding one, snatched up a sock that he'd found wadded up in the corner and dashed in a circular path through the house, seeing if anyone would give chase.

"That's it," Susan said with a sigh. "Time to move this kit 'n' caboodle outdoors."

Fortunately, for I still hoped to glean information from her, Susan hadn't called me on my earlier excuse that I could only stay a moment. I silently followed her into the kitchen.

"Come on, Chelsea. Want something to eat?"

The child nodded, and Susan grabbed a lunch box off the counter and we all headed to the backyard, which was spacious and lovely. The lawn and gardens were in considerably nicer condition than the house. A garden on the incline of the side yard had tiers built with railroad ties and layers of hundreds of beautiful irises that must have come from Long's Gardens, a world-renowned seller of iris bulbs in north Boulder that had been in existence for longer than I'd been.

I brought out the piece of magenta-colored paper in my

pocket and showed it to Susan, who was seated on the redwood picnic table bench across from the little girl. "Your
parents gave me this note. Is it from your notepad?"

She gave me an all-too-familiar-looking sneer. "No. Why
all would you want to know?"

Not wanting to divulge my true reason for asking, I felt my
cheeks warm and offered a feeble explanation. "I was just
trying to find out whose notepad it was. It didn't look like
your parents' typical color scheme."

She shrugged. "My dad, probably—" She stopped, then
said abruptly, "It isn't mine. Didn't you say earlier you could
only stay for a moment?"

She was suddenly hostile, either because I'd annoyed her
or because the subject matter made her tense. "Yes, I do have
an appointment at noon. I'd better be going." While we
spoke, the dog tore around the yard, chasing a butterfly.
"Boris must be, what, ten months old?"

"A little over nine months. How'd you know?"

"He's approaching his adolescent phase."

She snorted. "Runs in the family. My husband's stuck in
his adolescence."

Based on my desire to work with a schipperke, combined
with the thought that my suspicions about Susan and her parents might be best resolved by getting to know her better, I
tried to think of how to offer a trade of services. I couldn't
think of any particular construction projects that I had going
at the moment, and having seen the condition of their house, I
had doubts as to how motivated her husband really was. "So
you take care of your parents' lawn?"

"Yeah."

"If you do decide you'd like me to work with Boris, maybe
we can trade services. My mom's been talking about hiring
out the job of mowing for a while now. Maybe we could
work out some sort of equitable arrangement."

Boris tore through the yard and crashed into the glass door,
apparently not realizing it was shut. He yelped, then raced
back toward us. Before any of us could move, he leapt onto

the picnic table, snatched the girl's sandwich right off her plate, and dashed off. The little girl, in the meantime, burst into wailing sobs, pointing at the dog.

Susan turned toward me as she rose to console the child. "How soon could you start?"

Chapter 6

We set an appointment for the next day, and I left for my house visit in Boulder. I often go to the dog's residence, though sometimes, depending on factors such as the particular behavioral problem, the dogs are brought to my office. I charge more for the house visits, and they are usually much more advantageous for the dogs and their owners.

Maggie, my client, was a gorgeous, albeit exuberant, golden retriever. I'd grown up with a houseful of goldens, so they were one of my favorite types of dogs—although my list of favorites often seems to correspond with whatever type of dog I happen to be with at the moment.

This particular golden had become a hoarder of unreasonable proportions. She was "burying" her things—chew toys, rawhide bones, and other items she'd decided she wanted for herself, such as her masters' shoes—in all sorts of inconvenient locations in the house. She was then constantly either scratching up the doors in pursuit of her various "bones," or trying to defend them from anyone else touching them.

The burying instinct can be a very difficult one to overcome. To *not* bury bones goes against the innate survival instincts that dogs are born with. Owners can opt to have me help train the dog to use acceptable limits, such as burying bones only in certain areas of the property. However, prior to my being hired, Maggie's owners had put an end to all digging, which Maggie had translated to mean "no digging *outside*."

My advice to Maggie's owners had been to spritz Bitter Apple on their shoes, take away her toys and put them out of her reach, and give her only one item to play with at a time. When playtime was over, they would immediately collect her one toy, regardless of whether or not she'd "buried" it. This regimen makes it very clear to the dog that the human owners and not the dog itself are in charge of the various belongings.

We had been in the intermediate stages of the behavior modification regimen, which meant that Maggie was spending quite a bit of time whining at the base of the refrigerator, staring up at her box of toys with forlorn eyes. The owners were already discouraged. They had decided that they didn't want to indefinitely maintain the practice of having to limit her toys to one at a time. Instead, the final stage of Maggie's training, which we were now dabbling in, was to teach her to return her own toys to one location. Dogs can actually be trained to pick up after themselves in this manner, which makes for a nice parlor trick.

During this session, I had Maggie's owner bring down the box of her toys in my presence. Poor Maggie acted overjoyed and, as I'd fortunately forewarned, immediately set about laying claim to the rooms of the house by spreading out her things. Naturally, we had to do repeated fetching and returning of the toys to the box, until she gradually got the idea. Though I never admit this to my clients, the truth is, I appreciate these more stubborn canines. The eager-to-please and quick-to-learn ones mean fewer repeat sessions, and I charge by the hour.

Afterward, I drove to south Boulder to meet with an obstinate poodle that didn't tolerate strangers in the house. The owner's grandchildren were coming for a visit next month. This was a matter of getting the poodle to make more reasonable concessions on where his particular turf boundaries were. I was working on reducing the boundaries until they were defined as his dog bed and the immediate perimeter.

Once the poodle appointment was finished, I drove to my office, anxious to see Russell. The building we were in was a two-and-a-half-story limestone structure on the corner of Ninth and Mapleton, just north of the Pearl Street Mall. We were in the half story, a walk-out basement built into the steep incline. Though real estate agents would call this location "nestled in the foothills," our view through the small windows just below the ceiling went no higher than the ankles of sidewalk pedestrians. Russell didn't need two full rooms and had given me the front room, so that he and his clients had to go through my office to get to his. The access to the bathroom was through his office, so it was something of a trade-off.

His car was parked in the two-car parking lot that came with the rental, and I immediately got butterflies in my stomach at the prospect of seeing him. However, as soon as I went inside, the deep murmurings through our common wall told me that he was with a couple of male clients. Russell is a contract electrical engineer, so from my vantage point, this was likely deadly dull stuff they were discussing.

My thoughts soon turned to the missing Shogun. If Trevor or Edith had had any luck finding Shogun, they surely would have contacted me by now. Nevertheless, I decided to call them and share my concern. I dialed Edith's house, but there was no answer. I called Trevor, thinking I had no chance of finding him, that he'd be at work. To my surprise, he answered.

Trevor began by telling me that Shogun still hadn't surfaced and that he was "really worried." Oddly, he didn't sound even remotely worried, in contrast to his behavior last evening, and yet the dog had now been missing for almost twenty-four hours.

"I'm so sorry to hear that, Trevor. My mother and I haven't seen him in the neighborhood at all. I was thinking that, since your sister raised Shogun, he might have gone there. Where does your sister live?"

"Oh, uh, she lives . . . way north in Campion."

That was odd. He'd said it as if she lived in North Dakota, and yet Campion was closer to Berthoud than Longmont, where Trevor lived. "I'd like to speak with her. I'm trying to introduce myself to dog breeders in the area to help my business anyway, and it might be helpful for me to talk with her about Shogun."

"Why would you want to do that?" he snapped. For some reason, Trevor sounded affronted at my suggestion.

"When I last saw Shogun, he was acting more high-strung than usual. Sometimes it's helpful to talk to the breeder to get the full background on a dog. And I'd also like to be sure to enlist your sister's help in finding him." Furthermore, though I didn't want to come out and say it, I was afraid that Shogun might have run away after all, and if those prints in the blood were his, he could be badly traumatized.

"Oh. I see. That makes sense, except she hasn't kept up with Shogun enough for him to know where she lives. She and Edith don't get along, you see, so she practically never visited."

"It's worth a quick check, though."

"Okay. I'll call her and ask her. If you don't hear back from me, that means she hasn't seen Shogun."

"I don't mind calling her myself, Trevor."

"But . . . I . . . this isn't a good time. She's very distraught at our losing the dog."

"Distraught? I thought you said she hasn't stayed in touch with Shogun."

"I . . . that's . . . what I meant was that Shogun hasn't been back there. She hasn't kept in touch in terms of taking the dog to her place for visits. Let me get you her phone number. Uh . . . just a moment."

I pondered the nervous vibrations I was picking up over the phone. Trevor was giving me the distinct impression that, for some reason, he didn't want me to contact his sister. Maybe he hadn't really told her that Shogun was missing and didn't want her to hear the news from me.

He got back on the line a moment later. "I can't seem to find her address or her phone number. Tell you what, I'll keep looking, then I'll give her a call and tell her you'd like to speak with her, and she'll get back in touch with you."

"Okay. That'd be great. Thanks. What's your sister's name?"

"Luellen. Listen, I've got to get back to work. I'll have

her call you." He hung up without as much as giving me her last name.

There was something very weird going on. Why didn't Trevor want me to contact his sister?

I called information to check for a Luellen Cunningham in Campion. There was none. I flipped through the yellow pages of my Berthoud-Loveland directory, which included Campion, and spotted an advertisement for silky terriers. The ad listed both the address and phone number. I decided to forgo the phone call and go for the direct approach.

Campion was farther from Boulder than Berthoud, but having hit traffic at an off time, I was at the house that I presumed to be Luellen's just an hour later. It was a two-story home in a new, very suburban neighborhood, with only the mountains in the distance making the setting at all unique.

A wooden cutout in the shape of a silky terrier was fastened to Luellen's door. The cutout featured a cartoon dialogue bubble emerging from the dog's mouth with the words, "Luellen is OUT." The final word was written on a sliding panel. Just below the dog was a small hook holding a cardboard sign with the words, "I'll be back at:" over a clock face. The hands were set to a time five minutes in the future.

All of this signage could well mean that Luellen wasn't home, I thought, but I rang the doorbell anyway. To my mild amusement, the doorbell sang out, "Arf, arf, arf," in ascending tones. This set off a cacophony of live barking, but brought no human response. I took a seat on the bench beside her front door, keeping an eye on my watch to test the accuracy of Luellen's door postings.

With almost two full minutes to spare, a dark blue minivan pulled into the driveway. I half expected to see a mural of a silky on the side paneling, but the only doggie doodad was a little stuffed dog that swung from the rearview mirror.

The driver, an attractive fortyish woman with shoulder-length dark hair, rolled down the window and called pleasantly to me, "Hi. I'll be right with you." Then she pulled her van into the attached garage.

Unsure of whether or not she was going to come through her house or up the front walkway to meet me, I stepped down off the brick porch and peered around the corner. She trotted out of the garage toward me. She was dressed in slacks and a plaid blouse, rolled up at the sleeves. She wore the wrist braces typically worn by those suffering from carpal-tunnel syndrome. "Hi," she said to me. "Are you here to fill out an application?"

"Application?"

"Yes. For a puppy from the next litter. I'm afraid I'm very picky about whom I sell my dogs to. And I must warn you that I don't have any puppies available for sale at the moment."

Not wanting to broach the subject of Shogun too abruptly, I said, "Oh. That's too bad."

"You're welcome to come in, though, and see what fine animals these are."

"Sure. I'd like that. Can I give you a hand with your groceries?"

"That would be nice. Thanks."

Whatever physical problem caused her to wear the wrist supports didn't seem to slow her down when it came to carrying grocery bags. She thrust the two bags that she'd been holding into my arms, grabbed a couple more bags, then we did an awkward dance getting the inner door to the garage open while I introduced myself. My name clearly meant nothing to her. If her brother had already called to tell her about me, she must have been at the grocery store at the time.

Luellen's house was like entering a different world, where most of its inhabitants were less than a foot tall and very hairy. With excited long-haired dogs swirling around our ankles, we proceeded down a short hardwood-floored hallway and set the bags on the counter of her kitchen. I noted that her answering machine nearby had a flashing red light. Assuming the message would be from Trevor, I would have loved to overhear it. With luck, she might listen to it in my presence.

"These are some of my favorite babies," Luellen cooed,

sweeping two nearly identical-looking dogs into her arms. All told, there were eight silky terriers who'd followed us into the kitchen. "This is Lucas and Candy. Silky terriers are just the perfect dog. They're not too yippy and not too big. At the same time, they're a dog's dog. You know what I mean?"

I'd never really heard anyone refer to a "dog's dog," so I merely smiled. All toy breeds are dismissed by a certain subset of dog lovers as being for folks who really want a housecat but, for allergies or other reasons, wind up with a dog. You put a silky up against a Saint Bernard, and I suspect the Saint Bernard would be considered the doggier dog.

"Do you have any dogs, Allida, or will this one be your first?"

"I have two dogs," I replied, glancing again at her answering machine. I gestured at it with my chin. "I see you have a message."

"Yes, it's a regular madhouse around here." She nuzzled the dogs in her arms, then set them down. She grabbed a small stack of what looked like frozen vegetables and jammed them onto an already crowded shelf in the freezer. "Were you looking to get a puppy right away?"

"No, not really." There was no sense in delaying my telling her the real reason for my visit any longer. "Actually, I'm not here to ask about purchasing one of your puppies. I'm a neighbor of Trevor's."

There was a barely perceptible hitch in her motions, then she continued to put away groceries. "When you say you're a neighbor of his, do you mean in Berthoud?"

"Yes, I live across the street from the house he and Edith shared."

Her face grew somber. "You must have known that poor woman who was murdered, then."

"Cassandra Randon. Yes."

"That's such a tragedy. Trevor always spoke highly of both her and her husband. Do the police have any theories about who the murderer is?"

"Probably, but they haven't shared their opinions with us civilians."

She swept her hair behind an ear, her dark eyes focused on mine, a thoughtful expression crossing her pleasant features. She shared Trevor's pointy nose, but overall, she was quite a bit more attractive than her brother. "Wait a minute. Allida. I remember the name now. You do something with dogs, don't you?"

"Yes, I'm a dog behaviorist. In fact, Edith had recently hired me to help determine custody of Shogun."

She smiled. "That's right. Trevor mentioned that to me just yesterday afternoon. He said Edith had hired you. I told him that if you knew what you were doing at all, he'd wind up with custody."

"Well, Luellen, I have to say that I do think it's quite possible that your brother would have wound up with custody of Shogun. However, right now all I care about is locating Shogun. I was thinking that it was possible that he came here once he got frightened and left his home."

"Oh. I see. He's not here, though." An anxious look flitted across her features and she jumped back a little. "Oh, shoot. I forgot to get something critical at the store. Was there anything else you wanted to know, Allida?"

I wasn't certain, but I had gotten the impression that she'd seen something behind me that frightened her. I turned and watched as a ninth dog came toward us. The dog walked with those cute, perky little steps as he padded across the kitchen.

Could this be Shogun? Where had he come from? I silently answered my own question: In this strange—to him—environment, he would be lowest-ranking dog and therefore the last to enter a room to investigate new visitors. He came up to me as if returning to an old friend.

"Sorry to kick you out, Allida," Luellen went on nervously, "but I'm afraid I've got no choice but to run back to the store."

I knelt and let Shogun climb into my lap. "Shogun! Hi!" In my intense relief, I realized how frightened I'd been that Shogun had gotten killed in yesterday's tragedy. "What a good boy Shogun is. Thank goodness you're all right!"

Luellen was staring in unabashed horror at us, her

face pale. "That is not Shogun, Allida. That's his brother, Krumpet."

I studied her features. "Then why does Krumpet know me and respond to the name Shogun?"

"He's just a friendly dog, that's all. Krumpet, come." She slapped her thigh as she called him. After a moment's hesitation, the terrier headed toward her.

"I stand corrected. What an embarrassing mistake. I guess I was just so relieved to think that I'd found him that my imagination got the best of me."

"No harm done. I'm just going to put all the dogs . . . outside now. They need their exercise." She gave me a pained expression, then carried "Krumpet" out of the room, patting her thigh to signal all of the dogs to come. The remaining eight dogs trotted obediently after her.

What a perfect place to hide a silky terrier. Not unlike hiding one particular needle in a packet of needles. But why would someone hide Shogun here? Or anyplace else, for that matter?

Luellen returned empty-handed. Her cheeks were crimson by now, and she averted her eyes. She knew I was on to her.

There had to be an explanation for her trying to hide Shogun, and if it had anything to do with Cassandra's murder, I wasn't about to force her hand.

At least, not until I was relatively certain it wasn't holding a dagger.

I said good-bye, got into my car at what I hoped was a casual enough pace, drove a few blocks, then pulled over to consider my options. My hunch was that Trevor was trying to pull one over on Edith by helping to hide the dog at his sister's. And yet I'd told Trevor that, if he was Shogun's main caregiver, he was likely going to retain custody.

So why would either Luellen or Trevor hide Shogun, unless their doing so was related to Cassandra's murder? The dog was almost certainly at the murder scene, at least until the killer opened the gate, likely during the murder itself. How, then, could the dog have wound up at Luellen's, if not on his own four feet or having been brought here by the killer?

I needed to cross my name off the police's list of suspects. Maybe the best way to go about doing so was to enlist their help now. I could tell Sergeant Millay that Shogun was in the home of the sister of the man who owned the property where Cassandra Randon was killed. Getting the officer to believe that this was Shogun—and, therefore, could have been brought here by the killer—was going to be a challenge. Despite my best efforts, the sergeant had remained convinced that Shogun was likely to have simply run off, never to return, the moment the gate was left open.

I could picture Sergeant Millay, his hooded, emotionless gray eyes staring at me as I explained that, yes, this really was Shogun, in spite of what Luellen might say to the contrary. It would be more effective to have him witness Shogun running up to Edith or Trevor, but that meant convincing the sergeant to insist that they accompany us to Luellen's home. Plus I wasn't sure that either Edith or Trevor should be entrusted with the dog until all of this could be sorted out.

I drove to the nearest public phone, outside of a gas station on Highway 287, and called the Berthoud police, asking for the sergeant. He was out, and the dispatcher asked if I wished to speak to another officer instead. Not really. Hard as it was to imagine Sergeant Millay believing me—or caring about the dog—it was even less likely that some policeman I'd barely met would act on such an odd request. I gave my name and said I'd call back.

Time was of the essence. Luellen had not bought my act of pretending to realize that my identification of Shogun had been a mistake. She would call her brother and have him hide the dog someplace else.

How could I prevent Luellen from secreting the dog away a second time? I could stand guard at her house, but then what? Follow her if she left with a dog under her arm? Even at that, she was likely to spot me following her and could simply outwait me. And there was no chance of enlisting immediate help from the police. Even if I could prove that she was harboring Shogun, that wasn't a crime. Especially not when Trevor, Shogun's owner, knew that Luellen had the dog and that he was safe.

As I pondered the matter, I realized that there was simply no way for me to control Luellen's actions with Shogun. I could, at least, take comfort in knowing that the sweet little dog was safe and being well cared for. The same couldn't necessarily be said for Suds and her litter, however. An animal shelter was a good temporary home for a stray—better and safer than the streets—but it wasn't any place to house a nursing dog and her five puppies.

Before I could dismiss the notion that the husky and her puppies were suffering, I had to see her. Perhaps another foster home had been located. If not, I could think about taking them in myself.

The thought of Suds and her litter brought Melanie to mind. I wondered how she, at her young age, was handling such an immense, monstrous thing as the violent death of her mother. I barely knew Melanie and didn't know how to go about reaching out to her. Maybe I could at least talk to her father about the possibility of their adopting one of the puppies.

The animal shelter was in Loveland, due north of Berthoud and a short drive from Campion. Loveland is a nice little town, several times the size of Berthoud, though that's not saying much. Its biggest claim to fame is that, before Valentine's Day, people all over the country route their cards through the city to get their "Loveland" postmark on the envelopes.

The shelter was privately funded and operated out of a converted house. I pulled into the parking lot and walked toward the single-story brick building. The warm breeze carried the distinct odor of manure from the cattle feedlots that surrounded this part of the county. The stuffy air within the shelter smelled even worse, but I knew that my nostrils would soon adjust. The young woman at the counter looked to be a teenager at most. She was clad all in black, except for the series of silver rings on her ears and through her nose. It strikes me as comical that we humans intentionally poke holes in our bodies to supposedly make ourselves more attractive, yet call dogs stupid for pleasing themselves by rolling in something of foul fragrance.

I asked her if I could talk to someone about a husky named Suds, and she pointed to a half-open door next to the counter while she answered the phone. I took this to mean that I could go on in, and did so. There, to my pleasant surprise, sat a man holding one of Suds's puppies in his lap.

He grinned at me. He was thin and tan with a distinctive, high-bridged nose and a particularly appealing smile. His eyes were darker than his light brown hair, some errant locks covering the slight hint of wrinkles on his forehead. His good looks were augmented by the fact that he was cradling a puppy. A dog-loving man is infinitely more attractive to me than, well, someone like Russell, though he had other qualities that made him attractive.

"Can I help you, miss?" he asked. I couldn't help but notice that he gave me an appraising look, eyeing me at length as he spoke.

"Yes. Hi. My name is Allida Babcock. I wanted to ask you about Suds and her puppies."

"Ah. Great." Still seated, he held out the puppy to me. "This is one of her puppies I've got now. Would you like to hold him?"

I did, of course. Soon I was sitting in a desk chair and cradling a warm fuzzy body in my arms. I nuzzled his soft fur, and the puppy licked my cheek. His sweet, milk-scented breath was warm and pleasant on my skin.

What was a bit worrisome to me was that Suds had allowed the dog to be taken out of her sight. Mother dogs are almost always far too protective to allow a stranger to remove a puppy until the offspring are at least five or six weeks old. Perhaps Suds was becoming too stressed by being bounced from place to place in the past couple of days to maintain her mothering role.

"We're calling him Fez because of his pattern of darker fur on his head. I'm John White. I'm the kennel supervisor."

"Kennel supervisor? So you decide which dogs are adopt-able." This was a particularly lame comment, but I was distracted by his looks and my concern for Suds and family.

"That's right. Among other duties."

"Ah," I said, nodding. The trouble with starting down a particularly dull conversational path is that it's hard to leap gracefully on to a better one.

I turned my attention to the puppy in my lap and looped the circle of my thumb and index finger around Fez's paw. This was just about the right paw size for the prints I'd seen. Holding the wiggly puppy, though, it occurred to me that puppies this young weren't steady on their feet and tended to take frequent rests. The tracks I'd seen had appeared to have come from a surefooted canine.

When I looked up from my study of the puppy's paws, John was watching me, and I realized I wasn't being much of a conversationalist. "How is Suds doing?"

"She's fine. Though she'd be a lot happier if we could get her into a homier environment."

"I can imagine," I murmured, weighing the pros and cons of volunteering my own residence.

He searched my eyes, that marvelous smile of his catching my attention again. "You . . . sound as though you're personally familiar with her."

"Is she nearby?" I asked quickly, wanting to deflect further questions for the moment, until I'd had the chance to assess Suds's status for myself.

"Yes. We're keeping her in the office for now, where it's quieter, but we're hoping to get her foster-adopted again very soon. Today, in fact."

He rose and held out his hands for me to return Fez to him. I stood up as well and reluctantly returned the little ball of fur to him. John was taller than I would have guessed him to be—an inch or two over six feet. Ah, well. Nobody's perfect. "We need to return this little guy to his mom."

I followed as he rounded the corner in the L-shaped room. This part of the room was sectioned off, and there sat Suds and her other four puppies. Suds looked at me and got up on all fours long enough for me to give her a quick pat. She was panting and began to pace the moment I stopped petting her. This was too small a quarters for such an active breed as a husky. She needed to get out of here.

The fifth puppy wiggled his way over to his brother and sisters. John showed me where the sink was, and we washed our hands with an antibacterial liquid at the sink in the office. Diseases such as kennel cough can spread so easily. He walked me back over toward his desk afterward.

"Allida Babcock," John said, again eyeing me at length. "That name sounds familiar to me."

"So does the name John White. Isn't that some sort of a wild bird?"

He chuckled. "No, that would be my brother, Bob White. Are you familiar with dog foster-care programs?"

"Yes, I am."

"Would you be willing to consider fostering Suds and family? We had a foster-adopt for them, but that didn't work out. I should tell you right off, though, that the mother is not up for adoption, only the puppies."

"I'm at least partially aware of these dogs' backgrounds. I live in Berthoud, directly across the street from Cassandra Randon."

He stiffened and lowered his gaze. "That was such a shock. Mr. Randon brought the dogs back yesterday. He told me about the circumstances."

"Did you know his wife?"

He lifted one shoulder in a half-spirited shrug. "Met her briefly, is all. She was at one of the lectures I gave the volunteers. But still, it's such a shock. This has never happened to us. Not since I've been here, anyway. To have a death in one of our adoptive families."

He was staring at me intently and looked away the moment I met his gaze. Just then I got the slightest sensation of something being wrong or off-kilter in his attitude. The feeling passed as quickly as it came, and I dismissed it as being the result of the subject matter. "Before I agree to foster the dogs myself, there are a couple of questions I'd like to ask."

"Fire away," he said, gesturing at the chair behind me while he reclaimed his own.

I pulled up a green upholstered desk chair on wheels that matched his own and sat down. Though this animal shelter was said to be better funded than others, this room, like the office at the Humane Society in Boulder, was furnished with secondhand furniture. The desks were old and scuffed, and the shelves that lined one wall had seen better days. The old metal file cabinets were open and in a state of some disarray. The computers, though, appeared to be in good shape.

"Cassandra told me that Suds's owner was currently in prison, and that's why he couldn't take care of her and the pups."

He raised an eyebrow. "That's not true. I wonder where she got that idea."

So did I. Perhaps Paul Randon had deliberately lied to his wife.

Chapter 7

Cassandra had told me that she'd gotten her information secondhand, from her husband, Paul, but there was no reason for me to bring him up now. "You mean the owner *isn't* in prison?"

"Not anymore. He was. Now he's at a halfway house. Mrs. Randon must have gotten the wrong impression. I thought I made it clear that he was in the process of getting reestablished after his release. His new landlord didn't mind putting up with the one dog, but objected to the five puppies."

Maybe Paul had simply slanted the information so that Cassandra would feel safer in thinking that the man was behind bars. "What was he in for?" I asked, my choice of phrasing making me sound to my own ear like some character on a cop show.

"Burglary, I think was the charge. Nothing . . . violent, if that's what you're thinking." John gave me a sheepish smile. "Not to put thoughts in your head. You have no reason to worry about Suds's owner ever coming into contact with you."

Now that he said that, I *was* worried. "What's Suds's owner's name?"

"I'm sorry, Allida, but we don't give out that information. All of our adoptions are handled confidentially. Every now and then we get someone who changes his mind about a pet he's put up for adoption after it's too late. We can't allow the new owner to have to risk getting harassed by the previous owner, or vice versa."

I studied John's handsome features. Something was bothering me, but I couldn't say what. Maybe it was John's nervous mannerisms, the way he kept shifting his vision to the door behind me as if he expected some monster to burst in at any given moment. "You did tell the police about him, though, didn't you? I mean, just in case he had anything to do with Cassandra Randon's murder."

"Of course. I called them the moment Mr. Randon came back with the dogs yesterday and told us what happened." He ran a hand over his tousled hair. "I have to admit that I was relieved when I spoke to the police again this morning and learned that Suds's owner had an alibi. I'd have felt partly responsible if he'd been involved in the murder somehow, knowing we had to have let security slip for Suds's owner to have been able to locate the Randons."

"The police told you that he had an alibi?" That was surprising to me. They seemed reluctant to tell *me* anything.

John raised his eyebrows at the question. "Come to think of it, they might've just been telling me that to appease me so that I'd stop bugging them." Again he was looking at the door as he spoke. He rose, and I started to get up myself, thinking he was leaving the room. He opened the door a crack, then sat back down. "Sorry. It's getting a bit stuffy in here. The sergeant from Berthoud . . . Millay, isn't it?" I nodded as he continued, "He assured me that the alibi was ironclad."

"And so you're absolutely confident that there is no risk whatsoever in allowing Suds to be foster-adopted again?"

"Absolutely. That the Randons happened to have recently gotten these dogs was nothing more than a horrible coincidence."

"Okay."

"So you'll foster them?"

"I'd be happy to."

"That's great, Allida. Thanks!" He gave me another of his wonderful smiles, his white teeth accentuating his even tan. "I'll get the paperwork together."

He started to walk me to the front desk. "What do you do for a living, Allida, if you don't mind my asking?"

"I'm a dog behaviorist in Boulder. Though I'm not technically making a 'living' at it. More like scraping by till I'm established."

His eyes lit up. "No wonder your name sounded so familiar. You do volunteer work for the shelter in Boulder, right?"

I was flattered that he'd heard of me. "Yes, I just recently started there."

"I hear you're excellent. How lucky for them."

He waited with me while I quickly filled out the forms and handed them to him. He scanned them for a moment, then asked, "You say you live in Berthoud?"

"Temporarily. I'm staying with my mother for a few weeks till I can find a rental in Boulder. In fact, I'll need to let my mother know we're having canine company for a few weeks."

"Is that going to be a problem?"

"Not with my mother. When I was growing up, she was every bit as likely to use the look-what-followed-me-home routine as I was."

He fidgeted with the papers in his hands, then smiled and said quietly, "Here's a thought. How about if you discuss this with her, and if she's game, I'll drive the dogs out to your place myself after work? Then maybe after they're settled in, you and I could go out for a drink or a late dinner. Are you interested?"

Was it just paranoia on my part, or could he be asking me out because he wanted to learn how much I knew about the murder? If I went out with him, I was either going to spend time with a handsome man who'd dedicated his life to working with dogs, or perhaps learn how much *he* knew about the Randons and Suds's ex-con owner.

"Sure. That sounds nice."

"Let's say I'll swing by around . . . eight o'clock tonight?"

"Okay. See you then."

He smiled, his brown eyes sparkling. "Super. I'm looking forward to it."

Something was dampening my spirits, though, as I drove away, and I found myself thinking of Russell. He and I had never discussed exclusivity, and our relationship was too new to even broach the subject. Still, he'd been such a doll last night, and here I was, not even twenty-four hours later, making a date with another man. Should I tell Russell about John?

This is why I'm just not cut out for dating. I don't enjoy it enough to warrant all of the baggage that comes with it.

In case my next destination needed to be Luellen's home in Campion, where I hoped to drag Sergeant Millay with me to help me retrieve Shogun, I pulled up to a public phone and called for my messages. I had one from Sergeant Millay, returning my call, and another from Russell, who said it was important, so I called him first.

He sounded so happy to hear from me that I immediately felt guilty. He said, "Allida, I just scored two tickets for a concert tonight that's been sold out for weeks. They're for the—"

"I'm not free tonight, Russell. I'm sorry. I've made plans."

"Plans?"

I could feel my cheeks growing warm. " 'Fraid so."

"Should I be worried?"

"Probably not."

"That's not quite the answer I wanted to hear. I was hoping you'd say it was a girl's night out tonight."

"It's not. Sorry. But you really have nothing to worry about."

After a pause, he said, his voice lower, "Let me ask you something. If I told you that, since you said no, I was going to ask someone my friends have been trying to fix me up with, would you be worried?"

"Yes, but I wouldn't change my plans. I don't let myself be that insecure."

"Fair enough."

"I hope whoever she is turns out to be a . . . cat, since I'm too fond of dogs to use the word as an insult."

Russell chuckled. "Have a miserable time tonight, Allida." He hung up.

You, too, I thought, feeling inordinately sad. I didn't want to hurt Russell and didn't want to string him along. Perhaps it was just as well that he meet someone he had more in common with, someone who enjoyed rock climbing and . . . cats.

Why was it that other people seemed to have such an easy time finding their life's mate?

I called Sergeant Millay, and this time I reached him. In tones as unapologetic as I could muster, I explained about locating Shogun at Luellen's house.

"You want me to come with you to a house in Campion just because you think the missing terrier is there?"

"Yes. I think that this dog might have left the paw prints at the murder scene."

"Even so, Miss Babcock, he's not going to be what we'd call a reliable witness."

I gritted my teeth and felt like giving the phone a good whack just because I couldn't do so to Sergeant Millay. "True, but you see, it's possible that whoever brought Shogun to this house in Campion was Cassandra's killer. Otherwise, why wouldn't Luellen admit that the dog was Shogun?"

After a pause, he said gruffly, "All right. But I'm only doing this because you're Marilyn's daughter and I realize you got some vested interest in finding this dog. There's no need for you to come with me. If the dog's there, I'll bring him back with me."

"You won't recognize him."

"Yeah, I will. Looks like a scrawny, hairy fox. I've got a picture. Mrs. Cunningham gave it to me."

"Luellen is a breeder. She's got twenty-some-odd silky terriers at her place. To the casual observer, they all look virtually identical. It'd be like recognizing the original out of twenty copies."

"Okay," he said somewhat curtly. "Meet you there in half an hour." He hung up.

The sergeant was in his car out front when I arrived, his head bent down as he hunched over his paperwork. I knocked on his window, and he slowly looked up. He got out of his car without a word and gave me a little you-first gesture. I rang the doorbell and noticed the sergeant's frown at the canned rhythmic barking that resounded instead of a bell.

Luellen opened the door. She was wearing the same casual outfit as before—slacks and a plaid blouse—including the wrist splints. She gave no indication of surprise at seeing me, nor at seeing Sergeant Millay, though he was in full uniform. A policeman at my door would have surprised me, had I been in her shoes.

I could tell by the ease in her mannerisms when we explained what we wanted that this was going to be a waste of time—that she'd relocated Shogun. She led us through her house and out back where her heated dog pens were located.

I studied each dog, looking for the same subtle variations in markings that Shogun boasted. There were a couple of dogs that were close, but not exact.

"That's all of my dogs. You've met every last one of them," Luellen said as we circled back and returned to her living room, where the eight dogs that she kept in the house were located.

"You were right about them all looking alike to me," Sergeant Millay muttered under his breath. "Did you find this dog you say belongs to the Cunninghams?"

I shook my head. "He's not here now."

"That's because he was never here in the first place," said Luellen. "I'm telling you, I haven't seen Shogun since I last visited Trevor, prior to their separation."

"Then where is Krumpet?"

"Krumpet?" she asked, maintaining her smile.

"That's right. Where is he?"

"He's right over there." She gestured at a dog sitting at the base of a brass floor lamp. "Krumpet, come," she said sternly.

The little dog ventured out hesitantly, then sat back down, clearly confused.

"That's not this dog's name," I said.

"It most certainly is."

Sergeant Millay, appearing half asleep, looked from me to her and back. I clicked my tongue and told him, "He didn't behave as though that was his name."

"He's not particularly well trained," Luellen countered.

I narrowed my eyes at her and she averted her gaze. That was nonsense, and she and I knew it. Few things were easier to teach a dog than his name.

"Watch this, Sergeant." I turned my attention to the dog she'd claimed was Krumpet. "Bingo, come," I called, hoping Sergeant Millay was paying close attention. "Krumpet" looked at me and cocked his head, dog-speak for "Huh?" Then he sat down, which was a sure sign that he didn't understand my command; almost without exception, dogs revert to the first command they learned—sit—when they're asked to do something they can't interpret.

"Okay, Sergeant, now contrast how this dog behaves with one who hears his real name being called." I looked over at the group of dogs across the room from me. Using a name she'd thrown out earlier during her cursory introductions, I called, "Toto, come." Though I hadn't been paying enough attention earlier to focus on which dog had this name, one trotted up to me with confidence.

"See, Sergeant? That's how a dog acts when you call him by his name." Just to drive the point home, I said, "Watch how he acts now." I took a couple of steps back. "Soapflake, come." He stayed put, looking at Luellen as if asking for her to translate for me. "That is how a dog behaves when summoned by a name other than his own."

"This is ridiculous, Sergeant. She's wasting everyone's time."

"Krumpet, come."

Still sitting on the floor, the dog made no move, but merely looked at me, then at his owner, in confusion.

"Did you notice how this dog's behavior emulated that of Toto's when I called him by the name Soapflake?"

Sergeant Millay rose. "Yeah, but Ms. Moore's got a point about this wasting my time." He pointed at the dog she'd claimed was named Krumpet and gazed at Luellen. "Is this dog Krumpet?"

"Yes, it is."

"And that's also the dog Miss Babcock here thought was Shogun?"

"Yes."

"Then we're sorry to have taken your time, ma'am. We'll be going now." I hesitated a moment, allowing Sergeant Millay to leave ahead of me.

"Where is Shogun now, Luellen?" I asked quietly, so that the sergeant couldn't overhear.

She fisted her hands and said through a tight jaw, "You bring a policeman to my house, accuse me of lying, hint at a connection to murder, then expect me to 'fess up?"

"I'm just trying to do the job I was hired to do."

She held my gaze, then said, "I hope that once Shogun reappears, you'll make the right decision and give him to Trevor." She ushered me out the door, where Sergeant Millay was waiting.

I strolled up to him. "Maybe I can't prove anything here, but I know what she did."

The sergeant turned on a heel and opened his car door. "I see. Well. Thanks for the information. We'll look into this matter further."

Sure he would. Sergeant Millay's face bore the same expression that had been so rampant on opponents' faces whenever I walked onto a basketball court in an unfamiliar setting. It was the look of not being taken seriously. I did the same thing now that I did then: smiled with knowledge that his expression would change once he realized I knew what I was doing.

The situation now was radically different. Then all I needed was the ball to show my opponents how badly they'd underestimated me. Now I needed to expose a killer and find a missing dog.

Before heading home, I wanted to get a take on Edith Cunningham. It would be interesting to see if she was as calm about Shogun still supposedly "missing" as Trevor had been.

I strained my memory to the maximum and recalled that I'd once heard the name of her clothing store. The name had the word "Country" and was on Mountain Avenue, the busiest street in downtown Berthoud.

I wasn't sure about Edith's logic in opening this particular type of a business in Berthoud. It wasn't that we Berthoudites don't buy nice clothes, it was just that, speaking for myself, anyway, clothing was not the sort of item that required the kind of convenience of a small, local place. There were excellent clothing stores in Fort Collins and in Boulder, which were both college towns and both within very reasonable drives from Berthoud.

I'd given Edith's business acumen more than enough thought by the time I found her sign on the front of a small building. The store was called Country Boutique Classics. I realized with a start that this building used to house the Haywoods' hobby shop when I was younger. I'd never ventured inside. You tend not to want to set foot in a store in which the proprietors act as though they would rather see you dead than alive.

Judging from the lack of customers, she might have been better off sticking with the Haywoods' hobbies. She was alone behind the oak and glass counter and mustered a smile when the little brass bell above her door jingled as I entered.

I'd never been in quite so uncluttered a store. Across a wide expanse of plush azure carpeting were only a few small display tables featuring a torso, invisible except for its blouse or sweater, and a small selection of items on each tabletop. Edith must have believed that seeing more than one of a particular item of clothing hinted at factory production. Along the back wall was the only actual rack, which again boasted only a few dresses, adorned with a sign that read, "The Latest from Paris." Why anyone in Berthoud, Colorado, would care about the latest Paris fashion was beyond me.

Edith, wearing a shimmery gold blouse and brown and

gold skirt, approached. Her short auburn hair appeared to have been recently curled. "Allida, hello. Before you ask, Shogun isn't here."

Her abrupt greeting surprised me. How did she know I was even looking for Shogun?

"Or are you here looking for something nice to wear? Maybe I can interest you in some designer clothing." She strode toward me. Suddenly she'd become a smiling sales-person, complete with the mannequin smile and movements. I took a step back.

"The clothes make the woman, Allida. If you want to run a successful business, you have to begin by looking the part. You want an outfit that says, 'I'm confident. Yet fun. Appealing.' After all, in your line of work, you have to be able to move freely."

I glanced at the discreet signs on the table beside me, which sported a half dozen styles of blouses. The small signs bore the names of the designers, which meant nothing to me. I pulled out the price tag of a blouse and nearly choked. "Sorry, Edith, but all these clothes will say on me is, 'I've overextended my budget.' I don't think I'd be able to afford this kind of quality. I'm just trying to get my business off the ground."

Just as though she'd decreased speeds in an internal blender, the intensity left her mannerisms and her face. She said sourly, "I know what that's like. Tell you what, though. We're just about to have an end-of-the-season sale. You'll have to come in then. All of our summer items will be marked down."

"Season-*ending* sale? But . . . this isn't even summer yet."

"You really are a newbie in the fashion world, aren't you? The things I could do for you, Allida. Image, as they say, is everything."

"Maybe I'd put more stock in that particular slogan if it were coming from a more credible source than Madison Avenue. Anyway, Edith, I *am* here to speak to you about Shogun."

"Good. I want to remind you that, despite the horrible

events at my house yesterday, I still need you to make a decision regarding Shogun's custody at the earliest convenience."

"Edith, I don't understand how you can ask me to decide custody of your dog when he's missing."

"Trevor kidnapped my dog. Probably even killed Cassandra in the process." She tucked the price tag of the blouse that I'd touched back out of sight as she spoke. "If committing murder and kidnapping aren't grounds for awarding custody to somebody else, I don't know what is."

"That may be true, but at this point, Edith, there is no dog."

"I'm sure he'll turn up." She realigned her display of sweaters, acting calm and blasé, as though she didn't have a care in the world.

"You don't seem terribly worried. It's almost as though you know where Shogun is."

"I do." She didn't look up from her compulsively neat sweater arrangement. "He's with Trevor."

"Not according to Trevor he's not."

"He's lying."

"You've seen Shogun over there? You know Trevor has the dog?"

"No, but I have it on very good authority. I spoke to a mutual friend of Trevor's and mine. She told me that she saw Trevor with Shogun at his place not even an hour ago." Her speech bore an undercurrent of barely suppressed rage that was more than a little daunting.

"Okay. In that case, I'll give him a call and see what he has to say about all this."

"No, don't bother, Allida. Everything is under control." She glanced at her watch. "Shall we reschedule yesterday's missed appointment at my place? Say, five-thirty tomorrow evening?"

"Are you sure you'll even be back in your house that soon? Last I saw, it was still cordoned off with police tape."

"I'll be back in tomorrow. And mark my word. I'll have my dog back from that lowlife I used to be married to by this time tomorrow if it's the last thing I do."

Chapter 8

As I left the "boutique," I realized I had plenty of time to see for myself if Trevor Cunningham had Shogun before I would need to get home for my date with John.

Trevor's current residence was a duplex just north of Longmont, some fifteen miles south of Berthoud. This particular section of town was a massive grouping of tan and brown cubes, one duplex a mere doghouse's width from the next. The yards were so small that the residents could water their lawns by tossing a glass of water out the window. If I were Shogun, I would certainly prefer Edith's spacious property in Berthoud.

I rang the doorbell. No answer. Also, no dog barks came in response to the ring. Neither Shogun nor Trevor was here. If Edith's "mutual friend" had given accurate information, Trevor could have the dog with him. At least equally possible, though, was the notion that Edith had been feeding me nonsense, and Trevor didn't have Shogun in the first place.

As I was leaving, Trevor's thirty-something female neighbor from the other half of the duplex emerged from her front door and padded down the concrete path toward me. She was thin—emaciated, even—with unusually wide-spaced gray eyes, and was exceptionally pale. She blinked and shielded her eyes as if she could barely tolerate the bright sunlight.

"Are you Edith?" she asked in a trembling voice, her face slightly averted as if she were afraid of me. She peered through her long but sparse bangs at me, her eyes wide. Despite the temperature of at least eighty degrees, she wore an oversized gray cardigan sweater that dwarfed her frail frame.

The woman's overall demeanor was so fearful that I was too curious to do the right thing and simply say no. "Hello, there. Trevor didn't answer the doorbell."

"No, he's still not home, just like I said. I'm so glad you got my message. I wasn't sure you'd check your machine before Trevor got back."

I made no comment, but gave her a reassuring smile.

She chewed on her lower lip and was a picture of nervous energy, still blinking almost compulsively as she watched the street as if primed to bolt at the first sight of a car. "He could be back any minute. I've got the dog, like you asked. But Edith, I've just . . . I'm so . . ." She paused, then shut her eyes and blurted, "I've got to tell you, I don't feel good about doing this. He doesn't even know I have a key to his place."

"You've got Shogun in your home?" I tried to keep my emotions in check, realizing that Edith, unlike me, would not have been taken aback by this odd bit of news.

She held up her palms. "I know you told me to wait and do it tomorrow, but if what you say about him is true, I didn't want to risk leaving the dog in his possession for another twenty-four hours."

"Huh. I can understand how you must have felt." Edith must have manipulated the woman into grabbing the dog, and the woman had done so a day ahead of Edith's schedule. Perhaps this was the "mutual friend" Edith had mentioned, who'd reported to her that Trevor had Shogun. If so, this "friend" didn't even know what Edith looked like. Edith must have gotten hold of the woman's number somehow and told her that Trevor had been abusing the dog. Though I didn't know either Trevor or Edith very well, I at least knew that Trevor Cunningham was not about to abuse his little dog.

"So can you take Shogun now? I did exactly what you said and opened a back window a couple more inches to make Trevor think the dog got out and ran away. But you've just got to get him out of here right away. Trevor's going to come over to my place the moment he sees the dog is missing. And sooner or later he'll hear Shogun bark through the common wall."

Though it was dishonest of me, there was only one way to make certain someone else didn't disappear with the dog. "Yes, it's fine. I'll take Shogun now."

"Oh, thank goodness." She smiled for the first time and straightened a bit. She went inside her place to get the dog.

I hated compounding Edith's deceit toward this kind-hearted, anxious woman with one of my own. As soon as she'd given Shogun to me, I would tell her who I was and explain that Edith had merely tricked her into believing Trevor was abusive to the dog.

Before I could give the matter more than a fleeting consideration, Edith's black Lexus came flying down the street. She must have heard the phone message that the woman had left for her.

Edith hit her brakes, the tires squealing in protest as a spray of dust went up. She left her car running and emerged from it without pausing to feign calmness or even dignity. It was probably too late for either pretense.

She gave a glance at the door of the woman's half of the duplex, then looked at me. Her facial expression made it obvious that the wheels were turning in her devious mind. "Oh, Allida. I see you're here. Good. I meant to tell you. Trevor's neighbor now has Shogun."

She gave a second glance at the neighbor's front door, where the woman was now emerging with Shogun in her arms, then force-fed me a smile. "So you and I can go back to our original arrangement. You can come over tomorrow to visit with Shogun and decide which of us gets the dog, now that I've located him."

She turned her attention to the puzzled-looking woman before us. "You must be Fiona. Hi. We spoke on the phone earlier. I'm Edith Cunningham. Thank you so much for rescuing my dog." She reached for Shogun.

Fiona stepped back, turning her shoulder to block Edith

from even touching the dog. "*You're* not Edith Cunningham."
She pointed at me with her chin. "*She* is."

Edith clicked her tongue and put her hands on her hips.
"No, she isn't. *I* am. Do you need me to show you my
driver's license?"

"She's telling the truth. I'm Allida Babcock, a dog psychologist."

Fiona seemed to shrink into herself, but continued to stare
at us through her bangs. She clutched the dog closer to her
chest.

"I'm very sorry, Fiona. The Cunninghams asked me to
determine which of them deserved the dog, and I let you
believe that I was Edith until I could ascertain that the dog
was safe. It'd be best, under the circumstances, if you gave
Shogun to me for the time being."

A car was slowing behind me, and I knew even while I
still had my back to the car that Trevor had come home.
Edith cursed, and indeed the driver of the approaching car
was Trevor. He took one look at the three of us standing out
front, deserted his task of putting his car in the garage, and
raced over.

He stepped directly between his neighbor and his estranged wife. "Fiona, what are you doing with Shogun? Give
him to me."

She started shaking her head, backing away from us. "You
people are crazy. You don't deserve this precious dog! None
of you do!" She shuffled into her home and shut the door. An
instant later, the metal click let us know that she'd thrown the
bolt. I'd have done the exact same thing in her shoes.

"Edith! What the—"

Edith whirled around and jabbed a finger at Trevor. "Don't
you even start! You tried to kidnap Shogun! I'll bet you even
killed Cassandra Randon!"

"I didn't kill anybody! Though I'd snap that toothpick
neck of yours like that"—he snapped his fingers in Edith's
face—"if I thought I could get away with it. And I *didn't*
kidnap Shogun. Luellen found him. I called her the moment I
found out he was missing. She drove out to look for him and

found him on Second Street a couple of blocks from the house." Trevor turned to me. "She'd already found him by the time I was talking to you and your mom, but I didn't know it at the time." He refocused on Edith and said harshly, "He was probably trying to find his way to *my* house to get away from *you*."

"You expect anyone to believe that?" Edith shouted, just as Trevor cried, "He could have gotten hit by a car!"

"As if it's my fault that *you* left the gate open!" Edith cried, opting to defend herself against Trevor's accusation of carelessness.

"How did you know the gate was open, unless you left it that way?" Trevor asked.

"The policeman told me, you moron! And I'm filing dog-napping charges against you!"

"There's no such thing. Even if there were, neither my sister nor I stole the dog. Luellen realized that Shogun would be best off with me, and so she kept him hidden away for a day. That's all there was to it. I was going to call you tomorrow and let you know that I had the dog, just as soon as the dust settled."

"Like hell you were!" Edith said with a snort. "You and Luellen stole Shogun. I was completely within my rights to ask your neighbor to help me get him back."

"You've got a lot of nerve accusing me of stealing the dog, when you coerce my neighbor into snatching Shogun out of my house!"

I'd heard more than enough of this and employed a seldom-needed talent I'd picked up as a kid and put two fingers from each hand in my mouth and let go with an ear-splitting whistle. The Cunninghams abruptly stopped arguing and covered their ears, wincing and eying me in surprise.

"Fiona is right," I said through a tight jaw the moment they'd lowered their hands. "You two *are* crazy for behaving like two-year-olds. And *I'm* crazy for agreeing to mediate this mess!"

For a blessed moment, they listened in silence.

I began again in calm tones. "Here is what we're going to do.

We're all taking a few deep breaths, then we're going to approach Fiona, on bended knee if need be, beg her forgiveness, and you are both going to assure her that you support my taking temporary custody of Shogun."

They both started to protest, but stopped when I held up my palms.

"If you don't agree to do exactly what I say, I am going to tell the judge at your divorce hearing that neither of you deserves this dog, and I'll insist that we find an alternative home for Shogun. Have I made myself clear?"

Since I'd given them no choice, they nodded and grumbled their compliance. I rang Fiona's doorbell. After a couple of minutes of groveling, we convinced Trevor's badly shaken neighbor to hand Shogun over to me.

Before anyone could change their minds, I drove off, telling the Cunninghams that they'd hear from me soon. Shogun, the poor dear, was so out of sorts that he was trembling in my arms. I broke a cardinal rule and allowed the dog to sit in my lap while I drove. I talked to him in soothing tones, but he was still visibly upset until he perked up as I pulled into my street. His little tail began to wag once I headed up the driveway, and he was clearly happy at being back in his neighborhood.

It occurred to me as I got out of the car that very soon John from the animal shelter was going to arrive with Suds and her five puppies, and here I was bringing home what would be guest dog number seven. I sure hoped Mom greeted my temporary canine housing with her usual good humor.

Leaving Shogun in the car for the moment so that I could give the dogs forewarning with what would be a powerful scent on my clothing, I entered through our garage. Mom's King Cab pickup was not there. I let the dogs in and allowed them to collect their data with their noses while I read the note Mom had left on the kitchen counter. She was at a friend's house and she'd be back soon.

I instructed the dogs to lie down and stay, then went out to the garage and got Shogun out of the car. The key to introducing a new dog to one's other dogs is to make it clear

from the start that this new dog is the bottom-runger. Therefore, rather than carrying Shogun, I put him down on the
garage floor, opened the door, and went in first, having him
follow me.

All three of my dogs—I considered Sage mine, though he
was technically Mom's—pricked up their ears, only Sage
badly trained enough to disobey my stay command and sit up.
With this being such a little dog, the trouble wouldn't come
from the dominant dogs, but from the lowest-runger, currently Sage, who had the least seniority in the house but was
rapidly gaining esteem because of Mom's clear preference.

Shogun shrank back against the already closed garage
door and began to assert his presence the only way a little dog
can—with loud barks. Meanwhile, I said, "Pavlov, okay,"
releasing her only from her position in the center of the
kitchen; then I greeted Pavlov with a big hug around her
strong shoulders. As top dog, if she accepted Shogun, the
others would likely follow suit.

With Doppler watching her every move, Pavlov sniffed at
Shogun and lay back down in her spot. Sage, too, seemed
willing enough to let him join the group, and Doppler was
generally gregarious with other dogs. They knew him
already, to an extent. Edith had been over with him yesterday
and they had met one another a few times during our walks
through the neighborhood.

I decided it would be best to leave the dogs alone for a
minute or two and went out front. I remembered then that I
still hadn't spoken to the Haywoods about the notepaper of
theirs and crossed the street to head to their home.

The curtains parted and Harvey looked out the second time
I rang the doorbell, his lips set in a frown that didn't fade
once he saw me. After a long pause, Mrs. Haywood came to
the door. She left the screen door shut and said, "Yes?"

I could see Harvey behind her, sitting at the kitchen table
in the background reading the paper, wearing his usual
sleeveless undershirt and brown slacks.

"I was wondering. This morning, you gave me your

daughter's address on a magenta sticky-pad sheet. Do you happen to remember where you got that paper?"

"Harvey!" she hollered over her shoulder.

"What?" he responded, equally loudly, not looking up from his reading.

"The Babcock girl wants to know where you got the paper you wrote that note on."

"What note?"

Betsy narrowed her eyes. "Harvey wants to know why you want to know."

Actually, that wasn't at all what "Harvey" wanted to know, but I wasn't about to challenge her on the point. Nor did I wish to divulge that their paper matched the note on the Cunninghams' door, so I said, "I just liked the color and would like to get a couple of pads for myself, but haven't been able to find it at any of the stationery stores nearby."

"You hear that, Harvey?"

"I don't know what she's yappin' about," he called back, rattling his newspaper in irritation.

"We wouldn't know where to tell you to go. We don't do our own shopping no more. Susan does that for us."

"So she bought the notepad for you?" I asked, knowing full well that Susan had said she *hadn't* bought it.

"Must have," Betsy said with a shrug. "It just showed up on our counter."

"Recently? Did you ever see it prior to yesterday afternoon?"

"I don't remember." She gave a heavy sigh at the overwhelming inconvenience of it all, then asked, "Harvey, you ever see that pad of paper in a drawer or something before the Babcock girl come over here asking about Susan?"

"I don't know, Betsy! I got better things on my mind than pads of paper!"

"So do I, Harvey! It's the Babcocks that want to know!"

This was getting me nowhere. Over the sound of the Haywoods' continued bickering, I called, "Thank you for your time, Mrs. Haywood."

Frustrated, I returned home and took the dogs out for their exercise and training, which was one of my favorite parts of the day—theirs, too. I decided it might be fun to include Shogun and see how he could do against their standards of training. I played a game of fetch with each dog in turn.

Sage still had some catching up to do as far as his training went; he hadn't been with us for long, but he was such an intelligent dog that he was making fast strides. Shogun would immediately run out after the ball, not understanding that he had to wait for his name. He would glance around nervously, eyeing the other dogs, understanding that there was something he wasn't getting about this game, but not sure what it was.

During his chase of the tennis ball, Shogun ran through a muddy puddle by the fence, which immediately gave me an idea. Knowing Mom would forgive me, I ran all four dogs through the mud, then up onto the back deck. I was studying the tracks they made when Mom arrived. She slid open the back door and, without comment, watched me studying the muddy mess I'd encouraged the dogs to make.

Finally I looked up at her. She smiled and said, "You found Shogun?"

"Yes, and I'll give him back to one of the Cunninghams in another day or two."

"I see we're studying animal tracks."

Seeing the deck anew, I realized what a muddy mess the dogs had made, thanks to me. "Sorry, Mom. I'll get the hose and rinse off the dogs' paws before I let them back in."

"Did this teach you anything?"

I laughed and said, "I hope you're not expecting me to answer, 'Neatness counts.' "

Mom rolled her eyes. "I meant about the paw prints you saw the other day. Were they Shogun's?"

"No. The paw prints over at Edith's place weren't Shogun's. They were from a larger dog, Doppler's size. Only they weren't Doppler's, of course. He was inside the house or our fence all day."

"Does that mean it was one of the puppies?"

"Could be, but I don't think so. The tracks didn't strike me as having come from an unsteady young puppy. I might know for sure once they're here."

She raised an eyebrow. "Once they're here?"

Oops. I gave her a sheepish smile. "Is it all right if we foster the husky and her puppies for three weeks?"

She spread her hands. "Just let me know if you're going to turn my bedroom into a kennel, so I'll have time to pack up a few mementos."

"Thanks, Mom. I really appreciate your being so under-standing."

"Ah, comes with the turf. Muddy though it may be. Let's get these dog paws washed off."

Mom was unusually aloof when John White arrived with Suds and her puppies. I didn't know if that was because she took some sort of instant dislike to John, or if she was feeling put out by suddenly finding herself with ten dogs.

Prior to their arrival, Mom and I had set up a nice area for them in the basement, giving them the run of the laundry room, and the three of us now watched them settle in. Suds was obviously a little worse for the wear, having been moved so frequently in the past couple of days. Her puppies, how-ever, seemed complacent, quickly curling up against one an-other to sleep on the fleece blankets we'd laid down for them.

"They seem to be happy enough," John said to me. "Are you still up for going out for a drink together?"

"Sure." I tried to feign more enthusiasm than I felt. Though he hadn't changed a bit with his rugged, tanned features and his hair somewhat in need of a trim, he somehow didn't seem to be as handsome as he had been just a couple of hours ago. He was still wearing the same casual clothes he'd worn at work, sans the forest-green employee vest he'd worn earlier over his striped shirt. Strangely, I was finding myself thinking about Russell, wondering how his concert was going. And what this woman his friends had wanted to fix him up with was like.

As we started up the stairs, Mom said to John, "My

daughter tells me you're the kennel supervisor up at the shelter in Loveland."

"Yes. Have you seen our facilities?"

"No, though I've given substantial financial donations to it."

He gave her one of his brilliant smiles. "Then I'm a major fan of yours. Come on up anytime, and I'll take you on a personal tour."

"I'll take you up on that sometime." Mom wore a feeble smile that faded quickly.

"Great. I promise we'll roll out the red carpet."

We reached the front door, which we'd left wide open. As John started to open the screen door, Mom said, "I'm concerned about the coincidence between Suds's previous adoptive owner getting murdered the very day she got the dogs. Did you ever meet Suds's owner?"

"No, he, or some concerned citizen, had just called animal services, and they contacted us." He hesitated as he looked at Edith's place, kitty-corner to ours, where the yellow police tape was still in place. He pointed with his chin. "That must be the Randons' house, hey?"

"No, that's the Cunninghams' house."

"Really? I assumed . . ." He didn't complete his thought, but turned toward my mother, who was standing back, watching us with crossed arms. "It was nice meeting you, Mrs. Babcock."

"You, too."

"Let us know if you have any questions or concerns about the puppies."

She nodded, but frowned at me. Her expression made me finally take stock of what I was doing. "Oh, Mom. I'm sorry. I wasn't thinking. I shouldn't have dropped all these dogs on you, then be immediately leaving you alone with them."

She chuckled. "Think nothing of it. My house is your . . . kennel."

"I'll be back soon," I said, feeling guilty.

"Don't worry." She gave me a friendly wave and closed the door behind us.

I instantly worried about her.

My date with John had all of the typical awkwardness of a first date. He was the opposite of Russell in terms of interests, a man who appreciated dogs every bit as much as I did and wasn't into rock climbing. Yet I found myself thinking of Russ and wondering what he was doing now. Probably enjoying his concert, with the bimbo date of his hanging on his every word. I spent some time considering the reasons that Russell was better off without me and quickly came up with a new one: I was selfish and unfair. It had been my decision, not his, to go out with someone else tonight.

John ordered us a pitcher of beer and we sat in the dark bar, the smoke stinging my eyes. Secondhand smoke was one thing I didn't have to deal with in Boulder, with its anti-smoking ordinance. I shot John an occasional question— "How did you get involved with dogs?" "What's your job like?" "How long have you lived in Fort Collins?"—and he would go on at great length.

He said several times how much more comfortable and better he was at communicating with dogs than people, which was a sentiment I could relate to, but seemed odd considering how loquacious he was. At least when it came to talking about himself. It occurred to me that I'd told him next to nothing about myself, but decided that that was okay.

As I'd expected, John eventually brought up the subject of the Randon family and the puppies. "I wonder why Cassandra was killed at your neighbor's house," he said. "That strikes me as strange."

"Me, too." I wanted to volunteer as little as possible to gauge how anxious he seemed to be to pump *me* for information.

He held my gaze as if waiting for me to go on, then said, "Your mom isn't superstitious, is she? She isn't worried about the puppies being cursed or something, is she?"

"Of course not. But we'll both feel a lot better once the killer is behind bars."

"Just assure her that there's no way anyone from the animal shelter will give out any info regarding Suds and puppies' new whereabouts. So you'll be perfectly safe from him."

"I'll tell her that."

He studied my face, then asked, "Did you know Cassandra very well?"

"No, just to say hello to."

"You didn't know who she hung out with? That sort of thing?"

"No. Why?"

"Just curious. This is the first time I've ever met someone who wound up being murdered. Must make you feel real . . . tense. Living so close to where it happened."

He flashed me what might have been intended as a casual smile, which I didn't return. Once again, I was getting strange vibrations from John. Now all I wanted to do was leave. He finished the last swig from his glass, then asked if we should get a refill. I declined and we left.

It was later than I'd thought. By the time we arrived at home, the porch light was on but the house lights were off.

We shared that miserable awkward pause as John walked me up to the porch. "This was fun," he said. "We'll have to do this again soon. Can I call you again?"

I studied his handsome features and assured myself that I'd merely been hypersensitive; he hadn't said anything at all to justify my suspicions. "That'd be nice."

"Do you need me to come in and check on the dogs or anything?"

That was the exit line I needed. "No, I'm sure they're fine. Thanks, though. I'll give you a call in another day or two to let you know how they're doing." I let myself into the house and gave John a good-bye wave instead of a kiss.

Doppler was in his carrier, which doubles as his bed, but I had to shush Shogun—loose in the kitchen—and Suds, who'd run upstairs from the basement to bark at me through the front door. This, in turn, got Pavlov and Sage barking. If

Mom had managed to sleep through my opening the door, she was certainly wide awake now.

Once they'd finally quieted down and I'd closed Suds and pups downstairs, I tiptoed to Mom's bedroom and peeked in, glad to see that she appeared to be asleep, after all. I settled down on the living room couch, stroking Pavlov's head while Sage lay down at the opposite end of the couch. Too wound up to go to bed myself, I flipped on the TV, keeping the volume low.

I was only half paying attention to a late-night talk show when I heard a noise in the kitchen. It sounded like the click of metal against glass. This was where Doppler's kennel happened to be, so he immediately started growling.

Beside me, Pavlov snapped to alert. I hit the mute button on the television.

There it was again. A metallic sound, coming from the direction of the kitchen.

My pulse started to race. I assured myself that it was probably nothing. A tree branch scraping against the window, perhaps.

Sage, who hadn't been trained not to bark, let out some loud woofs and raced off in the direction of the sound. Shogun began yipping at the top of his lungs and galloped after Sage. Meanwhile, Pavlov stood up and looked at me.

There was another noise, too metallic and deliberate-sounding to be a tree branch. A neighbor recently murdered, now someone was outside our house? Shit!

"Pavlov, guard!"

She instantly raced out of the room, giving her guard-dog barks as she went to join Sage and Shogun.

Doppler was whining, while I, heart pounding, crept around the corner into the kitchen. It was ludicrous to expect my cocker spaniel to be quiet in his kennel, and I didn't want to take the time to lock him in now. "Doppler, okay." My command put him in charge of his own behavior, and he immediately rushed out his unlocked kennel door to join the other two.

Leaving the lights off, I scanned the room. The dogs were

barking at the window. The moment they saw me, they rushed to the door to be let out.

Should I release them? What if this was just a raccoon? Mom had had more than a little trouble with raccoons over the last several years.

I stared at the window, trying to decide why something about it struck me as wrong. I realized with a start that the screen was now absent.

Mere inches from mine, a man's face popped into view from outside the kitchen window, then dropped back down.

Chapter 9

Startled out of my wits, I jumped and let out a little scream. My heart thumped so hard that I could barely breathe. The man's face had been dimly lit and he'd ducked down so quickly that I barely caught sight of his features, except to see that he was bald.

The dogs were barking at the back door, desperate to get out and at the man, Shogun adding his high-pitched yip to my dogs' more intimidating barks. Their noise had roused Suds as well, who'd run up the basement stairs, her loud woofs audible through the door. She, at least, was closed off in the basement, and I decided to leave her there with her puppies.

Despite his vociferous protestations, I swept Shogun up into my arms and slid open the back door. Doppler, too, would only get in the big dogs' way, but there was no time to grab him.

Baying, the dogs raced around the corner. Led by Pavlov who, though normally gentle, was a formidable watchdog, the dogs would put fear into any trespasser's heart.

What if this was the killer? And what if he was armed?

Standing to one side of the glass door, I listened fearfully for a gunshot. I'd never be able to stop myself from rushing out there to protect my dogs if the man actually were to open fire on them.

My hand was frozen on the handle of the sliding glass door, my other arm clutching Shogun tightly against me.

I heard the soft footfalls of my mother as she padded barefoot into the kitchen. Mom was pale, her braids undone so that her long brown hair hung loose around her shoulders. "Allie," she said in a half whisper, "what's going on?"

Outside, from the direction of the window over the sink, a male voice cried, "Hey! Get away from me! Get back!"

I was too scared about the possibility of the dogs getting hurt to pay attention to my mother. Still carrying Shogun, I raced back to the window over the sink and caught sight of a man running awkwardly toward the front gate. He was thrashing wildly at the air with some object.

"Oh, God," I said in a half whisper. "Please, don't let that be a knife."

"Who's out there?" Mom asked, now at my side.

Fortunately, the dogs were keeping a few feet back from the man, pursuing him and barking in wild excitement, but not preventing his progress as he made his way toward the gate in the front.

"I don't know. Some man. He was at the window just a moment ago."

The man slammed the gate shut. "Thank God. They chased him off. But maybe we should call nine-one-one anyway."

Mom rushed to the phone. "I'll call."

Just as she picked up the handset, someone started pounding on the door.

We exchanged glances, utterly confused. "Hold off on your call. I'll see who it is." I wondered if the trespasser could have run from the yard, only to knock on the front door. That was beyond bizarre, but the timing left few other possibilities.

Shogun was still agitated and struggling to get free. I didn't want to risk his darting out the door, and kept a tight grip on him as I looked out the peephole. Betsy Haywood was knocking on the door. She wore her standard housecoat and the scowl that made the deep lines on her face look all the harsher.

"It's Mrs. Haywood," I told my mom, who was waiting in the kitchen entranceway, receiver in her hand, for word regarding who'd been knocking. "Maybe she knows what's going on." Mom dropped the phone back into its cradle.

I released Shogun and swung open the door, with Shogun keeping up a rat-a-tat bark at Betsy Haywood, who ignored him completely.

Betsy pointed a bony finger in my face. "What the hell did you think you were doing? You had no right!"

"What are you talking about?"

"Siccing your dogs on my poor Harvey, that's what! He just got confused. I was on my way over here to fetch him and saw him running for his very life! If you'd given me just one more lousy minute, I'd have had him back home with me."

"You're yelling at me because I sent the dogs into my own *fenced* backyard? Give me a break! Someone was trying to pry open our kitchen window. I let the dogs out into the yard to protect us. If that was your husband, he's the one who should be explaining himself to *us*."

"Why, you little ingrate! You young people have got no respect for your elders!"

"Not when they're committing criminal offenses, I sure don't!"

Putting a hand on my shoulder to calm me, Mom said in placating tones, "Betsy, there's no need to get upset at my daughter. It sounded as though someone were trying to break into our house."

"It was just Harvey. He . . . sleepwalks."

"He pries people's windows open in his sleep?" I asked incredulously.

She continued as if she hadn't heard, "But you didn't have to go and have those monster dogs of yours try 'n' eat him alive!"

"Betsy?" came a raspy voice from behind her. Harvey appeared on the porch next to his wife, which caused Shogun to turn up his relentless high-pitched bark by another notch or two. Harvey's face was damp with perspiration and his cheeks were flushed. I noticed immediately that he was fully dressed, including shoes. If he was sleepwalking, he had to have been a sleep "dresser" as well, or have fallen asleep fully clothed. "What are you doing over here at this hour?"

Betsy didn't answer. Harvey turned his gaze on me and

shook his head sadly. "I'm sorry to tell you this, Marilyn, but you've simply got to control those kids of yours!"

"Harvey! This is Allida." Betsy's voice was rife with exasperation and her cheeks colored. "Marilyn is standing right behind her."

Though Betsy pointed at my mother, Harvey continued speaking to me. "If you can't control that son of yours, we're going to have to call the police. He put Super Glue all over my daughter's shoes. Did he tell you that? Did he?"

My mother looked at me in confusion, which I could only mirror. "I'm sorry about my son's behavior," my mother said kindly to Mrs. Haywood. "I'll make sure he never does it again."

"See? That's all we needed to do, Betsy! I tol' you. Even the Babcocks can be reasonable if you try to communicate with them."

Betsy turned in a huff and said under her breath, "Keep your mouth shut, Harvey! They'll have you thrown in the loony bin, if you don't watch it. Which is where you deserve to be."

We shut the door behind them, the Haywoods hissing at each other, but walking arm in arm back to their home. I turned and looked at Mom, who was staring after our neighbors with a grim expression.

His all-around bizarre behavior and his having mistaken me for my mother left me feeling slightly sick to my stomach. I retrieved the dogs and let Suds come upstairs. She'd been barking periodically throughout our dealings with the Haywoods. Once the dogs had quieted, I asked my mother, still standing in the living room, "Do you think Harvey could have Alzheimer's?"

"Maybe so, though that would have to be in addition to the alcohol. Harvey drank himself out of that store of his."

"He did?" Now that I thought about it, the concept of his having been a heavy drinker didn't surprise me in the least. "I always found it odd that he, of all people, ran a hobby shop. He didn't seem to have any hobbies of his own, plus he hates people, especially children."

"It is ironic."

"So you think he might just have been drinking too much tonight?"

"Maybe."

"Has he ever done anything like this before?"

"Not for years." Mom sank into the couch, and I leaned back against the arm of the upholstered chair near her. "When you and your brother were just young kids, you slept through a couple of incidents . . . times when he'd wander over here. I'd see him pacing around in the backyard. Stumbling around was more like it, really. It would upset the dogs, of course, and scare the dickens out of me. That was before the days of nine-one-one, but I told Andy Millay about it. He talked to Harvey on my behalf, and Harvey's nocturnal wanderings stopped."

"When was this?" I asked, slightly offended that she'd never mentioned this to me in all these years.

"A couple of months after your father had died. I got the impression that, once he got too full of liquor, Harvey was taking it on himself to act like he was running the entire neighborhood."

"But he hasn't done that in some twenty-five years? And now he's taking to trying to pry our windows open as well?"

Mom frowned. "It does sound more than a little odd. Maybe he's just acting drunk or incoherent to cover up his actions, once he's already been caught in the act. All I know is that his DUI charges led to his getting his driver's license revoked last year. Then the bank foreclosed on his store. That's when he and Betsy decided to close up shop."

"Huh. I guess that was pretty lucky for Edith. She got to rent his store, which was in a prime location."

"Yes. The retail space she'd been renting earlier had been half the size at twice the cost."

"I'm surprised that Harvey didn't resent Edith for that."

"Oh, he did. Still does, in fact. You know the way that man holds on to a grudge."

I silently wondered if he had any grudges against Cassandra Randon. And what possible motive he might have had for trying to break into our house.

The next day I got my first opportunity to work with Boris, the schipperke that belonged to Susan Nelson. My plan was that as soon as the opportunity presented itself, I would ask her about her father's behavior the night before.

Susan and I stood in her messy living room, watching the dog whip through the house like a Tasmanian devil. Although he would stop by Susan's feet, he seemed to think that "sit" meant simply touching his haunches down, then off he'd go again.

"First and foremost, Boris is in need of some basic training. I highly recommend that you buy a clicker and a Gentle Leader. I've got extras in my glovebox, which I'll sell you at cost, if you're interested."

"At cost? Meaning what you paid for them?"

"Right. They aren't expensive, and they are absolutely invaluable."

She came outside with me to look at the training items. Then we rounded her dilapidated house to work with Boris in the backyard. It was going to be a scorcher today; not even ten A.M. and the temperature was over eighty degrees.

I showed Susan the clicker, a rectangle an inch thick and wide and two inches or so long, with a circle cut out for the thumb to access the metal noisemaker inside. I rarely use the clicker for my own dogs now that they're well trained, though I don't admit that to clients.

"This method was initially developed by a trainer of dolphins at Sea World. It gives the animal immediate feedback, indicating precisely what you want. For example, the trainer can click the moment the dolphin reaches the highest point of its jump, so that the dolphin realizes the trainer wants it to go high."

"Huh," Susan said, snapping her chewing gum. "If only Boris were as smart as a dolphin, I'd be more optimistic. Unfortunately, he's dumb as a doornail." She knelt and stroked his black fur good-naturedly as she spoke. "You saw him trying to catch the rainbow from the crystal."

I had also seen that Susan hadn't even figured out that the rainbow was what Boris was trying to catch, though that had struck me as obvious. It was something of a matter of opinion regarding which party was the less intelligent. But no sense in alienating a client, even though this one wasn't paying. "I've heard the clicker method works on almost all species, except snakes and other deaf animals."

"Snakes are deaf? That can't be true. What about snake charmers that get 'em to dance?"

By now Boris was trying to get into the shade for a nap, and I couldn't say that I blamed him. When would I learn not to delve into mini-lectures about my techniques? "Snake charmers use vibrations, I think. Anyway, let's do a few minutes of basic training here."

I took a couple of steps, then said, "Boris, come." He took a step toward me, mostly out of curiosity, but I clicked, then gave him a treat. I did the same with the sit command. "Notice how I made the noise the very instant that the dog rose, then again when he sat down. Dogs need immediate feedback."

I ran through a quick come-sit, come-sit routine a few times, using the clicker and tidbits. "Pretty soon, Boris will catch on that good things happen every time he hears that click. Then he'll put it together that he hears the click each time he does what his trainer tells him to."

"That's pretty simple. I think I can handle it."

"Next I'll show you how to get the Gentle Leader on him. That's really important when you're training, because it fastens around the muzzle and controls the dog's head position. Where the head goes, the dog necessarily follows. It's an outstanding way to teach leash training, as well as to teach the dog not to jump up on you, and so forth. Some dogs are so easily distracted that this is about the only way to keep them focused. A gentle tug on the leash forces them to look straight at you."

I went through the procedure of putting on the collar using

tidbits to get him to put his muzzle through the leash, and we waited through the typical period of the dog struggling to pull his collar off. Some dogs are so persistent with this that they flop around like a hooked fish, but the Leader doesn't hurt and is in no way a muzzle.

Once he'd calmed down enough, we resumed the training. At the same time, I explained, "The keys to successful training of a dog are consistency and putting the time in each day. I wouldn't overdo it with him, though. Just a couple of fifteen-minute-a-day periods should work wonders with his behavior. But don't allow anyone else to get hold of the clicker and play with it or use it for anything other than training Boris. Dogs can't extrapolate the way we humans can and conclude that the click means nothing unless x and y are also happening."

"Yeah, yeah. I get it." She watched me as we expanded into a lie-down-and-stay. I was really pleased with how quickly Boris was catching on, but just as I handed the clicker to Susan, she gave me a haughty sneer. "So, this is what you do for a living? You click a little plastic thing at a dog and you charge people a pile of dough?"

"Yes," I shot back, "and the benefit of working with dogs instead of people is that my canine clients never insult me."

She shrugged. "I'm in a foul mood, I guess."

"Which shouldn't qualify me as a target. If you would rather not continue with our agreement, we can end this right now."

"Nah. Sorry. Like I said, it's just that I'm in a bad mood. The parents of that little girl who was over here yesterday canned me. They found a day-care center that could save them a few bucks."

At the mention of a "little girl," I thought of Melanie and worried about her, but replied only, "That's too bad. I know you needed the money."

She shrugged and pushed at her curly head of hair. "It's a dog-eat-dog world."

An expression I've never cared for, but I said nothing. Drat. I wouldn't have minded if she'd said to forget our agreement. Sure, I'd been anxious to work with a new-to-me breed, but Susan herself was every bit as uncooperative and demanding as she'd been more than twenty years ago. On the other hand, she and her parents were perhaps the likeliest suspects in Cassandra's murder, and my continuing work with her and Boris might just lead me to uncover some clue that I could pass along to the police.

Boris was an interesting character, I thought as I removed the Gentle Leader. He had a real stubborn streak when it came to taking direction and yet was also playful. As was so often the case, I liked the canine much more than the owner.

Partway through my supervision of Susan's use of the clicker, a squirrel ventured into the yard behind Susan, and Boris tried to go straight through his owner in his anxiousness to get at it.

"Your dog shows strong aggressive tendencies."

"Do tell," Susan said with a sigh. "That's probably the main reason the girl's parents canceled. After you left yesterday, Boris grabbed hold of the skirt on her dress and wouldn't let go. I had to pry his jaws apart, and the fabric got torn. I wound up having to offer to sew her a whole new one for free, but they wouldn't hear of it. Their loss. I'm one hell of a seamstress."

A dog grabbing on to a little girl's dress was a much more serious problem than anything I'd witnessed so far and my mood immediately switched accordingly. Nothing bore the potential for disaster like a small child versus a badly trained or aggressive dog. "Boris's behavior has to be curtailed immediately, especially if you intend to baby-sit at your home. That means you've got to train him not to give chase, such as to squirrels or to cars."

"How?"

"The instant you spot something he's going to chase, you distract him with something he enjoys more. Next time you see him spot a squirrel, before he can chase it, call him to you, use the clicker, give him a treat. Or you engage him in a favorite game, so long as it's not tug-of-war. That's only encouraging him to grab and pull, like he did with that girl's dress."

"But I always win when we play tug-of-war. He's just a little dog, and I'm stronger."

"And once you get the item from him, what do you do with it?"

"I toss it and won't grab it again."

"Then, by Boris's way of looking at the world, he's won. He who winds up with the toy wins."

"Huh."

"Furthermore, even if you consistently 'win' at tug-of-war, Boris might seek to challenge a smaller, inferior opponent, such as a child. And you've got to be consistent with the rules. Dogs are eager to please their owners; they just need to know exactly what they're supposed to do."

I needed to make sure both Susan and her husband understood the importance of curbing Boris's aggression. "Is there a good time for me to come back to speak to your husband?"

"No, he's . . . out of town for the day."

She spoke so hesitantly that I began to wonder if she was telling the truth. "It would be best if I could work with him and Boris at least once. Is there a good time for me to come back and find him?"

She shrugged. "You could try tomorrow afternoon. It's possible he'll be back by then."

Boris finally gave up on his pursuit of the squirrel and returned to us. I worked with him with renewed interest. When Susan's eyes seemed to be glazing over from my dog-behavior talk, I said, "By the way, your father scared me half to death last night."

Her eyes widened but she made no comment.

"He was over peering into our kitchen window and had removed the screen. Your mother said he was sleepwalking, but—"

Susan furrowed her brow. "Dad's having a hard time accepting his retirement."

"I hear that's quite common with retirees. But what would

his adjustment problems have to do with his poking around our property?"

"Mom says he goes on a lot of walks at night these days. He fancies himself as something of a vigilante. He's harmless."

"But Susan, our neighbor was murdered a couple of days ago. It isn't safe for him to be wandering around like that." Nor was it safe for anyone else, when no one knew for sure that Harvey wasn't the killer.

"I'll talk to Mom." She glanced at her watch. "Listen, Allie, I gotta get going. I promised a girlfriend in Boulder I'd come over ten minutes ago. I'll call your mom before the end of the day to schedule when she wants me to mow your lawn."

"No rush. The grass isn't that long yet."

"I want to keep even. But this had better be the last time. I think I have changed my mind, after all."

"Excuse me?"

"I think we'd better cancel our arrangement. I don't know if I want to keep the clicker and the special dog collar yet. I'll either pay you for them or give 'em back in a couple days."

"Is this sudden change of heart because of what I told you about your father's actions last night?"

"No. Jeez, what gave you that idea? Listen, I really have to get out of here."

"Okay. Sorry things didn't work out."

Susan locked her front door while I got into my car, surprised and confused by her rapid change of heart. Her mood swing seemed to occur directly after I'd mentioned her father's behavior last night.

Feeling suspicious, I drove to the nearest intersection and parked to watch for Susan's car. My discomfiture only increased moments later when I spotted her. She turned not toward Boulder, but toward Berthoud.

Chapter 10

Susan had given me the impression that she knew more than she was telling. I replayed our conversation in my head as I drove to my office. Could she know what her father was up to last night? Could he have been trying to steal something out of the house, such as some piece of evidence that he thought I had? Or was he after the puppies? None of the possibilities made any sense to me.

When I got to my office, the phone was ringing. I answered.

"Allida," my mother said excitedly, "guess who just called me."

"Uh, Michael Jordan?"

"No," she said testily. "Your friend Tracy Truett."

"That's nice. What's she up to?"

"Well, the new owners of KBXD are reviving her show."

"Great. I'm glad to hear that." I'd met Tracy when she'd hosted me once on her talk show. She was the sort of person who enjoyed stirring up trouble, but she was basically a good—albeit loud—person with a great sense of humor, and I enjoyed her company. At least, in short doses.

"She wants you to be on her show. She thought she might be able to generate a little extra business for you if you'd be her first guest."

"Really? I'm honored. When is she on the air?"

"Today. Right now, in fact. She said you could just pop your head in there anytime."

Today? This began to strike me as suspicious. It sounded as though Tracy was awfully eager to have me on the show, given that she merely wanted me to talk about general dog-behavior tips. "I wonder why she didn't call me at my office."

"She said she already tried and couldn't reach you there. Oh, and she also wants to recruit both you and Russell for the softball team that the station is sponsoring."

"Okay. Thanks for the message. Listen, Mom, maybe you can do me a favor. I got some odd vibrations from Susan Nelson, the Haywoods' daughter. She got really flustered when I told her about Harvey's behavior last night, and I suspect she's going to confront him. I wonder if you can watch for her car and tell me if she shows up there soon."

"A beat-up Galaxy 500? She just arrived a moment ago in such a hurry that she got the dogs barking."

"Already? She must have been doing eighty miles an hour. You haven't had any more incidents from the Haywoods since I've been gone, have you?"

"No. As far as I know they're sleeping late, as usual."

"I wish I knew what was going on with that family."

"Me, too. I called Sergeant Millay and told him about our confrontation last night. He said he'd talk to him."

"Did the sergeant give you any signals as to whether or not he still considered me a suspect?"

There was a pause. "Allie, you've got to trust me when I say that Sergeant Millay is both intelligent and diligent. If he seriously thought you were a murderer, he'd be hounding you mercilessly."

" 'Hounding' me? He's a cat lover," I muttered. More likely he was the type to keep watch from a distance and pounce on me.

We said our good-byes, then hung up. My telling Susan about her father's attempted break-in had obviously upset her. The incident hadn't done much for my spirits, either, and I had a feeling we'd never learn what he'd been up to.

I turned my thoughts to Tracy Truett and pictured her strong, broad face beneath her short dyed-blond hair in its typical wet-looking kinky spikes. The thought of joining her softball team was appealing. Despite my lack of height, I'd played point guard on my college basketball team and enjoyed team sports. I'd never discussed softball with Russell, but maybe this would prove to be a common interest.

What hit me as odd was that this was a Thursday, yet now Tracy wanted me as a "first guest." The show had to have started on a Monday, and Tracy had not been so anxious to get me on the show as to have invited me then. She knew I lived in Berthoud, and she would have read the articles in this morning's papers about the murder. Was Tracy's sudden interest in me related to the murder?

I had three messages on my machine and pressed the button to listen. The first recording was in Tracy's deep, melodious voice:

"Hey, Allie. It's Tracy. Is it true that you found the body of that woman out in Berthoud? Call me. I've got something important to discuss. I think we can generate a lot of business for—"

I knew it. She wanted me on her show to talk about the murder. I pressed the forward button. The next two messages were from Tracy as well. Each was urging me to call her at the station right away, that she had a great idea for something that would generate interest in both her new show and my business. This was trouble.

My agitation already rising, I flipped channels on the portable radio I keep in my office and found KBXD. Tracy Truett was saying, ". . . got the fright of her lifetime yesterday when she not only found her neighbor dead in a grisly murder scene, but discovered paw prints in the blood that might allow the police to help solve this murder."

Paw prints? How the hell had she found out about that? Seething, I dialed her number at the station. Her producer patched me through. After a short wait, Tracy got on the line and said, "That you, Allida?"

"Yes, and you've—"

"Hang on." I heard a click on the phone, then she said, "We're on the air with Allida Babcock, who's consented to do a phone interview with me. Ms. Babcock is the dog psychologist who discovered the victim in the gruesome murder in Berthoud two days ago. Have you recovered from the shock yet, Allida?"

"I did not consent to a phone interview, Tracy. Now please take me off the air."

"Our listeners would like to know how it felt to suddenly find a dead body in the yard right across the street from your home."

"Tracy, take me off the air," I said, using the calm-but-firm voice that works wonders with unruly dogs.

"Sure, but could you just tell us how it was that you came to discover the body?"

The voice might work wonders with unruly dogs, but wasn't sinking through to Tracy. I'd have to resort to threats. "Off the air, now. Otherwise, I'll let loose with ear-splitting whistles into the phone till all your listeners change channels."

"Sounds as though our show's guest has woken up on the wrong side of the doghouse this morning. I'll see if I can do something to get rid of her bark. We'll be back after this break."

A moment later, the slight cavernous background sounds were gone as Tracy switched the phone back to a direct line and said, "Hey, Allie. Hear the one about why deejays have small hands?" Without giving me time to respond, she answered with a chuckle, "Wee paws for station identification."

"Heard it. Tracy, what are you doing to me?"

"*Doing* to you? I'm advertising your business. You should be thrilled."

"I'm not."

"I got that impression, but—"

"Tracy, listen to me for a moment. The police don't have anyone in custody. Nobody but me and the police knew about those paw prints. Furthermore, you've just announced my identity over the air. Till then, the media had only disclosed that 'a neighbor' discovered the body."

There was a pause. "Your mom's the one that blabbed to me. You should be mad at her, not me."

"She's not the one with the radio show that broadcast the word to half the state of Colorado."

"Half the state? I wish. More like ten people in the Denver-Metro area, but I get your drift. This could put you in a bit of jeopardy, hey?"

"Yes," I said, not bothering to cover my exasperation.

"Holy crow. Wish I'd gotten the chance to talk to you first. You should get yourself a beeper. Well, no problem. I'll get back on and correct this. Commercial's ending. Gotta go." She hung up.

I turned the volume back up on my radio. Tracy came back on and said, "Seems I was mistaken. Ms. Babcock, our dog-shrink friend, doesn't know anything about the bloody paw prints at the murder scene. I stand corrected. Let's go to another caller."

I hollered at the radio, "That's the best you can do, Tracy?"

"You're on the Tracy Truett show."

"Hey," said a man's voice. "I was wondering how come that last caller wouldn't talk to you on the air. Is she hiding something, or what?"

"She's shy. Spends a lot of time with dogs. Isn't used to talking much."

Too annoyed to listen, I switched the radio off and paced. This was going to be trouble. Sergeant Millay had specifically asked me not to reveal the information about the paw marks.

Rather than wait for the police to hear from someone else, I called the sergeant and told him what had happened—that my mother had talked to a talk-show host, who leaked the news about the paw prints over the air. He sounded annoyed, but no more so than I was.

While we were still on the phone, I heard the characteristic footfalls as Russell came down the front steps to our shared front door. My heart fluttered in response, which was ridiculous. I saw him constantly, after all. We shared an office. It wasn't as though it made any sense to get nervous whenever he was near. I thanked the officer, hung up, then turned to face Russell.

He was neatly dressed, as usual—khakis and a short-sleeved blue shirt—but wore no tie today. He must not have any client meetings on the day's agenda.

"Morning, Russell. How was the concert last night?"

"Oh, it was great. From what I hear. I sold my tickets to a friend at the last minute."

"You did? Why?"

He shrugged. "Just wasn't in the mood to go. And I got another rush job, so I wound up working instead." He smoothed his mustache, then asked shyly, "How was your evening?"

"Dull, actually."

"Really?" He brightened.

"Yeah. In fact, I spent most of the time—" I stopped, realizing what a huge risk I was about to take if I admitted to him how much I'd thought about him during my date with someone else. "Worrying about the murder." *Coward!* "As far as I know, there're no new leads, and—"

The phone rang. "Bet I know who this is," I muttered.

"How was that, Allie?"

I recognized Tracy's husky voice immediately. "Wretched." I held up my index finger to indicate to Russell to wait for me to get off the line, still determined to salvage our conversation.

"Well, hey, don't pull any punches."

"I won't."

"I'll make this up to you. How 'bout you meet me at the parking lot of Centennial Middle School next Wednesday at six P.M., and we'll discuss what I can do?"

"You want us to meet in a parking lot?"

At this, Russell raised an eyebrow.

"And bring your softball glove. Oh. And ask that guy that shares your office to come, too. Russell."

I grinned at him. "Shouldn't I find out first whether or not he has any interest in playing softball?"

"Sure. That'd be great. Ask him what position he wants to play."

"Anything else I can do for you?"

"Yeah. Bring a blank check. I'm not sure how much the entry fee to the league is." She hung up.

I found myself shaking my head in wonder. If the woman were a dog, she'd be a pit bull. With rabies.

"Russell, would you have any interest in joining a co-rec softball team with me?"

"Sure. I love to play softball. When do we start?"

"Next Wednesday's the first practice. Six P.M. At Centennial Middle School."

"See you there. Though . . . we'll probably see each other before then, too." His cheeks colored a bit, and I realized with a start that he was acting just as nervous around me as I felt around him. "We do have things in common. I . . . need to get to work."

"You might want to close your door. I have an office appointment with a miniature schnauzer mourning the loss of his life's mate."

"What are you going to do for him?"

I shrugged. "Try to distract him. The vet's opposed to doggie-uppers. Unfortunately, it's all too common for the surviving dog to lose his will to live. Other times dogs just have to be allowed to go through a grieving period, the same way people do."

"I'm sure he's in the right hands."

"Thanks. I'll see you later."

I watched him and we exchanged a little wave as he closed the door, my heart still fluttering idiotically.

A few minutes later, the owner and his lethargic miniature schnauzer arrived. Before coming to me for my services, the owner had rushed right out and purchased another female schnauzer puppy to keep his dog company. Depending upon the dog's temperament, this is not always advisable, and I felt strongly that the older dog should meet the puppy prior to making the decision. Indeed, it had backfired in this case and the owner had to return the new would-be mate to the breeder.

What I advised was that the owner gradually change the

daily patterns for the dog. Dogs love routine, but in this case, the dog was refusing to participate. I advised the owner to take him to different parks, making sure to keep his dog food exactly the same, which otherwise could add physical digestive upset to his broken heart.

I was finished for the day by seven P.M. and drove home, feeling that this had been at least a moderately successful day. My mixed-breed client with the fear of separation was making good progress, as was the fear-of-cars springer spaniel. However, as soon as I reached my street, I started remembering how Mom had blabbed everything to Tracy Truett. For once, it was my turn to take her to task for something she'd done, and I was going to make the most of it.

Mom's pickup was in the garage. I was mulling over my opening line—"Mom, how could you be so stupid?" versus "Do the words '*talk*-show host' mean nothing to you?"

She was standing fifth in line to greet me, behind our three dogs plus Shogun. Suds had rushed upstairs, too, but was darting around the kitchen as if she were a wild animal in a cage.

Mom held up her hands the moment we made eye contact. "Before you say anything, I'm sorry. I just didn't think. I can't believe how stupid I was not to realize that Tracy Truett was just pumping me for information to use on her talk show. I guess I was just so excited at the thought of my being able to help you get some exposure for your new business venture that I didn't use my brain."

Well, that was no fun whatsoever. "That's all right, Mom. I already called the sergeant's office and let them know what happened."

"I listened to the entire show, by the way—after hanging up with you, that is. If only I'd been listening from the beginning, I could have warned you."

"It's all right. Really."

"Did you listen to what went on after your phone call?"

"No. Why?"

"Tracy not only spilled the beans about the bloody paw

prints, but the fact that the victim had been taking care of a convicted felon's dog and her puppies."

"Oh, good Lord. She didn't say anything about the dogs still being in the neighborhood, did she?"

"No."

"It's probably fine, then." I wasn't sure if that was true, though.

"I tried to speak to the Haywoods today, by the way. They looked out their front window, saw it was me ringing their doorbell, and wouldn't answer."

"This is insane," I said, having surpassed my threshold for strained relationships. "Let's go over there now. Maybe if I apologize for the stupid Shoe Incident, they'll lighten up. Maybe we'll even find out what Harvey was up to last night."

There was no guarantee that they'd answer their door now, either, but they eventually did. They grudgingly invited us inside. This was my first time in their house and I looked around in curiosity. Every square inch of the furniture was covered with either a lace doily or a blanket. The lampshades still had the clear plastic coverings from the store, and plastic runners crisscrossed the green wall-to-wall carpeting.

"Hello, Betsy, Harvey," my mother said with a great deal of warmth. "My daughter and I wanted to come over and clear the air."

"Air looks pretty darned clear to me," Betsy grumbled.

"Not from our side of the street," Mom said with a sigh.

Betsy cleared her throat, looked at her husband, then said, "Harvey told me to apologize to you for his sleep-walking." Harvey merely blinked, but Betsy continued, "Didn't you, Harvey?"

"Oh. Eh, sorry if I scared you. Sometimes in my sleep, I get to remembering a time when I lost my keys and locked myself out of the house. Ever since that time, I hide a screwdriver in the bushes so I can get back inside. I must've gotten that screwdriver, but wandered over to your place."

"Which bushes do you mean?" I asked. "The ones nearest Edith Cunningham's house?"

He shifted his glance to his wife, but answered, "Uh, yeah. That's right."

"That's where I was looking for the note from Edith's house." All I'd seen back there were the paw prints, not a screwdriver, though perhaps this was insignificant. In any case, I didn't believe a word he'd said.

Mom said, "I understand you were quite upset by a prank one of my children played on you several years ago, involving a pair of shoes and some Super Glue."

"Don't remind me," Betsy said, the frown lines on her face deepening.

I was thoroughly baffled that they not only expected us to believe that Mr. Haywood had been sleepwalking last night, but that glued shoes were a feasible cause for upset decades later. However, when you're in someone's doghouse, the best-tasting selection on the menu is probably crow. "I apologize for my immaturity," I interjected. "I was only ten at the time. It was a nasty thing to do, though, and I assure you I won't do anything remotely like that ever again." Twenty-two years later, I silently added.

"Well, all I can say is it's about time you owned up to your actions and took responsibility for it. That's more than I can say for your brother."

I had to keep myself from laughing. "Mrs. Haywood, my brother David didn't apologize or 'own up to it' because he was innocent. He had nothing to do with it."

"Huh. Well. Yes, but he was your brother. He should have stood up on your behalf and taken your punishment like a man."

" 'Taken it like a *man*'?" I repeated. "He was *eleven*."

"Even still."

Mom said calmly, "I fail to understand why, if this has obviously upset you so much, you waited all this time to bring the matter to my attention. We're talking about something that happened over twenty years ago."

"Twenty-two," Betsy corrected.

"Was that the worst thing that anyone's ever done to you?" I asked.

"No, just the catalyst for what was to follow. You see, *Marilyn*"—she shifted her gaze to my mother—"when your son insisted he had nothing to do with it, Harvey and I just couldn't believe it was sweet little Allida. We accused our own daughters, and decided it was Susan. Things were never the same in our family after that. She was sixteen at the time, and she started to run with the wrong crowd, got herself into all kinds of trouble. Said her own parents wouldn't believe her when she told the truth." She looked back at me and lifted her wrinkled chin to peer down at me. "So, Miss Babcock, that may have just been a childish prank as far as you were concerned, but it destroyed our lives."

I couldn't respond to that and looked at my mother helplessly.

"Betsy, as one experienced mother to another, let's be honest here. Teenage years are difficult for everyone. We parents have already had all of the preteen years to impart a value system and judgment as best we can, then as you're forced to let go as they become adults, you hope for the best. But there's never only one particular incident that determines your teenager's entire future. It's human nature to think back that if only I hadn't done this one thing, all of my child's pain later might have been spared. But Betsy, we're talking about an argument over a pair of shoes glued to the porch. Do you really believe Susan made the wrong choices of friends and her grades slipped all because of that?"

Betsy sat in silent contemplation for a good minute or two. Finally, she rose. "I see what you're saying, Marilyn, but I think you're wrong. There is a pivotal point in everyone's life. Normally, it's just not as clear-cut as this one was for Susan. But I can see how you want to support your daughter by taking her side."

My mother and I exchanged glances, then got to our feet. "I'd be happy to pay you for the shoes. That would be the least I can do."

"Fine. At today's prices, they'd be worth a hundred dollars."

They were Keds, not Air Jordans, but at this point I wasn't going to quibble. "I'll bring a check over soon."

"Just leave it in the mailbox," Betsy said, then left the room.

Harvey, seeing everybody else was on their feet, got out of his seat as well. "It was good of you to visit. Be sure and say hello to Frederick for me."

I had no idea who Frederick was, but assumed Harvey meant my brother, so I merely said, "Thank you. I will."

We left. Mom put her arm around my shoulder and I said, "I'll bet she thinks the Shoe Incident is responsible for global warming and the national deficit, too."

"You're probably right. And it's nice to have a fall guy for whatever ails the world. Now I know that it's all your fault."

"I thought it was supposed to be a person's mother that was the root of all evil, not the person's daughter."

"Speak for yourself."

"I am."

We went back home. Shogun and our dogs joined us downstairs as we played with the puppies. Suds, however, roamed around upstairs and soon started howling at the back door.

As I let her out, I happened to glance through the glass and saw that there was a white cloth or paper hanging on the fence behind our yard. From this distance, it looked like a man's undershirt and did nothing to boost the appearance of our property.

"Mom, how long has that been out there?"

"What?"

"There seems to be someone's piece of clothing on the back fence."

Mom came up the stairs to see. "Must have gotten blown there at some point this afternoon. It certainly wasn't there the last time I looked."

"I wonder if it belongs to Mr. Haywood. He might have hung it there. Maybe he's taken to hanging his clothes on neighbors' fences, in addition to roaming through their yards in the middle of the night."

"Could be."

We watched Suds, who barked frantically at the cloth, leaping at it and pacing back and forth inside the fence. Suds then rushed over to whine at the back gate and looked back at us, tail wagging slightly, a canine's body language for "Come and let me out of the yard."

I slid open the door and called, "Suds, come!"

She ignored me completely. I called for her a second time and then a third. She stayed put by the gate, dashing back and forth in front of it.

"I think I'd better go check this out," I told my mother, and went outside and crossed the yard.

The cloth was indeed a white T-shirt and had been fastened somehow to the back of the fence. I couldn't get it off from inside the fence.

This felt like some sort of a weird setup to me. Suds was acting so frantic to get out of the fence area and at the shirt that I began to wonder if she recognized its scent.

Just to be cautious, I grabbed her collar and pulled her back inside the house with me. Some of the puppies came outside in the process of my dragging Suds through the back door.

"What's going on?" Mom asked.

"The shirt seems to be deliberately fastened onto the fence. I can't shake the thought that it's there to lure Suds over to it."

"Should I call Sergeant Millay?"

"To report a shirt? Keep Suds inside. I'm going to take Pavlov behind the fence with me." I called for Pavlov and put her leash on. There were few things as intimidating to people as a large dog.

Feeling only slightly ridiculous, I led Pavlov through the back gate. She immediately started barking at the irrigation ditch, and I knew someone was back there.

An instant later, Pavlov's hackles raised, and she started growling. A man stepped out from behind a copse of Russian olive trees and came toward us. He could have been a young-looking fifty, but I suspected he was an old-looking forty-year-old.

He was wearing a faded denim jacket that matched his jeans, a dark black T-shirt, and work boots. He stood only about five-foot-eight or so and had a decidedly wiry frame, but his protruding cheekbones, week-old beard, unwashed and greased-back hair hinted at his having led such a tough life that he had an advantage over me: This man had much less to lose than I did. To slam home the intimidation factor, he started trimming a hangnail on his dirty hand with an unusually large pocketknife.

I don't know how long he'd been outside, waiting for the perfect moment to let me know he was there. He smiled at the anxious facial expression that I couldn't hide.

Mom was inside and would be watching. She had perhaps already called the police, though I wasn't sure she could see the man from her vantage point.

"You Allida Babcock?" he asked in a voice that sounded prematurely aged by cigarettes and alcohol.

"How did you know my name?"

He stared into my eyes, not answering. His own were strangely hollow, as if there were something missing. He hadn't made one menacing move toward me, and yet I felt terrified.

"How did you know my name?" I asked again.

"I come for my dog," he said.

Chapter 11

Pavlov picked up on my fright. She quickly got in front of me, shielding me from the man. Though she didn't rush up to him, she let out a low, rumbling growl and assumed an aggressive stance—slightly crouched, hackles raised, and ears back.

He was an ugly man, pockmarked leathery skin, a nose that had been broken at least twice, a deep scar over his left eye. He pointed at Pavlov with his knife. "You better call off your dog."

"I will, just as soon as you put your knife away," I said with a confidence I didn't feel.

He grinned, revealing crooked, tobacco-stained teeth. "You mean this little thing?" He folded the blade, but kept it in his palm. "I got a much bigger one in my belt."

Oh, shit. Why did I have to come out here? I wasn't some macho crime crusader; I just wanted to live in peace with my dogs. The man was undressing me with his eyes. I needed to end this standoff as quickly and quietly as possible.

"Pavlov, lie down."

She hesitated, but obeyed. She kept her legs tucked under her in such a manner that she could spring up in the blink of an eye, though.

"Pretty dog you got there," he muttered. "Reminds me of mine."

"You're . . . the husky's owner?" I didn't want to give away Suds's name, wanting to make sure he really was her owner and knew her name.

"That's right."

"I'm just foster-adopting her, through the animal shelter." I wanted to find out his name and hoped that I could trick him into giving it. "You must be Sam Grant, right?"

He shook his head. "Carver. Craig Carver. Don't know nobody named Grant."

"We have no intention of keeping your dog. You're going to get her back in three weeks, at the latest."

He shook his head. "Can't wait." He was staring at something behind me. I followed his gaze. On the other side of the fence, one of the puppies was outside and making his way toward us.

"The puppies are too young to be separated from their mother."

"Can't help that. Timing's just bad." His large hand was in a tight fist around his knife. He and Pavlov locked eyes like prizefighters, each waiting for the other to make the first move. "I'm in a hurry." He gestured in the direction of the house, causing Pavlov to bark in protest. "Take your dog back inside and get me my dog."

"Okay. I'll just contact the kennel supervisor and tell him you needed to get the dog early."

"This is between me 'n' you. And Suds is my dog. Nobody else's got nothing to say about this."

At least he knew her name. He probably *was* her owner. There would be no reason for anyone to fake that and try to steal the dog. "How about letting me keep her and her puppies just one more week? That will give me enough time to wean them properly, which will be much healthier for Suds, as well as for her puppies."

He laughed without humor. "Lady, you got no idea what's gonna keep *you* healthy 'n' what ain't. But I guarantee it's got nothin' to do with you keeping my dog from me. Now stop stalling and get me my dog."

If only Mom would call the police and get them here before anything bad happened. "I'll be right back with her."

"You better be. Hate to have to go into your house and hassle the ol' lady."

I bristled and glared at him. He grinned. "I seen her

through the glass." He stared through the chain-link fence at the puppy. "This one of Suds's pups?"

"Yes. That's Fez."

He rounded the gate, grabbed the puppy, and held him up by the scruff of the neck, which made me wince, though I knew he wasn't actually hurting the little dog. "Hello, Fez."

I didn't want to go anywhere near him and stayed outside of the yard, keeping a tight leash on Pavlov, who'd risen and was again growling at Carver's having violated her territorial boundaries.

Carver eyed me and rocked on his heels, still holding Fez harshly as if to make certain I understood that he wouldn't hesitate to injure the poor little puppy. "Well? You gonna get my dog for me, or do I gotta go in after her myself?"

"I'll bring her to you. She's your dog, after all." I held out my free hand for Fez and stepped toward him. "Let me take him back inside."

He shoved me away, causing Pavlov to voice three sharp warning barks. "You get the puppy jus' as soon as I get my dog. You tell the ol' lady in the house to let Suds out back." He glared at Pavlov and pointed at her with his chin. "That police dog of yours acts like a junkyard dog every time I get near. You keep her inside your house. Let me take Suds 'n' you won't hear from me again."

With his free hand he plucked his shirt off of the fence. Then he grabbed a thin piece of white fiberglass rope six feet or so long that he must have lain by our fence when he'd first arrived.

"That's your leash?"

"It's Suds's. Yeah."

He didn't stop me from entering the gate, but still held the puppy in his one hand as if Fez were insignificant.

"Pavlov, come." I was too proud to break into a run, but I walked as fast as possible back into the house.

My mother was standing back from the glass door, with Sage at her side and her largest knife in her hand. From the whines and scratching noises, it was obvious that she'd put the other dogs in the basement.

Trying to keep my voice as unemotional as possible, I said, "Mom, Suds's owner is back there demanding I give him his dog, and he's scary. I'm calling nine-one-one."

"I already tried. He must've cut the phone line. I was going to dash out to a neighbor's, but I couldn't just leave you out there." She lifted her knife. "I also didn't want to run out there and provoke him. What do we do?"

"It's his dog. Let's just let him take her. Meanwhile, you go next door and call the police. Tell them what's happening. The man's name is Craig Carver. I think he's probably going to leave town once he's got the dog."

All of the dogs rushed into the kitchen when I opened the basement door. I grabbed a decent leash and snapped it on Suds's collar. The leash was the very least I could give her, at this point. I instructed the other grown dogs to stay, but the four remaining puppies tried desperately to follow as I led their mom out back. I slid the door shut on them, hating myself for my role in taking their mom from them before it was time.

Five-year-old Melanie lost her mother. Now the puppies were having theirs snatched from them. Was this the pattern of my life, all of a sudden, to watch young ones be separated from their mothers?

Suds quickly picked up on the scent of her owner, who was still standing just inside the back gate. Tail wagging, Suds strained against her leash, anxious to greet Carver. This was the irony of dogs' temperament; they love even the worst of owners. For my part, I felt humiliated and cowardly, but ultimately trapped.

I released my grip on the leash, hoping against logic that Suds would lunge at his throat. Carver dropped the puppy on the ground and gave his dog a hug. She leapt up and began licking his face. "Hey, girl. That's enough, now," he said through his laughter. I looked away, not wanting to see anything remotely joyful in what Carver was doing.

"Mr. Carver, I have to say that I'm opposed to you taking Suds like this. The puppies aren't fully weaned. This isn't going to be good for them or for Suds. Please. Let me keep her for another week."

He dragged his forearm across his face. "Got to leave the state. I hope the puppies'll pull through all right."

"So do I."

Suds rolled over in the submissive position and he started to rub her tummy. "Shit! She's still full of milk. What should I do with her?" He got to his feet and glared at me as if this were my fault.

"Normally you gradually cut down on the dog's food supply so that she'll stop lactating. We're still on a schedule to feed her the full amount till the end of the week, but you could get her to stop by not feeding her anything tomorrow, then over the next four days increasing her food by one-quarter amounts each day. She'll be pretty uncomfortable for the next couple of days, but will be back to full meals on day five."

He started to unhook my leash.

"Keep it."

He gave me a smirk but kept my leash on her. He ran his hand over her, shaking his head. "Isn't there some medicine I can give her to make her stop producing milk?"

To my knowledge, there wasn't such a thing for animals, but it would be best for Suds's sake not to tell him that. "Yeah, I think there is. You could bring her to a vet and ask for a prescription."

He shook his head. "You don't seem to get it, do you? I got my truck around the corner, all packed up. Got myself a job in Wyoming that starts at eight A.M., and I'm making a clean start for myself. Can you write up a prescription to get me some of that medicine for her to take with me?"

"I can't. I'm not a veterinarian. If you give me a minute, though, I'll call the animal shelter and—"

"Never mind. I'll get some from White on my way up north."

"John White? You know the kennel supervisor?"

He gave me a wink. "The two of us go way back." He started walking toward my front gate, with Suds in tow. I followed.

"Is that how you got my name and address?"

He merely kept walking without answering.

"My phone line seems to be down. You wouldn't know anything about that, would you?"

He chuckled and pointed at the gray-covered wire now lying on the ground. "Squirrel must have chewed through it."

I picked it up. The wire had been cut in a neat diagonal line. "Must have been a squirrel with a pocketknife."

He laughed and led Suds out the gate.

Angry and humiliated, I couldn't stop myself from calling after him, "If you had anything to do with my neighbor's murder, you'll be back behind bars in no time."

"I don't know nothing about no murder. Never even met the woman."

He headed around the corner, where I assumed he'd parked his truck so that we wouldn't spot it.

From the safety of my house, I watched out the front window for my mother, the puppies whining at my feet. Moments later, she returned, slightly out of breath.

"Sergeant Millay is on his way."

"Good. Maybe he can find out for us just how it was that this creep knew where Suds's foster owners lived."

"Do you think the animal shelter told him?"

"At first I assumed he heard it over the radio, but now I think he got the information straight from John White, the kennel supervisor."

"The man you had the date with last night?"

"Yes."

She paled a little, then laid a hand on my arm. "Is this a good time for me to mention how very much I like Russell?"

I was so tense at that point, it was a struggle not to snap at her, but I managed to say in an even voice, "I'm glad. I like him, too." A question occurred to me. "Whose phone did you call from?"

"The Haywoods'. They're always at home. If you can get them to come to the door, that is."

"How was Harvey behaving?"

"I didn't see him. Just Betsy. And she was as grouchy as

ever. As soon as I'd hung up with the sergeant, she said, 'Tell your daughter to mind her own business and not go talking to my Susan anymore about Harvey.' "

The next day, Mom and I went to Cassandra's funeral, held in the small Methodist church on Lake Avenue. We arrived a bit late. There were a half dozen or so family members, with Paul and Melanie up front. Really, though, there were far fewer people there than I'd expected. Only thirty or so. Most were from our immediate neighborhood.

To my surprise, both Haywoods were there as well as Susan, but I was beginning to wonder where this husband of hers was. We took seats directly across the aisle from them. They wore matching expressions of crabbiness. Meanwhile, Edith and Trevor sat at opposite sides of the church in an obvious attempt to avoid each other.

An elderly woman was playing indistinguishable music on the organ. Just as a man in a black suit rose to go to the podium, someone touched my shoulder. It was Russell.

"Russell?" I said in surprise. "Hi."

"Hello," he whispered into my ear. "I thought about how upset you've been by this, and I decided I'd come pay my respects."

Out of deference for our setting, Mom greeted him with a mere nod, but her eyes beamed as she looked at him and then at me. She seemed to be telepathing the thought to me, *See how great he is? Marry the man!* But that may have been my reading into things.

Throughout the service, there were periodic sobbings from the front, and the elderly woman I took to be Cassandra's mother was barely able to keep herself in check. The lecturer had the vocal vibrato of a Baptist minister, but I found myself blocking out the words, just trying to get through this without breaking down myself. What hurt me to the core wasn't the loss of Cassandra, whom I barely knew, so much as the loss of any vibrant person's life before her time. I was also acutely aware of the heat of Russell's body beside me, and I was grateful that he'd come.

Afterward, we rose and waited while the family left first. I felt a pressure in my chest and throat when Melanie walked down the aisle past me. She was holding on to her father's hand and a woman's who looked like a slightly older version of her mother. She must have been Cassandra's sister.

An old pain came back to me, suppressed but never quite absent. I saw myself in the same position, as a little girl at my father's funeral. I remembered how it felt to know that I was supposed to cry. To feel that everyone was disappointed in my heartlessness for remaining dry-eyed. I'd felt numb and empty, angry at my dad for leaving us and at myself for not being good enough for him to want to stay.

I realized with a start that I'd also been five years old when I lost my parent. I felt such a stab of regret for Melanie that it was hard not to cry out. Hers was a tough age to lose a parent, not really understanding what was happening. My face must have betrayed my emotions, for Russell took my hand and gave it a squeeze.

Back then, there never seemed to be any single-parent families besides our own. Mother never complained to us. There was a lot to be said for simply doing what needed to be done in this world. But much as I hate the "inner child" psychobabble, I've always agreed that if you scratch below the surface of any adult's veneer, regardless of how competent and strong the person seems to be, there is an injured child there. Mine had gotten through the toughest times with her arms wrapped around a dog or two. I wasn't sure who would be there for Melanie.

As we walked down the aisle, I realized that Sergeant Millay was seated in the back of the room. I wondered if his investigation had gotten anywhere. He seemed to be keeping a low profile, as if there were other things occupying his time, though I doubted that was the case. I stared at his face for a few seconds, hoping against logic that I'd see some indication of whether or not he still thought of me as a suspect.

We murmured our condolences to the family and made our way into the bright light outside, where most of the other mourners were lingering. The moment Edith spotted me, she ignored Russell and my mother to either side of me, marched toward me, and demanded, "Have you made a decision regarding Shogun's ownership?"

"Not really. But he's doing fine."

"I'm sure he is. But that isn't what I asked, is it? You have no right to keep him. And *I* have a right to know which one of us will get the dog permanently. And how soon."

"I'll let you know."

We walked away. Though I'd forced myself to be polite, I wanted to sock the woman.

"She was pleasant," Russell said as we continued on toward the car.

"She's our neighbor," Mom said. "She's hired Allida to decide whether she or her ex-husband gets custody of their terrier."

"The dog we were looking for in Longmont, right?"

"Yes. I found him at Trevor's house. Through a roundabout journey. But he was safe and sound."

We reached Russell's car. He shot a quick glance at his watch and said, "I've got to take off. I'll see you at the office. Good-bye, Marilyn."

"Thanks for coming," she and I both said in unison. I felt her eyes on me the moment we heard the solid thud of his car door shutting.

I was spared Mom's anticipated comments regarding how great Russell was when we spotted Trevor Cunningham waiting for me by my mother's truck. Unlike our conversation with Edith just moments earlier, he greeted my mother, then asked me kindly, "How is Shogun?" Two points to his side.

"He's fine."

"Has he been sleeping all right? I was thinking that he probably misses his bed. When my neighbor ransacked my house the other day, stealing my dog, she didn't think to take his bed, too."

"He's been okay. We put him on a pillow near my cocker spaniel's bed in the kitchen and he seems fine."

"Still. I'd feel better if you'd take his bed to him. I brought it with me in case I saw you."

"Okay."

"It's in my car. I'll bring it over to you."

We watched as he opened the trunk of a blue Honda Civic a couple of cars down and brought over a plaid doggy bed. I thanked him and stashed it behind the front seat. The bed was unremarkable except for the fancy stitching of "Shogun" on the front in shiny thread.

Edith had followed us. I knew by the sharp click of stiletto heels.

"What are you doing?" she demanded.

Trevor immediately stiffened and regarded her, his hands fisted. "I'm giving her Shogun's bed."

"Shogun doesn't need his bed. He isn't staying at Allida's house for more than one more night, and she certainly doesn't need that old thing cluttering up her house."

"Hello, Edith," my mother interrupted. "How are things going at your shop?"

"Uh, fine. Thanks."

"I was planning on stopping in. I'd love to get a new outfit or two."

"Really?"

I, too, looked at Mom in surprise, impressed that she was so intent on calming a potential altercation, she'd claimed she wanted to go shopping. Mom was whatever one would call the opposite of a clothes horse.

"Yes, are you going to be there tomorrow afternoon?"

"Absolutely. I just recently had to let my salesgirl go, so I'll be there from now on, at least until I can get some decent help."

"I'll be sure and stop by, in that case. Oh, and don't worry about the dog bed cluttering up our house. We have lots of room, and we'll be sure that the bed goes with Shogun from here on."

"Thank you, Marilyn."

She turned and headed back to her car without further word to any of us. His jaw clenched, Trevor watched her walk away and let out an exasperated sigh. "You have my work and home numbers, yes?"

"Yes. I'll set up an appointment with you and Shogun tomorrow."

"Great. I'll talk to you then." He said good-bye to my mother, then nodded to Sergeant Millay, who was watching Mom and me intently from a slight distance.

When the officer caught my mother's eye, he approached. "Mornin', Ms. Babcock. Marilyn."

"Hello, Andy," Mom said. "Did anyone have any more run-ins with that Carver person who was harassing my daughter last night?"

The sergeant shook his head. "Must have left the area, like he said he would."

"This is getting to me. Harvey Haywood suddenly acting completely crazy. This Carver person all but threatening my daughter at knifepoint. I see you haven't made any arrests yet. Tell me something, as one friend to another. Are we safe?"

Sergeant Millay dragged a hand across his thinning hair, visually focusing on some spot on the ground. "I don't know."

Chapter 12

Immediately following the service that morning, I drove straight to the Loveland animal shelter and marched into John White's office. He was sitting at his desk, going through paperwork, his light brown hair slightly unkempt. He wore an orange-red T-shirt that contrasted with the forest-green employee's vest. He looked a little startled to see me. "Hi, Allida."

"Okay, John. What's going on?" I leaned on his desk, glad that while he was sitting, at least, I had a few inches on him.

"With what?"

"You know exactly what I'm talking about. I called your office a couple of times and left messages for you. I had a visit last night from Derrick Carver."

"You mean Craig Carver?"

"Exactly. I was testing you to see if you knew his first name."

"I . . . never said that I didn't know his name, only that I had a duty to keep it from getting out to the public."

"Right. You wouldn't tell me who *he* was, and yet you or somebody else you work with must have told him who *I* was and how to find me."

"No, I . . . nobody told him your name."

"Then how did he find Suds? How did he know exactly where I lived and what my name was?"

"I don't know, Allida."

It was possible that he'd gotten my name and deduced my address from Tracy's radio broadcast, but Carver had also gotten John's name someplace. Carver could have called and asked for the director's name, but something told me it was John who was hiding the truth.

In a gentle voice aimed at defusing my anger, he said, "He shouldn't know where you live for the same reason I wouldn't tell you his name earlier. We have a strict policy protecting information like that, so he couldn't have learned it from here. Unless he's a hacker and got into our computer base somehow."

I shook my head. "The man is too stupid to tie his own shoes. He's no hacker. You know as well as I do that he has to use his fingers to add two and two."

"Allida, I don't know anything about him. I've never met him. Someone from Animal Control took the initial call."

"I'd like to believe you, John, but he called you specifically by name."

The color in John's face was rising and he couldn't meet my eyes. "He could have called here and simply asked what the supervisor's name was."

"Yes. He could have. But he says you two go way back. Do you?"

John raked his fingers through his hair and didn't answer.

"Listen to me, John. I'm more than a little fed up here. A woman gets killed right after she adopts a dog from your facility, then the dog gets taken from me at knifepoint, and you don't even return my calls to see if we're all right. Don't tell me you're an innocent bystander in all of this. I can't buy it."

"So you think I set you up? Why would I do that, Allida?"

"I don't know. Tell me. What was this? A burglary gone bad? Was he using his dog somehow to try to gain entry to people's houses?"

"Carver is an idiot. You said so yourself. He'd never have been able to think things through to cook up such a thing."

"How do you know him well enough to say something like that?"

"I don't. I just know his history." His cheeks were bright red and he could barely meet my eyes.

"You're lying, John, and I'm telling Sergeant Millay about you having a role in this."

I whirled around, intending to storm out the door, but John lunged forward and grabbed my wrist.

"All right, Allida. Yes, I did know him, at one time. He's someone I knew when we were kids. We happened to live near each other. And, unfortunately, back then I used some bad judgment. We used to shoplift together. He got caught and never fingered me, and I've always felt bad. Eventually he moved and we lost track. Then one day he ran into me in a bar."

His story was plausible enough. I prompted, "When was this?"

He shrugged. "A couple of years ago. He told me that he'd been through some tough times and asked me if I could help him find a job."

"You told him where you were working, or did he already know?"

"I told him then. And I said that, sure, I could get him a job, but it'd only be for minimum wage, that I barely made more than that myself. He got mad, said that that wasn't going to be nearly enough to get himself out of his jam. He said he had run up some pretty substantial gambling debts. Next thing I knew, I read in the crime blotter in the paper that he'd been arrested on some burglary charges."

"This was in Fort Collins?"

"Yeah. He disappeared for a while, then he resurfaced. He called here one day and asked if I could take care of Suds for a few weeks and find a good home for the puppies. That he wanted Suds back, though, as soon as he got out of jail. I watched Suds myself for a while, but my own dogs wouldn't accept the situation, and sooner or later there was definitely going to be a dogfight, so that's when Paul and Cassandra Randon happened to come in. I figured they'd be perfect; living out in Berthoud, they'd have all of this land for the puppies and everything."

"If that's the whole truth, John, why didn't you tell me that earlier? Why did you lie to me and my mother?"

He spread his hands. "A woman had just gotten killed. The woman I'd given the dogs to. My first thought was, 'What have I done? I hooked her up with a killer.' But then the times didn't jibe, so I knew Carver didn't do it."

"How could you know that for sure?"

"Because he was *here* all day. He came looking for me. I told him the dogs had been foster-adopted but that I'd give Suds back to him in three weeks. He said he was hurting for cash and needed to get out of town before he got into trouble, so I hired him to work here for a month, starting that Monday. I assure you, Allida, he didn't leave here long enough to get out to Berthoud and back, let alone hurt someone. End of my shift, he asked to be paid in cash, then he didn't show up in the morning. I never saw him again."

"You two grew up in the same neighborhood?"

"In Indiana. And before you ask, I have no idea how he found me in that bar. It had to have been a coincidence, or maybe he got hold of a reunion directory and was just desperately trying to find our old classmates, hoping someone would help him out."

"But this doesn't explain how he knew my address."

"No. It doesn't. And I swear to you on the lives of the entire canine population, he didn't get that from me. I have no idea where he did get it."

I finally arranged to have my appointment to watch Shogun with Trevor. Trevor was waiting out in front of his duplex when I drove up with Shogun. Shogun's tail began to wag and he perked up as soon as we neared. He ran over to my lap to get a view out the window, his little claws digging into the exposed flesh of my leg below my shorts.

I parked in Trevor's driveway, and by that time, Shogun was so excited and anxious to get out and see his owner again that he piddled on me. Now I was glad to be wearing shorts, as I could wipe his accident up easily and not have to be wearing urine, which is one of those things that tends to lower clients' estimation of my abilities.

Shogun leapt out of the car, raced up to Trevor, and then jumped straight into his arms.

"How's my big doggie?" Trevor said to him. "That's a good boy."

Watching the two of them, I soon verified what I'd already greatly suspected. Trevor loved Shogun far more than Edith did. Edith wanted Shogun primarily because she knew how much it would hurt Trevor to lose him.

All that remained for me to do was to see if Shogun was also so happy to be at his home in Berthoud with Edith that it was clear that I'd have to recommend "joint custody" and let the Cunninghams figure out the implications of that themselves. What struck me as most puzzling in this matter was, why would Edith be the one to hire me, when her spouse was so obviously more attached to the dog?

"I missed my big doggie!" Trevor was saying into the little dog's pointy muzzle, and Shogun was yapping back in mirrored excitement.

"Shogun is obviously delighted to be here with you. Would you mind showing me your home?"

"Course not. Come on in."

As he walked me up the driveway, I saw the curtains part at Fiona's, his neighbor's, place. They quickly shut again, and I was quite certain she'd seen me and wanted nothing to do with me. "Are things okay between you and your neighbor?"

"Fiona? Oh, sure. She explained the whole thing to me, and given what my bitch of a soon-to-be ex said about my treatment of Shogun, I can't say as I blame her. Fiona is a gentle soul, just needs to be withdrawn from the world."

With memories of all those interviews on news programs about neighbors of serial killers who said, "He was such a shy, quiet boy," my mind leapt to the possibility that Fiona was somehow involved in the murder. "How did you get to meet her?"

"I came over to say hi once I'd moved in next door. She's too shy to have made the introduction on her own."

"You never knew her while you were still living in Berthoud?"

"No. Not till I moved here a few weeks ago."

Whew. That let her out. The woman had been hassled enough already with the embarrassing ploy I'd used to glean information from her earlier.

Trevor took me on a tour of his two-bedroom duplex, which was really not my motive for asking to see the place, but rather to get the opportunity to watch Shogun's comfort level. He was content to trot along with us, often leading the way, and would settle himself in the doorway whenever we stopped to chat.

"Are you planning to stay here permanently?"

"Nothing's permanent for me anymore. I have a six-month lease, though, so it'll be at least that long."

"You're planning on staying in the general area, though?"

"Yes, my job's going well. I get to pick and choose my own hours. And I like Colorado."

"And how would you react if I decide to recommend a joint ownership of Shogun?"

He shook his head. "That just won't work. That's the one thing we agree on. Once this divorce is finalized, I never want to see that woman as long as I live."

"You loved her once."

"Hard to believe. I must have been out of my mind. She's a witch. Believe me, Allida, if you decide to give Shogun to her . . . well, I don't know what I'd do, but I guess I'd have to live with it."

"If I assign custody to you, what's to prevent her from breaking in here and stealing him back?"

"Nothing. And you're right. There's every likelihood that she would do that. That's why I'm installing a security system, even though I may only be here for less than a year. I'm not exaggerating about her. The woman is evil. If I were you, I wouldn't trust living so near her. You cross her, and the fangs come out." He swept his hair out of his eyes and stared into the distance.

He sighed and said quietly, "Allida, even though it's not in my best interest to tell you this . . ." His voice faded, then he met my eyes. "If you decide to give me the dog, you'll be putting yourself in danger."

* * *

I didn't have another client until late afternoon, so I drove home. Shogun came with me willingly, but watched Trevor out the back window as we drove off and spent the trip lying on the backseat with his chin on his front paws. He perked up again, though, as we made the turn onto our street. Mom was at work herself.

After I'd been home long enough to play with the dogs, someone banged on the screen door, which seemed odd, since we have a doorbell. I went to answer, my dogs beating me there. It was Paul and Melanie, Paul looking distressed. He was still wearing the black suit and striped tie he'd had on at the funeral. Melanie, though, was now wearing overalls and a T-shirt.

"Hi, Allida. Is your mom here?"

"No, she's not."

He grimaced, then said, "I need to ask an enormous favor. Can you baby-sit Melanie for a couple of hours? Something's come up at work that I can't get out of."

"Sure. You're . . . back at work already?"

"Not full-time. But I need to establish some normalcy, a normal pattern. I just have to . . . Can you watch Melanie till three or so? I should make it back by then at the very latest."

"I'd be delighted to," I said, though my brain was churning with the panicked thoughts that I had no experience with children whatsoever, let alone with children who'd recently been traumatized. But I did have plenty of dogs to help me. "Come on, Melanie. Would you like to see Suds's puppies again?"

"No!" She ran and grabbed her father's legs.

"Suds? You have Suds here?"

"No, the original owner took Suds, but I still have her puppies."

To my complete dismay, Paul was livid. His hands were fisted and he looked as though he wanted to punch me. His daughter was still clinging to a leg, but he seemed to have forgotten her presence. "How could you do that without asking me?"

"Without asking you *what*? Paul, I'm sorry if this has . . . rubbed salt in your wounds, but let's get a little perspective here. All I did was to foster-adopt a dog and her puppies that you had tried to foster, but couldn't due to tragic circumstances. It never occurred to me that you'd be upset."

He clenched his jaw and stared up and past me, at the roof eaves, if he was even aware of what was in his vision.

"I truly am sorry, Paul."

"Yeah, well, I guess . . . I guess there was no reason for me to blow up. You just . . . have no idea how hard . . ."

He broke off and stroked his daughter's hair. Watching him now, I felt like an idiot for just blurting out to little Melanie about the puppies. She probably could only associate those puppies with her mother's death.

"Melanie?" Paul asked in a tender voice. "Is it all right if you stay here for a couple of hours while Daddy's at a meeting?"

She nodded, said sadly, "I guess so," but let go of her grip on her father and approached me as if she were walking into the doctor's office for immunization shots.

"I won't be late."

"Good, because I do need to leave for an appointment with a client by four o'clock."

"I'll be back long before then."

He waved and rushed down the stairs. I turned to my new charge. "Could I introduce you to my other dogs? I know you've already met them through living across the street, but this is the first time you've been in their home, right?"

She shrank back, wrapping her sleeveless arms around her chest. "I hate dogs."

"Okay. Let's do something else then. And I'll go put all of the dogs outside."

This killed me. I felt that I'd lost a potential dog lover because of a horrible trauma that had nothing to do with dogs in general. I knew that I was wrong to think all people should love dogs. They were sometimes smelly, noisy, and messy— the dogs, that is, though the same can be said for people—and there were probably other flaws that I couldn't come up with on my own. But, by my experience, I wasn't sure how I could have coped with the loss of my father at Melanie's age if I hadn't had my family's golden retrievers to commiserate with.

She was staring at Shogun, who'd run up to greet her. "This dog belongs in that blue house next to me. How come he's here?"

"I'm just keeping him for a couple of days, then I'll give him to one of the Cunninghams."

"How come?"

I hesitated, not sure how wise this was of me to be sharing personal information with a little girl. "How come what? How come I'm giving Shogun to one of them?"

"Uh-huh." She gave me a big nod and stared straight into my eyes.

When I was a child, I hated the fact that people were always trying to keep "secrets" from me, and that I usually already knew them. "They're getting a divorce, so they won't both be able to keep him."

She nodded solemnly, in an adorable affectation of someone much older. "My parents were getting a divorce."

Melanie's poor enunciation must have gotten the better of me. Or else she'd misunderstood or was simply trying her best to make adult conversation. I'd been with Cassandra just a couple of hours before her murder, and she'd spoken about how she was fostering the dogs solely because Paul was a dog person. There was no chance that she was on the verge of divorcing her husband.

I realized, too, that this was going to cause Paul nothing but pain if his daughter was blurting out to people that he and his late wife had been getting a divorce. I had to set her straight. For emphasis, I knelt and got down to eye level with her, just as I might when establishing a bond with a good-sized dog.

"Melanie, honey, a divorce is when a marriage ends and . . . a mommy and a daddy don't live together anymore. Your parents weren't ending their marriage."

She looked directly into my eyes. "Oh, yes, they were. I heard them say so. That's why my daddy came home so early. He had to pack his suitcases. He was going to live someplace else."

Chapter 13

My reaction was a mixture of shock and almost horror, yet I immediately reminded myself that this was just a little girl. She might have concocted a scene in her head about her daddy packing up that day, or had gotten confused when he'd only come home to pack up for a business trip.

"Shogun is a nice little dog, isn't he?" I muttered to Melanie, desperate for a quick change in subject matter.

"Yes. I like little dogs. I just don't like big dogs."

"How 'bout we play with just Shogun and Doppler for a while, then?"

She thought about that for a moment, then nodded, her short dark hair bobbing. "Okay."

I brought Doppler inside, leaving Sage and Pavlov on the back deck. It was difficult for me to keep a calm exterior while my thoughts were in a whirlwind. I tried to decide if I should call Sergeant Millay later this afternoon when Melanie had gone and tell him what she'd said about the possible status of the marriage immediately before Cassandra was killed.

I had an image of the sergeant interrogating Paul Randon based on his daughter's one statement to me, and the scenario turned my stomach. I couldn't do that to him. It was just too likely that Melanie had fabricated the story. She was coping with the sudden death of her mother. She didn't need me or anyone else to put too much stock in her perceptions of her parents' marriage right now.

Surely Paul wouldn't have chosen to bring her over to my place if what Melanie had blurted was the truth. He'd have known that there was a possibility she would divulge such a potentially incriminating piece of information and would have found another sitter—some teenager who wasn't likely to report it.

We played a game of hide-and-seek, with the dogs as the seekers and Melanie as the hider. She laughed infectiously each time the dogs found her.

My big dogs watched us through the glass door with such obvious jealousy that their furry faces could have been green.

In the middle of our game, one of the puppies scrambled up the stairs. It was Fez, and though I hesitated, afraid that Melanie would be frightened at the sight of him, I said nothing as she spotted him.

"Look!" she squealed. "He made it up the stairs. All by his self!"

"Yes."

Though she hesitated for a moment, she knelt down and Fez waddled over to her. Melanie swept the little puppy into her arms and nuzzled his fur.

After a moment, she looked up at me. "Can I see the other puppies?"

The puppies were now five and a half weeks old and getting to the stage where it is important for them to socialize one-on-one with people, separate from their litter. Separation too early from the dam can lead the dogs to be too dependent on humans and to not fit in well with other dogs or animals. Too late a separation from the litter can be just as harmful in the opposite direction. Despite being taken from their mother a week and a half ahead of schedule, they had my dogs to teach them how to behave as an adult dog. I explained this to Melanie in the simplest of terms as we grabbed the smallest dog, a female I'd taken to calling Mrs. Smith, because she reminded me of my kindergarten teacher—they both waddled their cabooses as they walked. I'd also named the cutest puppy Little Russell. The two others were Dog-face and Fluffernutter, after my favorite sandwich as a kid, a name that sent Melanie into great fits of giggles each time it was used.

We played with each puppy outside, and Melanie was soon completely restored to her previous bouncing enthusiasm around the dogs. As time wore on, I started to glance at my watch a lot. Paul Randon was very late in spite of his promise.

This rapidly became one of the longer afternoons in my personal history. We watched TV, something that I'm loath to do during the day. As four o'clock drew near and I was fresh out of every idea for possible entertainment of a kindergartner—in a house with no toys—I began pacing. I realized that I'd made a big mistake, which showed my inexperience as a baby-sitter: I didn't know how to reach Paul.

"Melanie, do you know your dad's number at work?"

"No." Melanie clicked off the TV and flopped down on the middle of the living room floor. "I'm bored. I want to go home. When's Daddy coming?"

This was at least the hundredth time the question had come up, and this time I answered honestly, "I don't know. He should have been here by now. If he doesn't come very soon, you'll have to come to work with me."

"Okay," she said, ready and willing to drop everything and go.

I was running the possible solutions of what to do through my head. This was not going to be fair to my canine client, a mixed breed who had been so badly housebroken that he howled to get inside whenever he wanted to relieve himself so that he could go on a newspaper. That problem could be solved with a day or two's worth of attention from the owner and normally wouldn't have merited my services, but the dog had also become overattached to his owner and was starting to develop separation anxiety as well. The owners had no kids of their own and there was no advantage to suddenly throwing someone else's child into the mix.

Whatever planning I might have been able to do to accommodate Melanie was being circumvented by the rut that my thought pattern was in; I could only think about how inconsiderate this was of Paul to disappear like this. Melanie was enrolled in morning kindergarten. Why hadn't he arranged this important meeting of his to take place then? And what could possibly be more important than being with your child on the day of her mother's funeral?

We went out to the garage. I didn't have a car seat for her, but strapped her into the backseat of my Subaru. Just as we were about to pull out of the driveway, Paul drove up. He got out of the car, panting, his pale yellow tie askew. His dark hair was also mussed, as if he'd been driving with the window down, though that currently wasn't the case. "Allida. Hi. I'm a bit late."

"Yes, you are."

He ignored my tone of voice and got his daughter out of the car. "How's my princess?"

"Can I get a puppy, Daddy?"

Paul's eyes widened in surprise and he shot me a look that I hoped meant that he was impressed at how quickly I'd restored his daughter's appreciation for dogs. "We'll see, princess."

"Do they allow dogs where we're moving?"

He jerked slightly at the question, as if he'd gotten a jolt of static electricity, cluing me in that he'd rather not have had me overhear. "I'm sure they do."

"You're moving?"

He cleared his throat, his features drawing into a frown. "Soon, yes. There are . . . too many memories here."

"I can imagine."

"Thanks again for watching Melanie at the last minute like this." He got back into his car, Melanie on his lap, and he let her steer as they drove across the street to their own driveway.

It wasn't until I'd driven off myself toward my client's house that something puzzling hit me. Paul was now wearing a different tie than the one he'd worn when he dropped her off, supposedly on his way to work.

My work "day" ended at a house so far north of Boulder that I was almost in Lyons. I decided to swing by Susan's house. She'd made the decision to dump me so precipitously that I could claim to want to make sure that she hadn't changed her mind again about my working with Boris. I secretly hoped that she might be willing by now to tell me the whole story behind her father and his odd behavior.

There was a different car than usual in the driveway—a beat-up pickup truck. No sign of Susan's old Galaxy 500. Maybe this was her husband's vehicle and she'd been telling me the truth about his schedule after all.

A pleasant-looking, though overweight middle-aged man opened the door. He was average height—five-ten or so—and had curly brown hair and was wearing white paint-splattered overalls.

"Hi. I'm Allida Babcock. I've been working with your dog."

"Oh, yeah." He pumped my hand vigorously. "Hi, Allida. I'm Susan's husband, Fred. You live across from my in-laws. You own that great German shepherd and the collie, don't you?"

I immediately liked the man. "Yes. And the cocker spaniel, too. They are terrific dogs, aren't they?"

"Sure are. If it were up to me, I'd have five or six dogs, but Suzy says one's enough for her. Come on in." He held the door open for me, and I stepped inside their messy living room. Boris gave me a couple of territorial barks, but then allowed me to pat him. I'm sure his tail would have been wagging, had he had one.

Fred wore a bemused expression on his face as he watched me. "Susan told me she used to baby-sit for you and your brother. Said you were a pair of hellions."

I didn't want to get into a discussion of the past and quickly asked, "Is she here?"

"Don't know where she is, I'm afraid, but Boris is here, as you can see. We've got no plans for the next hour or so. I'd be happy for you to work with the two of us. Susan's here a lot more than I am, but I'll do what I can to help make Boris easier for her to get along with."

This was an unfortunate turn of events. Susan obviously hadn't told him about our last conversation, in which I'd been fired—though it's hard to consider oneself "fired" from a nonpaying position. "Susan didn't tell you that she doesn't want me to continue working with Boris?"

He studied my face as if to see if this was a joke. "She doesn't? Why not?"

"I'm not sure. You'll have to ask her."

He furrowed his brow, then shook his head. "No way. You must have misunderstood her. I gave her the fifty-dollar bill she said you needed just this morning."

"The fifty *I* needed?"

"Yeah. You only accept cash, right?"

"That's not true." I felt horribly uncomfortable, but I wasn't going to be a party to a lie between a woman I barely knew and didn't much like and her husband. "In fact, Fred, I'm afraid that you and she must have had the misunderstanding. I wasn't charging her at all for my work with your dog. We were going to work it out in trade. She was going to do yardwork at my mom's house."

"Whoa." He held up his palms and shook his head again. "That's crazy. Why wouldn't she pay you? I already told her I'd be happy to fork over the money if it made her happier with Boris."

I shrugged, embarrassed. "She said she couldn't afford it."

He averted his gaze, the muscles in his jaw working. "Damn that woman," he muttered under his breath.

He slammed his fist into his palm so hard that I was startled and instantly began to worry what her husband's anger might mean to Susan. What if I'd just set off an abusive spouse? She might have been hoarding the money so that she could escape from him.

"I'm sorry to have been the one who—"

"Hell, it ain't your fault." He gave me a lopsided smile. Though his cheeks were red, he met my eyes, and I had to say that his eyes portrayed only kindness. "She does stuff like this all the time. 'Fraid my wife has an expensive drug habit."

"I . . . had no idea. I'm sorry." I found myself making a quick appraisal of which scenario I believed—this man whom I'd only just met as a spouse abuser or Susan as a drug user. Susan hadn't struck me as the sort to be an addict, but then, I suppose I had a preconceived, naive notion of skinny, greasy-haired teens with dark circles around their sunken eyes. She did, however, have a fiery temper and rapid mood swings. Her husband was the more likable of the pair and, I decided, more credible.

"You're tellin' me. She'd been off the stuff for a while now, but she must be hooked again. It's all her damn . . . dieting that did it to her. She was obsessed with getting back to her old weight, and got into taking uppers to lose weight."

"If there's anything I can do . . ." I let my voice drift off, feeling stupid for starting to mutter the automatic response that nobody really expects to be sincere. Besides, I knew nothing about drug addiction or anything helpful to do toward easing his predicament.

"I'll bet Cassie's death pushed her right over the edge," he muttered to himself.

"Cassandra Randon?" I asked, surprised at the familiarity he'd shown. Susan had implied that she barely knew the woman. "Did you know her?"

"No. Only met her a couple times. I meant for Susan's sake, though." He studied my face. "Didn't Suzy tell you? She and Cassandra were running a business together—back before she and I met, that is."

"No, she didn't mention it. What kind of business was this?"

"Oh, they started up some mail-order thing—customized monograms or something like that. People could send in clothing and stuff, and they'd monogram it."

"Cassandra and Susan must have met when the Randons bought the house next to Susan's parents' place, then, right?"

"Yeah, and they found out about their mutual sewing talents. Then I guess Susan told Cassie about her idea for this custom monogramming business, and they gave it a go for a while. But Susan doesn't really do too well with other women, and they couldn't work together. So Cassandra was supposedly goin' to buy out Susan's half of the business."

He winced and ran his beefy hand across his curly brown

hair. "Suzy told me that she never did get her money out of Cassandra. Hell. Now that I think about it, she probably lied. Same way she lied to me about paying you. She probably bilked Cassandra for all she was worth. Maybe that's where she'd been getting her drug money, till now."

"Again, Fred, I'm really sorry that Susan's got such serious problems. I'd better go now."

"Hey. Don't be thinking that . . ." He laid a heavy hand on my shoulder. "Whatever drug problems Susan might have doesn't mean she had anything to do with Cassandra's death, you know. I promise you that. She'd never kill anyone. Not in a million years. She's had this drug addiction problem for years, off 'n' on, but she's never stolen or hurt anyone."

"I'm . . . glad. Have you talked to the police about your wife's troubles?"

"Oh, man. I shouldn't've got into all this. You're going to go straight to the police, aren't you?"

I hesitated and thought for a moment, then scanned the man's face. If he was lying about any of his convictions, including his insistence that his wife was innocent of Cassandra's murder, he was a skilled actor. I couldn't see the sense in my rushing to call Sergeant Millay. If Susan had a history of drug problems and was in the area when Cassandra was being murdered, he would know to check her alibi. He seemed to barely tolerate my dragging him over to Luellen's house to search for Shogun. Sergeant Millay was going to think I had nothing better to do than to tell him how to do his job.

"No, I'm not. But you and Susan might want to talk to them." Though I felt a bit Pollyanna-ish, I couldn't help but add, "If nothing else, the police might be able to help you get Susan into a good treatment program."

He breathed a sigh of relief and smiled. "I'll take care of my wife. Don't worry."

My heart sank into my stomach at the words, but his face stayed guileless. He surely didn't mean he'd "take care" of her in an evil sense.

I kept turning the phrase over and over in my head as I

drove home. As much as I believed my instincts that said Fred Nelson was a loving husband married to a difficult woman who perhaps had a drug problem, all I really knew was that Cassandra Randon had been murdered. Someone was playing for keeps.

Though I felt like a heel for having lied to the man, the moment I walked in my door, I went straight to my phone, ignoring my dogs and my mother, and called Sergeant Millay. I told him precisely what Fred had told me, including how his wife had claimed I was charging cash for services never rendered.

My mother listened to my end of the phone conversation in complete silence, her arms crossed as if she were cold. She was wearing my favorite blouse of hers, a black velvet collar and cuff on blue denim, which matched her jeans. After I'd hung up, she said immediately, "My God, Allida. How horrible."

"I know. And my last words to Susan's husband were that I *wouldn't* go straight to the police."

She shrugged. "That wasn't something you could stick with, though. You did the right thing."

"Did I? I have no idea if any of what Fred told me is true. I might have just made a load of trouble for Susan that she didn't deserve." I sighed. "Rest assured that Harvey and Betsy won't be nominating me for any Most-Beloved-Neighbor awards."

"Darn," she said, snapping her fingers. "And I know how much their opinion has always meant to you."

Despite my mood, Mom's comment made me smile, which soon faded as I considered more implications of Susan's situation. "Do you think it's possible that she and her father are both addicts? That Harvey was high on something when he came over here and tried to break in the other night?"

Mom ran her hand over her hair and down the length of her braid. Finally she said, "I don't know. I guess it's possible that she and her parents are up to their ears in debt because of drug problems. Maybe Harvey was trying to steal some petty cash out of my kitchen."

"Do you keep any petty cash in your kitchen?"

"No, not that I'd ever consider cash 'petty.' Which doesn't mean Harvey knows that."

The next morning was a Saturday, always my busiest day. Mom was up before me, but still wearing her robe. She was mixing milk replacement with water and puppy chow in the kitchen when I came in to grab a quick breakfast.

"How are the puppies doing with their new diet?"

"Pretty well. But they're making an incredible mess of things. Fluffernutter seems to think the food dish is the best seat in the house."

I tried to get the little puppy reoriented so that his correct end was in the bowl. Otherwise, they truly were taking to the food nicely, if messily. The phone rang. Mom was soon laughing and chatting with the caller, so I tuned out, assuming this was one of her friends. To my surprise, after five minutes or so she came over to me and said, "Allida, it's Russell."

She accompanied me to the phone, then realized when I gave her a significant look that she was intruding on my personal space.

"I'm going to take a shower."

"Hi, Allie," Russell said to my hello. "I was thinking of you and wanted to see how you were doing before I headed to the hills."

"Fine," I answered. My heart had started beating faster, though, and I felt a little out of breath. This was so annoying! I really, really didn't want to be finding myself getting so attracted to someone with whom I doubted I had enough in common to have a lasting relationship. "How are you?"

"Okay, but I wish you were coming with me."

"Ah, yes. My dream date. Scrambling up the face of a cliff till I get vertigo and pass out."

Almost as soon as the words were out, I regretted them, thinking Russell would assume I was making fun of him, but he chuckled. "Actually, I think we're just going to go for a few hours now, instead of . . ."

Someone started ringing the doorbell so relentlessly that Russell's words were drowned out. The shower water was already running, so I knew it was up to me to answer it. I apologized to Russell, but even in the short period of time that that took, the person outside was now also banging on the door. I quickly explained that whatever this was sounded too serious for me to get back to the phone right away, and hung up.

It was probably one of the Haywoods, who'd heard about my "squealing" to the police and wanted to get even by bringing a lawsuit against me for those glued sneakers. I reminded myself to get that check into their mailbox before I left for work. The visitor was pounding hard enough to rattle the door on its hinges. My temper rose with every step as I crossed the living room.

I glanced through the peephole and recognized John White through the distorted lens. I threw open the door and stared at his appearance in surprise. Despite his tan, his face had a waxy look to it. His forehead was dotted with perspiration. Something terrible had obviously happened to him.

Before I could say anything, he cried, "Thank God you're here. Allida. There's an emergency, and I need you to come with me."

"What?"

"There's no time. I need you to come with me. There's . . . I found a couple of dogs running loose just a short distance from here and I need you to help. It'll just take a couple of minutes."

"I don't understand. Why do—"

"It's over at the water tower on the edge of town. I'll explain the whole thing when we get in the car. Come on. We need to hurry, or else it'll be real bad."

"John, you're acting—"

"Come with me! Please! We've got to get over to the water tower before someone gets killed!"

"*Someone?* But I thought—"

"There's a child that's caught up on the water tower and an Akita that's acting rabid and won't let him climb down!"

"My God. We need to call the—"

"I already called the police, but they need help with the dog." He started down the steps back toward his car. "If you won't help me, maybe I can find someone else who will!"

My heart was racing. I wouldn't be able to forgive myself if some child was in danger and I did nothing. I trotted down the walkway toward him.

How on earth could a dog have trapped a child on a water tower? And how had they come to contact John about that? He must be working Animal Control and gotten the call. But if so, where was the van and its equipment? We needed one of those poles with the loop on the end so we could safely catch the dog.

I got into the passenger seat. The car had the familiar scent of dogs, but reeked of tobacco now, too. "John, tell me again. What's happening at the water tower? Why do you need me to—"

There was a sudden motion from the backseat, and I gasped and automatically lurched forward while twisting around to look. It was Carver, and he had a long-bladed knife in his hand.

"Howdy, Miss Babcock. The three of us are goin' for a little ride."

I looked at John, whose face in profile was beet red and damp with perspiration.

"Sorry, Allida. He said he had a gun that would be pointed at me the whole time we were talking. He didn't give me any choice."

Chapter 14

"Just drive," Carver instructed in a gravelly voice to John. "Get us out of here before her ol' lady sees us." He ducked down slightly, and John slowly pulled away from the curb.

"What do you want?" I asked Carver as calmly as I could, only the slightest tremble in my voice giving me away.

"Same thing everyone wants. A million bucks. A mansion with a batch of servants. But I'd settle for an even break. I lost my job, thanks to you shitheads. And now I lost my dog. I need you two to get her back."

Carver was talking nonsense. There was no way either John or I had anything to do with his failing to get some job that he wanted. Or with the loss of his dog.

His eyes looked wild, and I wondered if he was high on something. The thought of his being less than lucid while holding a knife to my neck was not a pleasant one.

I gave a little glance in John's direction, afraid to fully look at him for fear that Carver would see any communication between us as a threat.

John gave me the slightest of winks—some feeble attempt at reassurance—the perspiration on his forehead showing that he was far from relaxed. "He hasn't explained this to me, either, yet. He ambushed me at work and basically insisted I do what he says without explanation."

"I told you as much as you need to know. You're driving to the dog pound in Boulder."

"Fine, Craig. I'll take you to the Humane Society. I can get your dog back, no questions asked. We don't need Allida for that."

"Hey! Get this straight right now, John-boy! *I* decide what I need. And right now, I need her to do the front work for me."

"Front work?"

"You're going to go into the Boulder Humane Society with me and fetch me my dog. Meantime, John here is going to keep the car engine running, and we'll bring the dog out around back."

This was nuts! He was taking two people against their will just to get his dog out of the animal shelter? "Why don't you just go in and identify your dog and take her yourself?"

He grabbed a handful of my hair, pulled my head back, and held the knife against the skin of my neck. "That's none of your business, dog girly." His hot breath on my face reeked of alcohol.

My eyes filled with tears from the pain in my scalp. I automatically reached up and tried to pry his fingers loose, but he only pulled harder.

John's steering went wild. We were veering all over the road. "Calm down, Craig."

Carver chuckled. "Don't like me touching your girlfriend, hey?"

"You're hurting her. You're just getting yourself in deeper and deeper."

Not trusting my voice and unwilling to give Carver the satisfaction of seeing me cry, I tried to swat John to signal for him to pay more attention to his driving. He was barely staying in the lane. That blade was all too close for John to be making an unexpected swerve.

"Deeper and deeper, hey?" Carver snorted and released his grasp on me. "You got a way with words, John-boy."

"Are you okay?" John asked me quietly.

I turned my face to the window, not unleashing the four-letter words on the tip of my tongue. My head hurt horribly, and rage had me far too tempted toward taking a stupid risk than was in my best interest.

"Are you okay?" Carver mimicked, then laughed. "Shit. You are such an idiot. I'll let you in on a secret, John-boy. I don't have no gun. All you had to do back there was tell your little girlfriend here to call the police, and I'd've been up shit's creek."

I looked over at John, who grimaced and reddened. So Carver had fooled him into thinking he had a gun trained on him when he was at my door. Carver also must have gotten violent in his drunken state and had Suds forcibly taken from him on an animal cruelty charge, or he would be able to get her back himself simply and legally.

Most likely he was on the lam and had escaped getting arrested for whatever he'd done to Suds. He also might not want to take the chance of going in there after his dog, knowing that he might be recognized. There was often an inmate or two working in the exercise areas or outbuildings.

I desperately needed a plan, but had none. I couldn't do a damned thing to escape, with a knife against my throat. One thing was clear, though. Fair or not, I never wanted to see John White again as long as I lived. Which I hoped meant a long time.

It was a long drive into Boulder, and Carver settled back in his seat in silence. I considered my options: jumping out of the car, which wasn't going to work; crying hysterically, which might force Carver to think again about taking me with him into the Humane Society. Even at that, Carver could simply claim I was distraught over concerns for the dog. Most of the volunteers and staff at the Humane Society knew me. Could I get out of harm's way long enough to tell them to call the police?

The drive seemed both eternally long and far too short as we turned on 55th Street and neared the building. This was a Saturday. The place would be packed with families, children, looking at prospective new pets.

We pulled into the parking lot and found the last available space in front of the building. The long ride had only solidi-fied my fear. I honestly wasn't sure my legs would work. If I got out and ran inside to get someone to alert the police, Carver might kill John in his desperation to escape.

John rotated in his seat to look at Carver. "Listen, Craig. It's just not necessary for you to use Allida like this." John was making a second attempt at some measure of chivalry that could never compensate for his having tricked me into getting into his car in the first place. "I'll just go into the shelter and tell them that I'm taking Suds back up to Loveland with me. They won't stop me. I have all the necessary credentials in my wallet."

"Yeah. That'd work. Except for the slight problem that I don't trust you out of my sight. And that I'd feel a lot better walking in arm-in-arm with your little girlfriend than with you."

There had to be an easy way out of this mess. Even if I elbowed him and got away, I didn't want to put anyone at the Humane Society in jeopardy. Carver would just grab some other person to use as a hostage.

My mind was blank. He was right in assuming that no one would stop us. Though Carver couldn't possibly know this, the staff had seen me there frequently in the past few weeks working with the dogs. All I had to do was put on a volunteer's vest, walk straight in, locate Suds's cage, and take him out.

Carver got out and opened my door. He leaned in, his eyes roaming down the length of my body. "You do realize, don't you, John-boy, that if you try anything, if the car isn't right here, engine running, no police in sight when we get back here with Suds, this is the last you'll see of little Allida. I'll slit her throat on the spot. You got that?"

"I understand. I'll be right here." His face was pale and sweating profusely. He gave me the quickest of glances, then averted his eyes, not willing to face the part he'd played in dragging me into this mess.

Carver shut the door and grabbed my upper arm firmly, pulling me out of the car. "Come on."

"Listen, Mr. Carver. I'm no heroine. You obviously love Suds and deserve to keep her. There's no reason for you to go in there with me. I'll just tell the employees that I've located Suds's owner, pay the fine, and bring her to you."

He laughed and leaned down, putting his face inches from mine so that I got another whiff of his foul breath. "Guess what, girlie? I don't trust you out of my sight, either. Now let's go."

With slow, deliberate movements, Carver folded up his knife and stuck it in his back pocket. "Just to let you know, Miss Allie, this is a switchblade. I can whip the blade out before you can get to the letter *p* in the word 'help.' "

I was impressed that he knew how to spell the word, but held my tongue. As we turned to head for the entrance, I caught a glimpse of John through the windshield. He tried to give me an encouraging nod, but his face was pale and he looked stricken.

Carver opened the door for me. I'd deliberately chosen the door on the right side of the lobby so that we'd have farther to walk. The warm air inside the building was heavy with animal odors that normally didn't bother me, but under these circumstances made me gag.

There was what looked to be a family of three engaging a male volunteer in an animated conversation. A young woman named Skye was behind the counter. She looked up, caught my eye, and said, "Hi, Allida."

I indicated Carver with my eyes and said, "Hi, anathema," knowing that the word would be beyond Carver's vocabulary and hoping Skye would at least be alerted to keep an eye on Carver.

Unfortunately, it was apparently beyond Skye's vocabulary as well, for she chuckled and said, "You mean 'Skye,' don't you?"

Though I again tried to point with my eyeballs, she had already turned her attention elsewhere.

"Keep going," Carver said into my ear.

Nobody gave us a second glance as we pushed through the door into the hallway. Adult customers don't need supervision during the day to go back here, and given that the vast majority of employees had seen me before, there was no chance that anyone would stop us.

The hallway was empty. The dog kennels were to the left, but the exit to the exercise pens was straight ahead of us. I could run for it.

Just as the thought hit me, a young boy—seven or so—came bolting inside, followed by his parents. I hesitated, imagining Carver pulling his knife out of his pocket in front of the child, and the moment was lost. Carver laid a heavy hand on my shoulder.

"Let's find Suds. Right now."

"They won't let us take her out without a leash," I said, gesturing in the direction of the dozens of leashes hanging on the wall.

To get to the leashes, we would pass another area where there were always staff members and volunteers. If only some burly man would come out. That might distract Carver long enough for me to get away.

No one was near this door, nor by the laundry room on the other side. I grabbed a sturdy leash, torn between the hope that, if I went along with this quietly, Carver might just let me get his dog, perhaps he'd steal John's car, and take off, at which point we could let the police handle him—and the realization that Carver was acting so irrational now, there was no guarantee that I'd ever have another chance to get away from him.

We went into the kennel area. There were twenty large cages here, all chain-link. To my surprise, only two men happened to be in the immediate area. They were prospective customers, walking through ahead of us, checking out the dogs. They were young and athletic-looking. If things came down to it, it was unlikely Carver could handle both of them at once. This was going to be my one opportunity.

Carver sensed this, too, and grabbed my wrist, his other hand on my shoulder. "Find the dog and get us out of here."

The kennels were in their typical state of chaos whenever anyone walks through. The majority of dogs had rushed forward to bark at us, pleading with us in dog-speak to get them out of here.

My first thought was to throw open a batch of the cages to create a diversion, but Carver would pull his knife by the time I got one cage open. We passed the first couple of cages.

Carver had such a tight grip on me that I couldn't even reach a gate latch.

I finally caught sight of Suds. She would not be up for adoption yet because of her short time here. She was all the way at the end of the row. Even at this distance, I could see the bandages on her injured muzzle where Carver must have beat her. The sight filled me with rage.

Carver was looking around, as if concerned he had not seen her yet. One of the men checking out the dogs was coming our way.

"She's right over there," I said to Carver, pointing with my free hand. The moment he loosened his grip on me to follow my gaze, I whipped my wrist around and threw my shoulder into his midsection.

My sudden motion surprised him enough that he fell back against the cages. With the racket this caused, both men looked our way.

"Help! He's got a knife!" I yelled, hoping the man nearest the exit would go to get outside help.

Carver was struggling to regain his balance. I dove at him before he could get his knife out. His head banged against the white-painted cinder-block partial wall that separates the two rows of kennels.

I was too slow. Carver shoved me down as if I were a child and grabbed the knife out of his pocket.

The man just a few feet away from us took off running for the exit, saying, "I'll get help," as he scrambled out the door.

Shit! The second man had left as well, and now I was on my own with this creep and his knife!

I kicked Carver blindly, then sprang to my feet, but I knew there would be no way for me to outrun Carver to the exit. I threw open the cage of a rambunctious mixed breed I'd been working with—part dalmation, part springer spaniel. She rushed out of the cage, distracting Carver for the half second it took for me to whip the leash at Carver's face, the metal clasp catching him right in the eye.

Carver cried out in pain and brought his free hand up to his injured eye. I kneed him in the groin, and he dropped the knife.

I kicked the knife away, just as Carver managed to get his hands around my neck.

"You little bitch! I'll teach you!"

Just then, three men charged through the doors toward us. Carver loosened his grip on me at the sight, and I managed to elbow him in the Adam's apple and break free.

While the men nearly barrelled into me in their effort to grab Carver, I ducked down and snatched up Carver's knife. One man tackled Carver and another bent his arm back.

Carver growled and struggled to free himself, but the men had him firmly pinned. Meanwhile, the dog I'd freed was in a frenzy, scared by the men's struggle, and tried to jump up on me. I turned my back on her, which, as with almost any dog, immediately made her get down, then I grabbed her collar and pulled her back into the cage.

I tried to thank my rescuers, but my voice came out in a croak. I put a hand on my throat. My throat and voice box were in horrible pain. The memory of Carver choking me with his strong hands was not going to leave me anytime soon. "Police," I managed to utter.

"Skye's already called them," one of the men said.

The Boulder police arrived and took Carver away. Another officer drove me to the station house to make a report and later drove me home. My day's schedule had been shot to hell, but I was just glad to be alive and rescheduled everything for next week.

Ironically, Mom was feeling guilty for not having worried about me. When she found I'd left without saying good-bye— and without taking my car—she assumed Russell had picked me up to make my rounds with me, and had taken off herself shortly afterward. I changed into a turtleneck so that she'd stop staring at the red marks on my neck. She kept asking me if there was anything she could get for me, and, more to get her to stop than anything else, I sent her out for ice cream, claiming that would soothe my throat.

Moments after she'd pulled out of the driveway, the door-bell rang. The full menagerie of dogs, puppies included, accompanied me to the door, where I looked out the peep-hole. It was Trevor's sister, Luellen. I considered simply calling out to her to go away, but my voice wasn't fully restored and I didn't want to strain my vocal chords. I opened the door, but said nothing in greeting.

Luellen was wearing splashy-looking, predominantly blue pants augmented with gold lines and a scoop-necked T-shirt. "Hello, Allida. I was in the neighborhood and wanted to check on Shogun." She turned her attention to Shogun, who'd worked his way to the forefront. "There's my baby," she cooed. "How's my little man? Huh? How's my little man?"

Her "little man" promptly got overexcited and piddled on the floor. We were getting accustomed to accidents with the proliferation of puppies anyway. Shogun began scratching at the wooden frame on the screen door. I opened it a crack. He squeezed out, and while he and Luellen greeted each other, I slid a newspaper on top of the newest puddle. She picked up Shogun, and we locked eyes.

"Trevor called me this morning. He told me you still have Shogun. You know just as well as I do that that dog would be best off with my brother. What's the holdup?"

With a hand on my throat to soothe the pain, I answered, "If you or Trevor had told me that the dog was at your house the night after my neighbor's murder, this would have been resolved back then."

"We didn't *take* him, Allida. I went looking for him when he was first missing, and I found him."

"I'm supposed to believe you? After you tried to make me look like an idiot? After you lied to the police about your having Shogun?"

"Allida, I did some underhanded things, I realize. But they were all done in an effort to protect Shogun."

"Protect him from what?"

She glanced over her shoulder. "Can I come in?"

I herded the dogs back and shoved open the door, still too

exhausted and cranky to be the least bit hospitable. Luellen stepped inside, but neither of us moved toward a seat. She ruffled his fur, then set him down with the other dogs.

"When I found Shogun, Allida, he was frightened out of his wits. He didn't even recognize me, and he bit my hand when I first tried to pick him up. It was as if he were running for his life."

Only then did I notice that she wasn't wearing the wrist braces she'd had on the previous times we'd met. "That's what you were wearing the wrist supports for? To cover up your dog bite?"

"Right. I put them on to hide this." She showed me the characteristic puncture wounds across the fleshy part of her hand between the thumb and fingers. The bite marks could only have been made by a very small dog, such as Shogun. "I'm not exactly a walking advertisement for my dogs while sporting bandages from a bite wound."

"I can imagine."

"None of my dogs has ever bit me before. And Shogun's never bit anyone. This dog is as gentle as a bunny. He only bit me because he was in such a state of terror. I just couldn't let him go back there to Edith. I believe she killed that woman. That's why Shogun was so frightened."

"If she chased after him or hurt him, maybe, but I can't see Shogun having been capable of interpreting whatever he might have seen and concluding that he was in danger."

"Maybe not. But all I know is I've always warned Trevor about Edith. She's a self-centered, evil-minded woman. I think if Shogun had bit her instead of me, she'd have had him put to sleep."

I tended to agree with that assessment, and the sentiment must have been written on my features, for Luellen studied my face for a moment, then smiled. "Allida, I know you'll make the right decision. But believe me, Shogun would be safer with Trevor than here, so close to that woman. I wouldn't put it past her to . . . do something terrible to Shogun, just to keep Trevor from ever enjoying his company again."

On that note, Luellen turned on a heel and left.

I stared across the street. The police tape was down from Edith Cunningham's house, and I got a glimpse of her through her front window. As much as I wanted to curl up in the fetal position and stay safe for the rest of the day, Luellen was right. I needed to get this issue regarding Shogun resolved. I had already met with Trevor. I needed to do the same with Edith.

I called her on the phone. When she answered, I asked, "Would this be a good time for me to come over with Shogun and finally have our appointment?"

"As a matter of fact, this isn't terribly good timing. I only just now got back into my house. I shouldn't even be here; I'm supposed to be at my store, but there are some things I need to take care of." She paused and sighed. "However, I am anxious to see Shogun again. How long would you estimate that this will take?"

"Half an hour at the most."

"All right, then. Let's get it over with."

She hung up abruptly, which I assumed meant I was to come over posthaste. I wrote a note to my mom that I was at Edith's and would be back ASAP, and that I hoped she could just stick my ice cream in the freezer for me.

Though I now had that nicely personalized bed for Shogun, no one had given me his leash, and I wanted to test Shogun's reaction as we neared his former home. It would be interesting to see if he was anxious or reluctant to get there.

I foolishly grabbed Doppler's leash right while he was in the room. This, of course, immediately signaled to Doppler that we were going for a walk, and my snapping it on Shogun's collar instead of his was likely to lead to a power struggle between the smaller dog duo. Before leaving, I reached into my emergency supplies in the coat closet and gave Doppler a rawhide bone, which more than compensated for the temporary use of his leash.

Shogun and I left through the front door. To my surprise, Shogun had been leash-trained. He stayed right by my side and sat the minute I stopped at the roadside. "Shogun, heel," I ordered out of curiosity as we started out to cross the street. He hopped up and again walked perfectly at my left side, his pointy ears up and his mannerisms happy and proud.

To test his reaction, I slowed my pace and gave Shogun full lead as we headed straight for the Randons' walkway, which was directly across from mine.

To my surprise, Shogun started up the walkway as if this were a visit he was accustomed to making. And yet Cassandra had been so dog-shy, it would have been strange for either Edith or Trevor to bring the dog when going next door.

As soon as the leash got tight as I quit following the dog up the Randons' walkway, Shogun stopped, looked back at me with hunched shoulders and hanging head—the dog expression of embarrassment—and trotted back over to me. When I deliberately didn't move, to see which way he headed, he let out a little whine and started toward Edith's house, then sat down, waiting for me.

As soon as I took one step down the sidewalk in the direction of his former home, he started happily trotting ahead of me, pulling on his leash. This was a good sign, to my way of thinking. It was good news to everyone, in fact, except possibly Trevor, but for all I knew, Shogun might be hoping to see Trevor in his house. Dogs can be infinitely patient when expecting to return to their old routine, which meant, for Shogun, both owners at home.

I started getting the heebie-jeebies as we neared the Cunninghams' house. I immediately stared at the gate, noting that this time it was shut, and tried to blink away the hideous scene from a few days ago that had returned unbidden to my memory.

Out of curiosity, I removed Shogun's leash. The dog raced up the walkway and to the front door, which meant this was a common return route for him, as opposed to his heading toward the gate at the side.

I rang the doorbell, and Edith swung open the door, looking her usual elegant self in a tailored dress suit—predominantly rust-colored, which matched her lipstick and brought out the auburn highlights in her hair. As usual, her cosmopolitan attire struck me as incongruous with our rural setting, but maybe that was just me.

"Hello, Allie," she said, with her version of warm smile that struck me as more for show than heartfelt. Her use of my nickname was a bit offensive. Normally only my closest friends call me Allie, and she was far from that category. I noted, too, that she was focused on me and not her own dog, her vision not drifting down in the least.

She continued to pay no attention to Shogun even as she ushered us inside her house. The little dog rushed ahead as Edith led me to the center of her tastefully furnished living room, where we remained standing.

As a test, I wanted to keep her engaged in conversation not related to Shogun to see how long it would take till she even noticed her supposedly beloved dog. "Edith, I was wondering when that sale you were telling me about was going to start."

"Today, as a matter of fact, which is why this is so inconvenient." She appraised my attire and said, "I can do wonders for you. Give you an aura of professionalism."

"I'm sure my clients will appreciate that."

"Dress to the level to which you aspire. That has always been my motto."

"And what level would you suggest a dog behaviorist aspire to?"

She clicked her tongue and didn't answer. "How is my little boy doing?" she finally said, turning her attention to her dog, who quietly waited by her feet. She picked him up, his tail wagging as she stroked his fur.

"Fine. Edith, I'm curious about something. When you go out of town, who do you have take care of Shogun?"

"We used to take him with us, on those few times we traveled together."

"Did you ever ask Cassandra to watch him?"

She winced at the name. "No. Although we were close friends, I would never have asked her. She didn't like dogs."

"So you never, for example, brought Shogun over there when you were visiting Cassandra?"

"No. But I can't promise the same is true for Trevor."
Through clenched teeth, she added, "For all I know, he might
have been Cassandra's pimp."

Though I'd become inured to Edith's caustic comments
regarding her husband, her remark about Cassandra rattled
me. "Um, I don't think I want to get into this. Cassandra was
a nice lady and a good mother, and beyond that, I—"

"Yes, she was both of those things. And I considered her a
friend, despite her faults. Furthermore, I sincerely hope the
police find her killer and string the bastard up by his thumbs.
Unfortunately, though, by the sounds of it, I knew Cassandra
a good deal better than you did." She looked me straight in
the eyes and said firmly, "I knew that she should have put a
revolving door in her bedroom."

For just a moment, an expression of genuine sorrow
passed across her features. She added sadly, "And that my
soon-to-be ex-husband would have had his paw prints all
over it."

Chapter 15

I decided to ignore Edith's last remark as best I could. During our conversation, Shogun had rushed under the writing desk in the corner of the living room. He was obviously used to hiding out there.

Edith followed my gaze and saw where he was cowering. She managed to put her anger toward Trevor aside long enough to bend down and call, "Come on, Shogun," in a high voice with a you're-going-to-get-a-treat enthusiasm. He came up to her with only a slight hesitation.

Trying my best to give her the benefit of the doubt, I had her run through some basic training routines. This was always a good way for me to get a feel for how a dog and his owner relate, not so much by watching the dog's responses, but by watching the owner's reactions to the dog's responses. It's amusing to me how seriously the human contingent always seem to take this exercise. Invariably the owner reacts as though I'm sitting in judgment of his or her ability to properly train the dog.

In this case, Edith was clearly very anxious to please, and so was Shogun. The dog was enthusiastic throughout and obeyed very well, which was what I'd expected from my own experience with Shogun during the past couple days.

I clapped my hands once loudly when the dog was in the middle of a lie-down-stay routine. As I expected, Shogun was startled, leapt to his feet, and let out a quick series of shrill, scolding barks at me.

"What did you do that for?" Edith snapped in the human equivalent of her canine's reaction.

"Just testing his temperament. Can we step into the kitchen for a moment, please?"

"Certainly," Edith said with a hint of impatience.

Though Edith didn't question me, I had asked this last as a way to see how at home Shogun felt. Most dogs who consider themselves the alpha dog of the pack will dart ahead of their owners and lead the way into rooms. Less dominant dogs, however, tend to follow a few steps behind, then plant themselves in the doorway afterward.

"Shogun isn't normally this jumpy," she said to me as we entered the kitchen. Shogun rushed ahead of us, but—tellingly, in my opinion—stayed by my feet rather than by Edith's.

"I'm sure that's true." Which was what I'd tried to tell her the very first time she'd come to me with Shogun.

"It's all that he's been through, lately. Getting kidnapped by Luellen and then by my husband and then, well, pardon my bluntness, but by *you*. The poor baby doesn't know if he's coming or going."

That was an interesting, and very one-sided, interpretation of the facts. A bit of revisionist personal history going on there. "Not to mention his witnessing Cassandra's murder," I added a bit caustically.

She winced. "I try not to even let myself think about that tragedy. Cassandra was a dear friend of mine. It's too upsetting to think about her meeting with a violent end, right here in my own house."

Right. A "very dear friend" whom, minutes ago, she was calling a whore. My eyes were drawn to the deck. Everything looked normal there now; no hint of the horrid scene I'd stumbled upon a few days ago.

Edith lifted her recently sculpted nose and said, "I would like very much to think that Shogun somehow missed witnessing the actual murder. I'm quite certain it was Trevor. Some sort of lover's quarrel, I suspect. I'd like to believe that he at least put Shogun in his car beforehand."

I studied her face to make sure she was serious. Her lips were set in a firm, thin line. The prospect of anyone killing someone in the heat of passion, after first swooping his dog up to protect him from witnessing the act, was sheer lunacy. "Even if it *was* Trevor who killed her, he didn't have Shogun right after the murder happened. Luellen did."

"Oh, please." She gave me a dismissive wave. "Luellen worships the ground that Trevor walks upon. She'd lie to the priest on her own deathbed for her brother's sake."

"But Edith, it doesn't make any sense that Trevor did it. Why would Trevor have come here to your house? Surely he knows your schedule at the store. He would have expected *you* to be here, not Cassandra. Even if he did have a motive, why kill her at your house?"

"That answer's obvious. He lured her over here and killed her on my property to frame me."

I didn't know how to respond to that. This dark side of human behavior was so sickening to me. Wasn't it tragic enough that a woman, a supposed good friend of hers, had been murdered? How could Edith suspect her husband on top of everything else?

"Well, Edith, I know you have to run, and I think I've seen enough." I knelt and pulled Doppler's leash out of my pocket. "Come, Shogun."

The hum of a lawn mower resounded outside. The noise was coming from the direction of the Haywoods' property, and I wondered if that could possibly be Susan Nelson, out mowing her parents' lawn. My stomach was instantly in knots at the thought of facing her, but I'd have a guilty conscience forever if I didn't find out what had transpired between her and her husband, thanks to my report to the police. First, though, I had to complete the matter of the ownership of Shogun.

Shogun trotted over to me, and I fastened the leash on his collar.

"What did you decide? Which of us gets the dog, me or Trevor?"

That was not a question I felt like answering yet. I stood up and met the intense gaze from her gray eyes. "It would probably be best if I waited to discuss this until the two of you could be present. Why don't we set up an appointment at my house this evening? I'll call Trevor and see if there's a good time for him to come over tonight."

Her jaw dropped. "Why, you little . . . fool! You've chosen Trevor, haven't you?"

I tried to head past her toward the door, cutting a wide arc around her. Despite his owner's angry demeanor, Shogun followed in perfect heel position. My neck and throat still ached from my run-in with Carver. I so desperately didn't want to have a second confrontation the same day. "I didn't say that, though you're not helping your case any."

"It's obvious by the way you're behaving." She stomped her foot and put her hands on her hips. "You can't be serious. You seemed intelligent to me, but I totally overestimated you. You're planning to give my dog to a murderer!"

"The police will solve Cassandra's murder case, Edith. If Trevor is guilty, he won't have Shogun for long." I opened the door as I spoke. "The job you hired me to do was to determine which of you should keep your dog. While Shogun is happy here and you do a fine job with him, there is not a doubt in my mind that he is even happier with Trevor. So, yes, that's what I'm recommending."

I stepped out onto the porch, feeling as though I were running in front of a train, by the way she stormed after me.

"If you think that's the end of this, you've got another thing coming!"

She slammed the door behind me, barely giving Shogun time to get through it.

Shogun was badly frightened at nearly getting crushed by the door. Now wanting to go back inside and give Edith a piece of my mind, I knelt and reassured the sweet dog. Where did she get off hiring me and then treating me like dirt? Had she ever seriously believed that I would find in her favor?

The warm air carried the fragrance of newly cut grass. From my crouched position on Edith's porch, I watched Susan mowing the Haywoods' front lawn, a scowl deeply set on her face. I rose and waved and tried unsuccessfully to catch her eye. She was deliberately ignoring me.

While she took another pass across the lawn and moved toward the back, I coaxed Shogun to come with me. The little dog, whose fur was not unlike an overgrown lawn, was wary of the mower, but trotted along the moment Susan turned away from us. I truly did want to avoid confrontations for the rest of the day, seeing as how forever was decidedly unlikely. Yet I really did want to clear the air between Susan and me, once and for all. If such a thing was possible.

I waited by the junipers for her to make another pass with the mower and come toward me, Shogun sniffing the ground with avid enthusiasm, tracking a squirrel, perhaps.

I waved at Susan as she neared. Her expression didn't change at the sight of me. Considering how tense things had been when we'd last spoken, this was a good sign. It wouldn't have been all that far out of character for her to spit at me.

Shogun was tugging against my grip and I crouched down to see what had caught his interest. A patch of pink immediately caught my eye. My heart raced. I'd checked this area fairly thoroughly the day after the murder. How could I have missed this?

I grabbed the now-faded piece of paper, which looked as though it had been soaked with rain or sprinkler water. The paper was soiled and the ink had run so badly that the writing could no longer be deciphered, but as with the note on Edith's door the day of the murder, it had been written with a black felt-tip pen. This could only be the missing note!

"I found the note!" I cried over the sound of the motor to Susan as she reached me.

"What note?"

"The note from Edith's door." I didn't need, or want, to give any additional explanation.

She rolled her eyes. "Again with the stupid magenta paper? Like I said before, someone else must've left the note-pad at my parents' house."

I nodded, frustrated. Why did this note disappear and then reappear? Was this some kind of a sick game to someone?

"I was thinking of going over and working on your yard

after I finish up here. Would that be all right with you and your mom?"

I was surprised by her demeanor. She wasn't acting hostile or standoffish. It was as though neither her husband nor the police had filled her in about the fact that her secret drug addiction had been divulged. "Sure. That's fine. But there's something I wanted to talk to you about. Got a minute?"

The mower, though she'd reduced engine power, was still rumbling such that we were forced to raise our voices over the noise. There was no way I wanted to be at a half shout as I brought up the subject of money and her husband's theory about why she was hoarding cash.

She nodded and called, "Just let me finish this one section."

While we waited for Susan, Shogun settled into a shady patch of cool sand beneath the bushes. Seeing him there reminded me that I'd never followed through on my desire to restudy those paw prints and see what it was about them that struck me as so familiar. I rounded the juniper hedge and stared at the sandy soil.

Now there were no footprints—canine or otherwise— here. The impressions from my own shoes the day after the murder were gone, as were the paw prints. What was left in the sand were streaks, as if a broom had been dragged across it, wiping out all prints.

There was no way these markings could have occurred naturally. Someone had deliberately wiped out the tracks that were there the other day. Why? Was it possibly to cover up the dog tracks that had perhaps matched those that I'd seen in the blood? And yet, the only people who might have known about the tracks behind the bushes were the Haywoods . . . and Susan.

"What's up?" she said to me, raising an eyebrow as she watched me scramble back to my feet. "Looking for an entire stationery supply back there?"

"No, just . . . trying to figure out how the note could have been blown over there, and how I missed it the first time I looked."

"Huh. So you said you wanted to talk to me about something?"

"Susan, I don't like to get involved in a squabble between a husband and a wife, but I also don't like being a silent partner in a lie. What did you tell your husband about our financial agreement?"

The guilty look on her face gave her away. "Our financial agreement? But I thought we were doing this on trade."

"That's what I thought, too, but your husband seems to be under the impression that I'm still working with Boris, and that I've been charging you fifty dollars a visit."

"He is?"

"He certainly is. I'm surprised he didn't bring this up with you last night."

"Oh, yeah. I . . . I was saving up to buy him a birthday present, and that's the only way I could think of tricking him into giving me the money for it."

"And you thought it would be all right to possibly damage my reputation by not even having me *work* with Boris, yet to fool your husband into believing I was charging you."

"I guess I didn't think it through."

"Come on, Susan. Do you really think you're fooling me?"

She knelt and picked up Shogun. "This dog always reminds me of Toto from *The Wizard of Oz*," she murmured.

"Fred seems to be worried that you're using the money for drugs."

"Drug money? That's stupid." She spoke with confidence, but still seemed to be actively searching for anyplace to look other than directly in my eyes. She let Shogun leap down from her arms.

"I hope so. I'd hate to think of anyone getting messed up on drugs."

"I did have a problem with it, starting when I was in high school."

High school? That would be the drug dependency problem her parents felt I'd brought about with my gluing her shoes to their porch.

"I got off the stuff a long time ago. That isn't what I'm using the money for."

"A birthday present?" I asked derisively.

She shook her head. "The money is . . . going toward bailing my parents out of a jam they're in. My father did some damage at Edith's store one night. He used to own a business there, you know, and he . . . thinks he still does sometimes."

My interest was piqued, but she had a ways to go to convince me that this time she was telling the truth.

She glanced at the window of her parents' house and lowered her voice. "My dad's not always lucid. He broke some windows to get in and ruined some of Edith's merchandise, and we're trying to keep it quiet. We're paying her for the damage under the table. You can ask Edith, if you don't believe me. I'm surprised she's kept it quiet this long."

"Is it Alzheimer's?"

She nodded, her expression grim. "You might as well know the whole thing. See, I don't know for certain . . . Dad could've picked up that pad from someone's house. He's taken to wandering into places and grabbing stuff lately. A couple months ago, Cassandra had to call Mom to get him when he was insisting he lived at her house. When we brought him home, Mom found Cassandra's saltshaker in his pocket."

"Why didn't you tell your husband the truth?"

"I didn't tell Fred because he'd just use it against me. He thinks we should commit my dad, put him in some kind of an institution, but my mom thinks . . ." She paused and then sighed. "She's just not ready."

"I'd like to believe you, Susan, but you seem to have a problem with the truth. Why did you lie to me about your relationship with Cassandra?"

"Allida, I told you. I barely knew the woman."

"That's not what your husband told me."

Her eyes widened in alarm. "You talked to him about that? Why?"

"He told me that you and she used to have a monogramming business together."

In a flash, her demeanor turned stone cold. "Damn you, Allida. You really haven't wised up at all in all these years, have you?"

"What do you mean?" I asked, startled by her sudden outburst.

"What I mean is you're trespassing! You are sticking your nose where it doesn't belong! And if you don't watch out, you're going to wind up—" She stopped as suddenly as she'd started, then turned her back on me.

"You think I'm going to wind up as a second murder victim, Susan?"

She didn't answer, but returned to her mower and started up the engine with one furious yank of the cord. Though I stayed for another minute hoping she'd cool down enough to talk to me again, she was not even willing to look at me.

The curtains parted, and Harvey Haywood peered at me. I expected him to frown and perhaps even yell at me to get off his property, but he threw the window open and gave me a close resemblance of a smile. "Ellen, you go tell your sister to come on in now. You two have been out there for hours. You're going to make yourself sick, being out in the sun this long."

I didn't know what else to say, so I gave him a friendly wave and said, "All right. I'll tell Susan what you said."

A moment later, Betsy's angry face appeared beside her husband's. She shut the window with a vengeance and gestured at me with two flicks of the wrist to go away, as if she were shooing a fly.

I walked off with Shogun, and once again he did fine on leash until we reached the Randons' walkway. There Shogun trotted up the path as if that was where we were surely going. It dawned on me then that it was probably Melanie he was expecting to visit and that, since Edith wasn't the one to bring him there, Trevor must have been.

To test my theory, I let Shogun go ahead and lead the way, and I rang the doorbell. Shogun's tail began to wag as we waited. Not knowing whether or not anyone was even home, I found myself immediately hoping that the little guy wasn't about to be disappointed.

Paul swung the door open. He was unshaven and wearing a grubby sweatsuit, his dark hair uncombed. "Allida, hi. What's up?"

I picked up the waggy-tailed little dog. "Actually, we're here to visit with Melanie for just a minute. Is she home?"

Before Paul could answer, she popped into view, then bolted through the door. "Shogun! It's Shogun, Daddy!"

"I can see that."

She held out her arms for him, and seeing no unspoken objection on her father's part, I let her take him and give him a hug. Shogun licked her face and she giggled.

"As you apparently guessed, they're old friends," Paul said, indicating his daughter and his next-door neighbor's dog.

"Yes, he kept pulling on the leash to come over here, and I finally figured out that the Cunninghams must have brought him over here to see Melanie."

He nodded. "A while ago, Trevor used to let Melanie walk him." He stared at his giggling daughter. "Seeing these two together was the main reason I was so adamant about wanting to get a dog."

"That was nice of him." Though somewhat unfounded, I felt a surge of relief at the thought that maybe this meant that Edith's accusations concerning Trevor having had a sexual relationship with Cassandra weren't true. Maybe he'd innocently been over here to let his dog visit with Melanie.

"Trevor was a good neighbor. Listen, I'd invite you inside, but the place is a mess and—"

"No, that's all right. It really was the dog's idea to come, and I'd better be going myself."

"Can Shogun stay?" Melanie asked. "He can sleep in my bed."

"No, he can't, honey. Sorry. Shogun doesn't belong to Allida."

"Your Dad's right. I'm going to give him back to Trevor tonight."

"Tell him I said hello," Paul said.

"But you said you hated him," Melanie said, getting to her feet.

"I said no such thing. Come on inside." Paul all but chucked Melanie back inside the house. He gave me a sheepish smile and shook his head. "Kids. It's hard to know where their imaginations leave off and their interpretation of reality begins." He ruffled his daughter's hair. "Thanks for bringing Shogun over. Have a good day."

He shut the door, and I walked Shogun back across the street, feeling intensely uneasy. It had been my impression that Melanie had a fairly good grasp of her "interpretation of reality." And I remembered how Paul had said something to Trevor that all but froze him in his tracks the night after the murder.

Back home, my mother gave me a shoulder colder than the cup of ice cream she'd stashed in the freezer. When I asked why, she said, "You're obviously hell-bent on getting yourself killed, and I don't want to have to stand by and watch. For God's sake, Allie, a man nearly strangled you this morning! Then I see you over there talking to Susan, after you came out of Edith's house. One of those women might be a murderer! For heaven's sake, stay away from them. Let Andy handle things."

"I am. I just want to get Shogun to his rightful owner." Then I wanted to get the puppies and Suds adopted to good homes; I doubted Carver would be a free man anytime soon.

Mom was already in a huff, so I decided that I might as well go through with my idea of calling Trevor to invite him over to get Shogun. He wasn't home, so I tried his work number and reached him. The moment I said, "This is Allida," he blurted, "I just hung up with Edith. She tells me that she thinks you're incompetent and won't pay. Am I right in taking that to mean that you've decided to award me custody of Shogun?"

"Yes, and I was wondering if—"

"I'll be right over. And don't worry, I'll cover your fees myself."

Half an hour later, despite a rainstorm that had developed, Trevor arrived, soaking wet. He pumped my hand vigorously, picked up his dog and Shogun's bed, then handed me a check for twice what I'd planned on charging. He said he had never been so willing to pay for anyone's service.

Just as he was about to leave, I decided I had to address the niggling concern that Edith had raised about his relationship with Cassandra. "Trevor," I began, "I heard a rumor about Cassandra having been unfaithful to Paul. Did you ever hear anything to that effect?"

Trevor scoffed. "Cassie? Unfaithful? Never." He shook his head and met my eyes, his own filled with joy at having his dog back. "Someone got the story wrong." He beamed at me, said, "I can't thank you enough," and left.

That evening, John White called me to ask how I was. I said, "Fine," and asked how soon I could get Suds back with her puppies. He insisted on personally bringing Suds to my home. In a lame attempt at humor, he promised that this time he wouldn't have any knife-wielding passengers with him.

An hour or so later, he rang my doorbell. He was wearing brown cotton-twill slacks and a pale yellow T-shirt, and his hair was neatly combed. I wondered if he'd spruced up in my honor. Suds, her muzzle still bandaged but otherwise healthy-looking, rushed inside and straight to her puppies the moment I opened the door, but John remained on the porch.

"Thanks for bringing her." I was unable to make my voice more than barely civil.

He shrugged. "I really came over to apologize. I'm sorry I lied to you before. I never dreamed Carver would . . . I just wanted to tell you that I've turned in my two-weeks' notice at work. I'm leaving the state, getting a fresh start someplace else."

"Because of Carver?"

He nodded. "My past has been catching up with me. I need to get some distance between myself and . . . who I used to be."

"I don't understand." I didn't feel like talking to him

through the screen door, and even less like inviting him inside, so I joined him on the porch. "Who did you used to be?"

"A petty thief, for one thing. I've changed my ways, though."

Now I understood. "That's how you met Carver. In prison."

He nodded, not meeting my eyes. "I'm real sorry, Allida. I had nothing to do with your neighbor's murder, and I never thought Carver would come hassle you and try and take Suds."

"What's going to happen with him?"

"He's going back to jail. We'll be putting Suds up for adoption in a couple of weeks, once the puppies are fully independent. That'll be my last project for them before I go. We'll try to get the puppies adopted immediately when they're at seven weeks. They'll go fast. Puppies always do. You wouldn't want to make your fostering of Suds permanent, would you?"

"No. Sorry, not until I've got my own place. I think Mom has put up with enough of my decisions regarding the animal kingdom. She's probably getting pretty fed up with my taking my work home with me."

He nodded. "I'll be seeing you in a couple of weeks, then, unless something comes up in the meantime."

"No offense, but let's hope not. So far, anything that's 'come up' has been painful."

John sighed and searched my face. "I never intended to get you involved with Carver. You do believe that, don't you?"

I regarded him for a moment and realized that I'd been unlucky—or unwise—when I hadn't thought to double-check his claim that the police had told him that Carver had had an alibi. Otherwise, John's lies might have unraveled sooner than they did. "Yes. It's just that . . . you can't run away from your past, and lying about it doesn't make it go away."

"That, if nothing else, is one thing I've learned. Good-bye, Allida." He pivoted on his heel and walked back to his car, then drove away without a second glance.

* * *

Sunday morning, I accompanied my mother to church. She had seemed to have put our previous friction behind her, and I was more than willing to drop the matter. It was such a nice day that we left all of the dogs outside in our absence. Mom went out to the back deck to check on them the moment we returned. Suds and a couple of the puppies rushed in the instant she opened the door. She was looking pretty flustered when she returned from the backyard. "Have you seen Fez?"

"No. Isn't he with the others?" I asked stupidly.

"No. Not unless I miscounted and he already came inside."

"Okay. He's got to be here someplace."

We searched thoroughly, inside and out. Fez was nowhere to be found. But I did find a puppy-sized hole underneath the fence. Suds might have done the digging. My own dogs weren't diggers, and the puppies were too young to have taken up this particular activity. If Fez had dug this hole himself at his age, he was awfully precocious.

First Shogun was missing, then Suds was forcibly taken. Now a puppy was missing. This was a pattern that had to stop soon. One way or another.

Chapter 16

Mom and I decided that she would check with the neighbors on our side of the street and I'd check with those on the opposite side. The neighbors next door, whose property bordered the fence the dog had dug under, had been out of town this past week. Mom went there first to see if they were back home. She didn't return, which meant that, yes, they were home, and Mom would have all too much catching up to do on the recent grisly events befalling the neighborhood.

It was unlikely that such a young puppy would venture far on his own. Someone could have spotted him and picked him up, which would not have been a tragedy, for Fez would be old enough for adoption in another ten days anyway. The real danger, of course, was that he might eventually wander into the road at an unfortunate time. I couldn't forgive myself if that were to happen.

Fez was too young to respond to his own name, so I whistled a few times, but didn't bother calling. I went to the Randons' place first, because it was closest and because it was possible that Fez remembered his former temporary home, even though he'd been there for less than a full day.

The front door was open. "Hi, come on in," Paul hollered from a back room in answer to my knock.

That was a surprisingly friendly greeting, but I stepped inside his home.

He came out wearing only shorts, and his face fell at the sight of me. For my part, I had to say that Paul really wasn't the sort who should be showing off his torso. He had fairly substantial love handles and only a few scraggly-looking chest hairs on his pale skin. "Oh. Allida. I thought . . . I'm expecting my secretary to drop by with some work for me." He crossed his arms over his chest as he spoke.

Pretty casual relationship with one's secretary not to have put on a shirt for her, but that was his business, not mine. "I just came over to see if you or Melanie have seen any of the puppies this morning. One of them got out through a hole underneath the fence a few minutes ago."

"Oh. Er, no. Sorry."

"Could I ask Melanie?"

"She's . . . not here. She's staying with my sister for the next few days. I thought that would give her a chance to get—"

"Yoo-hoo," a woman called from the doorway. I whirled around and faced a pretty young woman with blond hair. She appeared to be startled to see me. Her eyes darted between Paul and me. "Oh. I didn't realize you had company."

"Uh, yes," Paul said. "This . . . is just a neighbor looking for her lost puppy."

"You lost a puppy? Oh, dear." She cast a glance in Paul's direction, then said with clasped hands, "I do so love little puppies."

Spare me, I thought. She was obviously playing up to Paul.

Paul disappeared into the room he'd emerged from, muttering, "Let me get a shirt on."

I couldn't wait to get out of there, but Paul's visitor was still standing in the doorway. The young woman had a smile plastered on her face.

"I'd better check with some more neighbors."

"So you live in the neighborhood?" she asked, still smiling.

"Across the street."

"I'm a real estate agent. Helping Paul to find a new home. I don't know if he told you this, but he'll be moving to Boulder."

I was embarrassed for my own sake and for theirs, being caught in their lie. "That's nice. Boulder's a great town."

Paul reentered the room just then and chuckled nervously.

"Yes. She is not only my secretary, but has her real estate license."

"That's . . . very industrious of you."

Paul had a dog-caught-with-his-nose-in-the-garbage look on his face when I turned back toward him. "Please let me know if you see the puppy."

The woman, still smiling but now with crimson cheeks, stepped aside, and I left quickly. I now had to choose between visiting Edith next door and skipping that house to go to the Haywoods'. Not that the Haywoods were such a treat, but I sorely wanted to avoid seeing Edith again this soon.

I started to head past Edith's house on my way to the Haywoods' and glanced directly across the street to see if my mother was still over there, hopefully with the dog. Mom was on the front porch chatting with the neighbor. No puppies in sight. She apparently wasn't overly concerned about Fez's whereabouts.

I heard a screen door bang and turned to see Edith Cunningham standing on her porch with a puppy in her arms. She was watching me, a haughty expression on her face. I changed directions and slowly headed toward her, wishing someone else had found Fez.

As usual, she was impeccably dressed, in a long white pleated skirt and a gold silk blouse, augmented with pearls. To her credit, she was cradling Fez with seemingly no regard to his getting her clothes dirty. "Why, Allida. Look what I found."

"Yes. Thanks. I've been looking for him."

She nuzzled the puppy, but kept her eyes on me. "Seems as though the Fates are trying to even things out between us, wouldn't you say? I have your puppy, you took my dog. Of course, there's no real comparison between your puppy, which you intend to give up for adoption in a couple of weeks, and my beloved Shogun. Is there?"

"No, there isn't. Could I have the puppy, please?"

"I found him scratching at my gate, trying to get in. So, naturally, dog lover that I am, I let him in. I cannot believe that you, who teach people how to handle their dogs' behavior problems, would actually allow a young puppy in your charge to get loose like this and run across the street. Such news would hardly help your business if someone were to spread the word around."

"Is that a threat?"

"No, my dear. I'm hardly the sort to engage in neighborhood gossip." She fixed her eyes across the street, where my mother and next-door neighbor were still talking. "Unlike some people I could name."

Her thinly cloaked insult of my mother set my teeth on edge. "Odd that you make these insinuations about my care of the puppy just after I informed you that your husband and not you would be getting custody of your dog."

"Are you accusing me of stealing your puppy?"

"No, just of not being sincere about the source of your hostility toward me."

"So call me small-minded, but you are not one of my favorite people. And if I can cause you the same kind of pain that you caused me, I would not hesitate to do so. Unfortunately, I am not about to take your cocker spaniel or your shepherd to teach you that kind of a lesson. I cannot stand to hurt even you that deeply."

She thrust Fez into my arms, then whirled on a heel and shut the door.

Somehow, I doubted she would be offering me a special low price at her store anytime soon.

Mom and I wedged a rock in the hole underneath the fence, and I took off for work. My mind wasn't fully focused, and the day seemed to drag. Late that afternoon, I went into my office to catch up on paperwork and the like. Sundays were typically quiet and offered none of the distractions that I readily looked for while trying to avoid this type of work.

To my surprise, Russell trotted down the steps into our walk-out basement office. He was dressed casually, jeans and a purple collared short-sleeved knit shirt. He gave me a big smile that immediately warmed my heart. "Hi. I was hoping I'd find you here. How's everything going?"

"Fine." I suddenly realized that the last time we'd spoken, I'd had to abruptly cut short our phone conversation. "Oh, jeez. I just realized I never called you back yesterday. I . . . got into a bit of a mess with Suds's former owner, but he's safely locked up now."

"Locked up? What happened?"

"He beat Suds, who had to be rescued by Animal Control, then he decided to take matters into his own hands and get Suds back. Using me to run interference. Anyway, it's over now."

He studied my face for a long moment, then said, "I have a feeling you left a lot of details out of that story. Which maybe we can remedy. Are you doing anything tonight?"

"No, I'm free." I didn't want to seem too anxious, but held my breath in anticipation, hoping he would ask me out on a date.

"Would you be interested in going out for dinner with me tonight?"

"I'd love to."

"Great. I'll come pick you up at your house around seven." He gestured at the door behind us and took a step backward. "Think I'll go now, before you have the chance to change your mind."

"I won't change my mind."

His smile broadened, his dark eyes sparkling. "Great," he said again. "Still, I'd . . . better go. See you at seven."

"I'll be looking forward to it."

"Me, too," he said, and pushed out the door.

Seven o'clock just couldn't seem to come fast enough that evening. I got dressed up—heels and a blue knit dress and scarf—then finally decided that, rather than watch the clock, I'd spend time with my dogs. To my surprise, partway into some brush-up obedience training with the three of them, Russell stepped through the gate.

His face instantly grew pale at the sight of Pavlov, currently off the leash.

"Russell. I'm sorry. I didn't mean for you and Pavlov to

cross paths. I didn't realize it was so late. Plus I thought you'd ring the doorbell."

His eyes still on Pavlov, he said, "I'm a little early. I saw you back here as I turned the corner."

To my horror, Pavlov forgot her manners and barked at him and started to trot toward him.

"Pavlov! Sit! Stay!"

The poor man had already broken into a sweat. One of Russell's earliest memories, he'd once told me, was of his brother being mauled by a German shepherd. He had such a strong fear now that it was physically painful to have to watch him near my beloved shepherd.

"Pavlov, lie down. Stay."

Russell blushed and averted his eyes. "Sounds idiotic, I know, but I forgot your dog was going to be here. I didn't prepare myself, or I'd have been fine."

"That's okay."

From inside the house, Mom threw open the screen door. Suds barreled out, barking at Russell, who shrank back and cried, "No. Stop. Get back!"

"Suds, come!" I yelled, but Suds jumped up on Russell. "Suds, down!" The dog ignored me, and I tried again, thinking she might know the other frequently used command for this. "Suds, off!"

Russell looked nearly apoplectic and was shielding his face with his arm.

"No! Bad dog!" I grabbed Suds's collar, and for the first time in my life, I was so angry at the dog—despite her injured muzzle—that I was sorely tempted to step on her hind paw to discipline her.

Mom had heard the commotion and came out, joining me in my apologies to the beet-red Russell for the dog's behavior. She took Suds back inside, talking sternly to her as she went.

"Not exactly an impressive entrance," Russell said. "I'd have rather tripped and fallen on my face."

I felt too inhibited to reach out and touch Russell's cheek reassuringly, though I knew that would have driven home my words more effectively. "It's not your fault, Russ. Lots of people are afraid of dogs, and with much less reason than you have."

"Do you still feel like going out with me tonight?"

"Of course I do." Truth be told, if anything, I still felt like throwing my arms around him to compensate for the miserable greeting he'd gotten from my dogs.

I glanced back and saw that Pavlov was dutifully lying down, watching all of this with big worried eyes. I was torn between wanting to give both Russell and my shepherd hugs, but the dog got preference because she was likely to stay in this position forever, awaiting my command. "Pavlov, okay. Good dog." I called to Russell, "Just let me get my things and I'll meet you out front."

The moment I heard him click the gate latch so that I knew he wasn't watching, I gave Pavlov the reassuring hug that Russell was probably more in need of, then said good-bye to the dogs and rushed inside to wash my hands, grab my purse, and say good night to my mother.

Mom murmured, "I feel so bad for all but siccing Suds on Russell accidentally. Is he all right?"

"A bit of injured pride is all. I've got to run."

"Tell Russell again how sorry I am."

Russell was waiting in his avocado-colored Volvo, but he promptly got out and opened the car door for me. I decided the best option was not to mention the dog incident and hope that we could put it behind us. We made small talk during our long drive to Boulder, the atmosphere charged, at least for my part, by nervousness.

We wound up parking in one of the lots nearby and walking through the west side of the Pearl Street Mall to a Mexican restaurant just a couple of streets away. The mall is a touristy section of downtown Boulder a few blocks south of our office. It's a pretty red-brick street where sidewalk acts of jugglers and musicians play for coins from pedestrians.

Our hands brushed together, and he took mine, giving it a squeeze. I began to worry that my palm was really sweaty and found myself babbling to cover my nervousness. "I'm really glad we got the chance to take a rain check on dinner. I'm so looking forward to a margarita and a chance to relax."

"Me, too."

"How are you doing on that big job you've been working on for your client?"

"Finished, thanks. I finally get some free time again."

"Maybe we can spend some of it together," I said before I could stop myself.

He gave me such a winning smile that my heart seemed to flutter. He had the softest dark brown eyes I'd ever seen on a human being. If only he weren't terrorized by the one thing I loved most in this world.

We reached the restaurant, where the aroma of salsa and spices greeted us. We were soon seated. His arm brushed against mine as he held my chair for me, and I found myself wanting to linger in the warmth of his body.

The waitress was saying something about the specials, but she might as well have been speaking a foreign language as far as my ability to listen. I found myself scanning the menu without reading it, wondering if I was really feeling this attracted to Russell or was just drawn to him as a safe harbor from all the hateful things I'd recently stumbled upon.

"Does anything look good to you?" he asked.

My cheeks warmed. This was ridiculous. I needed to get a grip on myself. "Yes, but I haven't decided what I want yet. I'll be back in a moment."

Halfway to the restroom, I saw a familiar-looking man sitting with a woman and was so incredulous that I stopped and stared at the man in profile. There was no doubt, though. Paul Randon.

He was holding hands across the table with the woman I'd met earlier, his secretary-cum-real-estate-agent. She was gazing into his eyes with unabashed love, or, at least, lust.

I had seen enough and turned on a heel and headed back for the table before Paul could spot me. I sank into my seat and snatched up my margarita, wishing at the moment that I could drown myself in it.

"That was quick," Russell said with an engaging grin. "Did you miss me?"

I wanted to smile at his joke, but couldn't. "I just . . . saw a neighbor that I didn't particularly want to see."

"Are you all right?"

I nodded, not mentioning that my stomach was churning and that I'd lost what little was left of my appetite.

Just then, if I had any doubts about the nature of Paul's relationship with this woman, they were put to rest as Paul and his date left their table and headed past ours toward the exit, his arm wrapped around her. His eyes widened when he caught sight of me. He immediately drew away from the other woman, but walked past us without a word.

"That's Cassandra Randon's widower. He has a child, Russell. A little girl, five or six years old, who's just lost her mother."

What Melanie had blurted out during my baby-sitting had been the truth. Paul Randon was in love with someone else, and he and Cassandra probably *had* been arguing about their getting a divorce.

Had their argument ended when he killed her?

Chapter 17

Russell's gentleness and charm during dinner helped me put Paul into the recesses of my mind, but the vestiges of our encounter lingered throughout our date. Even if Paul was innocent, even if he and Cassandra had been on the verge of separating, how could he treat her memory this way? How could he hang all over some woman, when his wife had been murdered not even a week earlier?

Years ago, Paul had to have been in love with Cassandra, had to have taken her out on dates and believed his feelings for her would last forever. How was I supposed to have faith in this courtship ritual when its victims and failures were so readily apparent? Maybe the Fates were trying to tell me something. Maybe I was one of those people who was truly meant to be alone.

Russell drove me home. The windows in the Randons' house were all black and the place had a deserted aura to it. Paul must be at his female companion's place. No wonder he'd changed his tie at some point during his "meeting" the other day.

Only the porch light was on at my home. Mom must have gone to bed early, or at least had deliberately given that impression by turning the living room lights off. The instant we parked, Russell launched himself out of the car and around to my side to open the door for me. I smiled in spite of myself. The man really knew how to make me feel as though he were fully in the moment and focused on me, even if, sadly, the reverse wasn't quite true.

We walked to my front door in silence, but I was acutely

aware of the warmth of his body by my side, of the way his hand brushed against mine. The crickets were chirping, heralding summer's rapid approach.

I turned toward him at the door, intending to apologize for dampening the evening with my moodiness. The porch light cast soft highlighting upon his face and dark hair. He looked incredibly handsome, and I suddenly felt as though I couldn't get a deep enough breath of air. In a strained voice, I muttered, "Thank you, Russell. I had a nice time."

He was staring into my eyes, and I felt myself being drawn closer to him. A moment later, his lips were on mine, his arms around me, and my senses reeled in a desire that I was not at all ready to give in to, leaving me dizzy.

When our lips parted, Russell held me for another moment, and I rested my forehead on his shoulder. "You're shaking," he said quietly. "Are you okay?"

"I'm fine. It's been a tough week." I pulled away, hoping my motion wasn't too abrupt, but needing some distance. I found my key and fumbled with the lock until I got it open.

"Can I call you soon?"

"Yes. Please do. Anytime. Good night, Russ."

"Night."

I quickly stepped inside and shut the door, leaning back against it and trying to catch my breath. It felt as though I were toying with the *L* word here, and that wasn't what I wanted.

Why did this have to happen now, when I really and truly only wanted the chance to reestablish myself back in Colorado in this new job? I was doing fine on my own. I didn't want to get hurt again; didn't want to hurt someone else.

"I'm scared of heights," I whispered to myself. "I don't want to *fall* in love."

For a minute or so, I stood there in silence, trying to get a grip on my feelings, then realized that I still hadn't heard Russell's car engine, or even his footsteps as he left the porch. Curious, I swung the door open. Russell was standing there, facing the door, looking only slightly embarrassed at my seeing him there.

"You still haven't left the porch."

"And you still haven't turned your lights on."

"I . . . like the dark."

"And I like your porch."

The inanity of our exchange made me smile. "Just the same, you'll scare the milkman away if you stay there too long."

He chuckled. "I don't have a comeback for that. So I guess I'd better go. Are you doing anything tomorrow, or would that be too soon?"

"No. I mean yes. I mean, I'm probably not busy, and it's not too soon."

He smiled, stuck his hands in his pockets, and trotted down the steps.

The next morning I found myself smiling for no reason, happy just to be alive and in good health. My mother, too, seemed almost giddy before she left to "do some shopping," and I wondered if she had been listening to my conversation with Russell last night. If so, she was too smart to say so or even to ask me about my date.

I decided to indulge myself by walking the three dogs—leaving Suds with her puppies, much to her howling despair, but I had no desire to attempt walking four dogs at once. We walked down to the park, known to the local teenagers as "stoners' park," in reference to the clientele after school hours. The place was peaceful now, only a mother pushing her two young children on the swings, their high-pitched chatter the only sounds.

Having the three dogs on their leashes was a juggling act, despite their good training. One dog or another was changing pace or being distracted by a scent or a noise, but the challenge proved a welcome distraction from my worries.

By the time I managed to quiet my thoughts and relax, it was time to return home. I headed up our street, past the Haywoods' and Edith Cunningham's homes. The rumbling sounds of a lawn mower came from somewhere in the vicinity of my house, and I wondered if that could be Susan mowing our yard. The brief rainstorm just after we'd spoken that Saturday had probably delayed her plans to do the job then.

Suddenly the sight of a recent, familiar-looking muddy paw print on the sidewalk chilled me to the core. I instructed the dogs to sit, and I knelt to examine the print. My mind flashed back to the vision of the paw prints in the blood. For the first time, I fully realized that there had been an unusual aspect to some of the bloody prints—a merged digit pad in the left front paw, as if the dog's middle two toes on that paw were poorly separated. That same unusual pad was present in these prints, which were heading right up Edith Cunningham's walkway.

I glanced at my watch, realizing that it was already mid-morning. She was unlikely to be home, her shop having opened by now. In any case, if I'd double-checked those prints behind the Haywoods' bushes when my instincts had first told me to do so, maybe there'd have been one less mystery surrounding the murder. I sure wasn't going to let this new opportunity pass me by.

I told the dogs to stay, dropped their leashes, and went alone up Edith's porch, studying the pattern of the prints. It looked as though the dog had come as far as the top step, circled, and then jumped off the porch. Rarely do dogs run up uninvited onto strangers' porches, unless there's another dog inside. On the other hand, some dogs have an I'm-lovable-so-you'll-want-to-pet-me attitude that wouldn't preclude their doing this, plus Shogun's scents would still have been strong to a canine's nose. I'd learned nothing. A little discouraged, I collected my dogs' leashes, and we crossed the street.

Susan was, indeed, halfway through mowing my front lawn. She was wearing cutoffs and a black tank top and had been moving at such a clip that her frizzy hair was damp with perspiration. I waved to her and she called over the engine's loud whir, "Started raining the other day and I didn't get to this till now. I've got Boris in your backyard. Hope you don't mind."

I gave her the okay sign and went inside. It *was* completely okay with me, but the dogs begged to differ. My three canines immediately joined Suds and puppies by the glass door and barked their heads off.

I went out alone. Boris greeted me eagerly, and it was easy to imagine him wagging his nonexistent tail. It was nice to see him.

Boris's paws were all muddy. Maybe those prints at Edith's were his. This was so obvious that I should have instantly picked up on it.

I checked his left front paw. Where most dogs have two middle digit pads, Boris had one figure-eight-shaped pad.

I walked along the fence, checking for clear prints and curious to find the source of the mud. Boris trotted alongside me, while Susan's mower was still sputtering along in the front yard. To my annoyance, the source was a new tunnel, right next to the old one, which Boris had been digging.

"So you're a champion digger, hey, Boris?" Taking into consideration the length of time the dogs and I had been on our walk, he could only have been working at this new tunnel for half an hour or less, and he was nearly all the way through.

Seeing the two tunnels side by side demonstrated something else that was so obvious, it was inane of me not to have noticed before. My mind, however, had been elsewhere then. The loose soil from this tunnel was inside our fence, because that's the direction Boris had been digging from. In the older tunnel that Fez had likely passed through to escape our yard yesterday, the loose dirt was outside of the fence. The dog that had originally dug that tunnel had been breaking into our yard.

A couple of the indentations in the dirt bore a familiar distinguishing pattern. I ran around the fence to check the paw prints on the other side. Though the prints here were mostly obscured, I was relatively certain that they, too, were Boris's.

By now Susan was mowing the adjacent corner of the fence. Curious, she cut the motor and came over to me.

She immediately focused on the loose soil. "Oh, man, I'm sorry about the hole. Boris is a real digger."

"It looks as though he tunneled under our fence to get in the other day. That's pretty unusual."

She grimaced and nodded. "That's Boris for you. He's pretty social. When he sees a dog he wants to play with, he just tunnels under the dog's fence." Her eyes widened with alarm just for an instant, as if she'd realized she'd let something slip, then her customary haughty expression returned. "Guess I should have had you work on that problem when I had the chance."

"Was he friends with Shogun?"

"Nope. Not at all," she answered quickly. She shrugged. "You think he might have been in the Randons' yard when Cassandra was murdered?"

"Yes."

"I doubt it." She started to walk away toward her mower. "I'd better get back to—"

"How did you know the name of the Cunninghams' dog? Are you and Edith friends?"

She froze for just a moment, then glared at me. "No. My parents have mentioned it repeatedly. They've lived next door to Shogun ever since the Cunninghams bought him."

That was plausible, but didn't explain the signals I was getting from her regarding how upsetting she found the possibility of her dog having been in Edith's yard at the time of the murder. "Think back," I said, letting my impatience show. "Did Boris disappear on you for a while the day of Cassandra's murder?"

She cleared her throat. "I guess so. I had to call him a couple of times. But believe me, he didn't come in with bloody paws or anything. I would have called the police."

"So you're saying it's possible that Boris was in the Cunninghams' yard right around the time that Cassandra was killed there."

"Anything's possible," she snapped at me, "but who cares? If he was there, I didn't see him. Nobody did."

Nobody did? How could she speak for anyone else? Was she protecting her parents? "I need to cut through your parents' yard to take a look at the Cunninghams' fence. Do you want to come with me?"

"No. I'm going to finish up here and take off."

I nodded, but she'd already turned her back to me.

I dashed across the street and onto the Haywoods' lawn, relieved that for once they didn't seem to be watching me from behind a curtain. I examined the length of fencing between their property and Edith's.

There was no tunnel underneath the fence, but there was loose soil on the Haywoods' side of the fence that made it all too clear that this had been patched back over. I knelt by the tunnel and looked through the chain-link fence. I had an unimpeded view of Edith's deck, where Cassandra had been murdered. The patch job of Boris's tunnel had been fairly recent; no grass or other plants had had the chance to reclaim the soil.

Someone knew that a dog had burrowed under the fence. It could be that Edith had discovered this, but she hadn't had Shogun in her yard since the murder. She might not have had reason to even suspect that the tunnel existed.

More likely this was the work of one of the Haywoods or Susan, who'd been out here dutifully covering up all signs that Boris had even been in their yard that day. The paw prints behind their bushes, too, had been swept away, and that could only have been the work of one of them.

To my mind, this meant that Susan or one or both of her parents had, at the very least, witnessed the murder. But if that was the extent of their role, why sweep the prints away?

Just then, Betsy came out and gave me the evil eye. "Whatcha doing trespassing on my property?"

"I'm looking at a tunnel a dog dug under Edith's fence."

Her frowned deepened, though I wouldn't have thought that possible. "You got no business over here, young lady. You don't go poking into my daughter's— Haven't you messed things up for my family enough?"

"Susan's dog was in Edith's yard when Cassandra was killed, wasn't he?"

"No!"

"Did you see the murder, Mrs. Haywood?"

"No, and I don't like your impudence! If you was my daughter, I'd have you shot!"

I raised my eyebrows and caught my breath at the severity of her statement. "Nothing has ever made me more appreciative of my own mother than that particular remark."

Harvey came outside and stood beside his wife, a look of confusion and impatience on his pale face. "What all are you carryin' on about, Betsy?" he demanded. When his wife didn't answer right away, he turned his eyes to me. He ran his palm over his bald pate. "You're that Babcock girl. What are you doing over here?"

"I was just leaving, Mr. Haywood."

"The faster, the better," Betsy growled, and slammed the screen door behind her.

Susan had been rolling her mower back across the street to her parents' garage, but stopped as she witnessed our exchange, her eyes wide with alarm.

Harvey smiled at the sight of her. "This is my daughter Susan," he said to me, his voice phlegmy. "Susan," he called, "this is Marilyn's daughter from across the street. Have you two ever met?"

"Yes, we've met, Daddy." She shot me a look that, I thought, was protective of her father. "Go back inside," she told him. "I'll be right there."

We waited a moment till he was out of earshot. "I'm sorry about your father, Susan," I said.

Her grimace was my only acknowledgment as she dragged the mower to the garage.

I went home and called Sergeant Millay and relayed the information to him that I'd located the dog who'd left those prints, and that the dog belonged to Susan Nelson.

There was a pause. "You're certain?"

"Yes. Susan says she didn't see the murder, that she just called her dog and he responded, but I'm not sure how that's possible."

"That's interesting," he said in a tone that indicated he

found my news anything but interesting. "We'll follow through on it," he murmured. "Anything else?"

"Haven't I made myself clear? If Boris was in Edith's backyard during the murder, it was possible that Susan or her parents were there, too. Or, at the least, that one of them witnessed the murder and isn't telling."

"Possible, sure. But it's hardly what anyone would consider evidence."

"Don't you see? Susan had to have been lying to me when she told me how she got Boris back. That is, unless someone managed to chase Boris out of Edith's yard unseen by Susan, which seems unlikely, considering the yards are adjacent to each other. Susan said she called him a couple of times, then he finally came running up to her. But getting a dog to go back through a tunnel he's dug is almost impossible, if you're anywhere in the vicinity of the tunnel."

"Why? The tunnels are one-way only?"

"No," I snapped in exasperation. "Because, provided he's been scolded for digging—which is the case with Boris—the dog thinks: Owner plus tunneling equals punishment. He thinks he's going to get punished for being seen going back through the tunnel."

Sergeant Millay said nothing, so I continued, "The dog will avoid the tunnel, act like he doesn't know it's there. He thinks as long as you don't see him go through the tunnel, he won't get punished. Instead, the dog will typically bark along the fence till you open a gate. In which case, Susan or a substitute dog-master, such as her parents, would have witnessed what had happened in Edith's yard."

"But the dog already did the digging, and that's what he's getting punished for."

"Right, but dogs don't have the lengthy cause-and-effect perception that we do. They can only associate something that's occurred within the last few seconds as having caused the resulting punishment."

The sergeant let out a puff of air into the receiver. "Okay. I see what you're saying. Like I said. We'll look into it." He hung up.

I felt frustrated at having to accept Sergeant Millay's patronizing attitude. Bad enough that I knew so little about anything in this world. Not being taken seriously on the one subject in which I really was knowledgeable was the proverbial "adding insult to injury." I read the paper for a while to get my mind off the conversation.

A half hour later, Mom rushed in carrying a turquoise-colored plastic bag with a clothing store's style of built-in handle. She smiled at me and was so focused on me that she didn't even greet the dogs. Today her hair was back in a ponytail, and she wore black jeans and a casual-looking black-and-pink-striped blouse. At a quick glance, she looked to be in her forties, though she was pushing sixty. "Oh, great, Allida, you're still home."

"Yes. I've given myself an actual day off."

She set the plastic bag on the table and started to remove its contents. "Guess where I was?"

"The Budweiser plant on I-25?"

"No, but only because I didn't think of that first. I went to Edith's clothing store." She pulled out a light blue long-sleeved blouse in some thin man-made material. "Edith helped me pick out something especially for you. She says it's by some fancy French clothing designer who's all the rage right now. Edith and I both thought it would look perfect on you."

I was a little disconcerted at the notion of Edith's picking something out for me. I half expected it to look and smell like a skunk hide. Was there such a thing as a gag-gift blouse? I was pleasantly surprised when I examined it. The blouse did look lovely, at least when neatly folded and being worn only by white tissue paper. "Oh, great. Thanks, Mom. It's very nice."

"Aren't you going to try it on?"

"Of course." She kept her eyes on me, and I realized she expected more from me. "You mean you want me to try it on now?"

"If it's not too much trouble. If it doesn't work out, I want to take it right back to Edith. Despite all of her ravings about the incredible bargains of her sale prices, it wasn't cheap, believe me."

"Oh, I'm sure of that. I've been in that store myself, and nothing in there is inexpensive."

"True, but Edith assures me that's the price one pays for these fancy designer labels."

I glanced at the label, which bore a name I didn't recognize. A kinked-up piece of red thread dangled from one corner. "It's a pretty lousy label," I said. "The thread is unraveling."

I dutifully tried the blouse on. It felt really tight on my shoulders and upper arms, but looked nice enough. Just not as nice as it had on the tissue paper. I came back into the kitchen to show her. "What do you think?"

"Pretty," Mom said. "I like it."

"Doesn't it look as if it's a size too small? It feels a bit tight under the armpits. I'm afraid that it'll be uncomfortable to move around in when I'm working." I stretched my arms out in front of me as a test and immediately heard a rip as one of the shoulder seams gave way.

Mom stared in surprise, and I joked, "There. That's much better. Downright roomy now."

"Good Lord! You pay all that money for a blouse, you certainly expect the seams to hold for more than five minutes." Mom got to her feet, grabbed me by the shoulders, and turned me around to look at the tear.

"I guess even these fancy clothiers can get defective merchandise," I said. "I'll take it back to Edith and exchange it for a size larger." Eventually, I silently added. Once enough time had passed that Edith might be able to be civil to me.

"You shouldn't have to do that. It's my gift to you, after all. Maybe it would be best, though, if you came in with me so you can try everything on right there."

"Okay."

Mom took my "okay" to mean "this minute" and snatched up her car keys. Not wishing to argue, I changed back into my unprestigious but unripped blouse and climbed into the passenger seat of Mom's pickup. We were soon at Edith's store and found her rifling through her merchandise in something of a Tasmanian devil mode, her back to us. She was the most casually dressed I'd seen her, wearing black stretch pants and an oversized sweater.

To my utter surprise, she looked relieved when she turned and recognized us. I would sooner have expected her to show me the door at once.

"Marilyn. Allida. How did that blouse work out for you?"

I studied her for a moment and decided that she must be one of those gung-ho types who would never allow personal feelings to interfere with a potential sale. "Not too well. In fact, a seam ripped out when I was simply trying it on."

"Did it really?" she replied, clicking her tongue and shaking her head.

"Yes. For a supposed original from this fancy designer, it sure wasn't well made. I mean, even the label itself is deteriorating."

Edith snatched the blouse away from me as if it had been about to combust in my hands. "This is totally out of keeping with my high-quality merchandise. They must have made a shipping mistake and I inadvertently sold your mother a factory-second at full price."

"Then you won't have any trouble getting reimbursed by your suppliers?" Mom asked.

"Not at all. I'll be right back with a perfect blouse."

I glanced at the table beside me and immediately spotted the blouses from which Mom had chosen. "Can't I just pick up another from the display here and try it on?"

"No, I . . . want to make absolutely certain this doesn't happen again. I'm going to pull one from a newer shipment that I haven't had time to restock."

"Okay. Thanks."

I idly flipped through the other blouses on display, while Mom examined some sweaters. The label on one particular blouse caught my eye, so much so that I unfolded it. There was a black thread sticking out from underneath the corner of the label that didn't match the tan thread used on either the label itself or to sew the label onto the garment. I gave it a tug, just as Edith returned, peering over my shoulder with a pained expression. I grinned in embarrassment and returned the blouse to its table.

"Here," Edith said, thrusting the blouse into my hands, all of her salesmanship forgotten. "Try this one on. It's a slightly different shade, but I think it will work for you."

I looked over and caught my mother picking at something on the window ledge. "What're you doing?"

"There's a glass shard here, Edith. I wouldn't want anyone to cut themselves."

"Oh, thank you," Edith said with a sigh. "We had an . . . accident here a few weeks ago and a plate-glass window broke. I'm still picking up little pieces, after all of this time."

"Susan told me about that."

"She did?"

I nodded.

"I'm surprised. She made it clear to me that it was a family secret." She gave me a conspiratorial nod as she looked at my mother and said under her breath, "Alzheimer's. There but for good fortune go any one of us."

Mom's hearing was excellent and she said, "I can't imagine anything worse. Honestly, Allida, if I get something like that in my old age, you have my permission to shoot me."

"I'll remember you said that. I'm going to go try on the new blouse."

There was no comparison between the two blouses. This one felt wonderful against my skin, fit perfectly, and was somehow much more flattering than the other. I came out of the dressing room to show my mom, suffering through a flashback on my sometimes painful visits to clothing stores with my mom when I was a teen.

"Wonderful," Mom said, turning to Edith. "I love it. If I weren't already getting this for my daughter, I'd buy it for myself."

"I thought you'd be impressed," Edith said, still looking peeved for some reason, but making a great effort to be gracious. "This blouse is actually a newer design and my cost was nearly three times what the other was, even though it's the same manufacturer."

"Oh, dear," Mom said. "Do you need more money from me?"

Edith forced a smile and held up her palms. "No, no. Consider it my compensation to you for your trouble. Just be sure to recommend my store to your friends, and we'll consider it even."

"Thanks, Edith," I said.

"Yes, thank you," Mom chimed in.

"Do you want to wear that home?" Edith asked. "I can just snip off the price tag."

Mom was beaming at me. I'm not the easiest person in the world to shop for, and for her sake, I said, "Sure."

Edith gave me a plastic smile and came at me with those scissors with such a venom that I nearly jumped back, but she did simply snip the price tag off.

We left. There was something bothering me. We rode in silence for a while, then Mom said, "You're so quiet all of a sudden. You do like the blouse, don't you?"

"Yes. Very much. Thank you. I'm just thinking, that's all."

"About what?"

"Did you notice how all of the clothes in the store had those anti-theft devices, except for my new blouse?"

Mom shrugged. "Edith said something about not having this one in her inventory yet. She probably didn't have the chance to get it ready for sale."

I looked at the label of my old blouse that I held on my lap. Suddenly I knew.

Chapter 18

Mom pulled into the garage. She had been talking to me during our drive back from Edith's store, something about a flying student of hers she was having trouble with, but I was too lost in thought to listen.

Although things were starting to add up, there were still some big holes in my theory. If only I could fill them, I could talk to Sergeant Millay and, if my theory proved correct, give him the additional evidence that might help him make an arrest. Heaven knows I would rest a lot easier once that happened.

We let the dogs inside, upon their insistence. Pavlov, Doppler, Sage, and Suds and pups had been outside enjoying the glorious weather. We were soon knee-deep in dogs, and I was beginning to think for the first time that it would be something of a relief when we got to put Suds and puppies up for adoption.

Mom said over the sound of yipping puppies, who had very recently discovered their vocal cords, that she was going to "return some phone calls" from her bedroom. That was unfortunate, as I'd intended to make some calls myself, toward resolving some of the inconsistencies that I'd uncovered. She was probably finding me to be lousy company, so I merely said, "Okay, Mom," and left it at that.

The puppies were clowning around, their energy and their desire to wrestle with one another boundless. They were staging their puppy fights, important in establishing their ranking but even more important in establishing needed aggressiveness. Too subordinate a dog becomes too dependent on his owners.

A pair of them tried to engage Doppler in their game, which quickly escalated into a potentially dangerous situation when Suds threatened to square off with Doppler. I needed a distraction to safely break this up, so I flung the nearest unbreakable object—a phone book—against the wall. The noise startled the dogs enough for me to scoop up Doppler and take him to another room.

He was in something of a snit when I set him down, immediately walking away from me as if angered that I'd interfered. He was actually relieved at my rescuing him from engaging in a fight with a much larger dog; even dogs have their reputations and pride to protect. Without Shogun here, only the puppies were smaller than he, but Suds wouldn't let him near them, and he probably missed having Shogun to boss around. Doppler wanted to be let back outside again, which was very unusual for him; he rarely wanted to be separated from the other dogs in the pack.

While the other dogs were finally quieting down, the phone rang. Suds trotted along beside me as I went to grab the phone. Pavlov, who was starting to have some struggle with Suds's territorial rights, admonished Suds with a warning growl. The moment I picked up the phone and said hello, Pavlov sat down by my feet, her ears back as she staked her claim on me. This really was starting to get to be a bit too much like being a den leader, for my taste.

"Hi, Allie."

I recognized Russell's voice immediately, and my demeanor instantly softened. "Morning, Russell."

"Good morning. What's left of it. I know Mondays are supposed to be your day off. Are you coming into the office anyway?"

"No, I really am taking the day for myself. How're things going for you?"

"Better, now that I'm hearing your voice."

I rolled my eyes, but smiled. "That's flattering. Thank you."

"Are you doing anything for lunch?"

"Well, no . . . but I was planning on staying in Berthoud."

"I don't mind taking a long lunch and getting something up where you are. Is that French restaurant in Berthoud open for lunch?"

"No, just dinner. And not on Mondays."

"Do you have another suggestion?"

"There's the Summit in Loveland."

"Sounds great. I'll come pick you up as soon as my Volvo and the traffic let me."

We said good-bye and then hung up.

"Who was that on the phone?" asked Mom, who'd emerged from her room partway through my conversation and who, come to think of it, couldn't have been returning calls on our one line. She must have just wanted some solitude.

"Russell. He's taking me to lunch at the Summit."

"Lucky you. Have I told you how much I like your Russell?"

"Yes, you have. More than once. And he's not *my* Russell." Although I was rapidly becoming more and more keen on the idea.

She swept up her purse and headed to the garage. "Have fun. I have a meeting this afternoon at the airport. See you tonight."

" 'Bye."

She stopped and gave me a visual once-over. "For heaven's sake, Allida, when you see Russell, don't . . . be so on guard. Relax and live it up a little."

"Fine. I'll put on a leather miniskirt and ride to the restaurant on the hood of his car."

"Pardon me for offering a little motherly advice."

"You call 'relax and live it up' *motherly*?"

"For you, yes. See you tonight."

" 'Bye, Mom."

I watched her drive away, thinking that this was good timing. I needed to make some calls to verify my theory, and I truly didn't want her listening in, especially since I was still so unsure of myself.

I called Trevor at work. Unfortunately, I had to go through his secretary, which made the whole reason for my calling seem more serious than I'd wanted to portray.

"Allida, hi. Is everything all right?" He sounded tense, and I regretted bothering him, but it was too late to hang up now.

"Fine. I just have a couple of questions to ask you."

"That's a relief. Whenever I hear your name these days, I assume Edith has run off with Shogun again or something to that effect."

"Actually, I just wanted to ask you where you got Shogun's bed. I'm thinking of getting one for my cocker spaniel."

"Edith bought it from PetsMart, I think."

"And she paid extra to have them put Shogun's name on it?"

"Oh, no. Cassandra did that for her as a favor. She used to do excellent embroidery work."

"Does Edith do any embroidery work herself?"

"Now she does, as a matter of fact. She had Cassie give her lessons and bought this fancy sewing machine from Cassie's former partner, but she didn't really get the knack of it. Her threads were always unraveling and it looked pretty amateurish. I wouldn't hire her, if I were you."

"Where is Shogun now?"

"He should be safe at home. Why?"

"Just making sure. Thanks, Trevor. Let me know if Shogun has any trouble adjusting to his new home."

"You'll be the first person I call. And thanks again for straightening everything out with Edith."

"What do you mean?"

"She called me and said that you and she had made your peace and she realized that you'd made the right decision in letting me keep Shogun."

"That doesn't sound like her."

"You're telling me. But I don't look a gift . . . dog in the mouth. Take care." He hung up.

I paced, trying to make sense of all of this. I was now quite certain about the scam that Edith was running. She was

selling cheap knockoffs of designer-label clothing, removing
the actual labels from the cheap knockoffs and replacing
them with her imitation labels.

Mom had told me that Edith had once asked Cassandra to
be her business partner. Could that somehow have led to Cassandra's murder?

I called Susan, but hung up when the machine answered.
Just in case, I dashed out front and down the block a few steps
till I could see the Haywoods' driveway. Susan's car was still
there.

I knocked on the door, and fortunately, Susan answered so
that I didn't have to deal with her parents.

"Susan, I was wondering. Did you sell your sewing
machine to Edith Cunningham, by any chance?"

Susan averted her eyes and stuck her hands in the pockets
of her cutoffs. "Stay away from this, Allida. You always
were a pain in the butt."

"Edith was sewing expensive labels onto cheap clothing,
wasn't she?"

She still wouldn't meet my eyes, but her rapidly reddening
cheeks gave me my answer. "I don't know. Not for sure."

"But you mentioned your suspicions to Cassandra Randon, didn't you?"

For the first time I saw a genuine look of sorrow on her
face. She looked up and sighed. "Cassie and I . . . had our differences. She was always yelling at me for smoking cigarettes while sewing . . . claimed it made the cloth stink. By
telling her about Edith, I thought I was doing her a favor. I
thought maybe she was getting mixed up in it. I just . . . I
wanted to tell her that she wasn't going to get away with it."

"Only she didn't know anything about it, right? Because it
was all Edith's doing."

"I tried to warn you off her, Allida."

"Why didn't you go to the police with this?"

"Like they'd believe me? With my drug-abuse record? I
want nothing to do with the police. Anything happens near
me, and I look the other way."

"That's why you covered up your dog's prints, isn't it?

Because you knew your dog was the one that left the bloody footprints. And you didn't want to be implicated in the murder."

"You're reading into things, Allie. I didn't do anything wrong." I held her gaze, and at length she continued. "He'd burrowed under the fence and into the yard. I had to go through the Randons' gate, but he came then. I didn't see anything. And I heard Edith arguing with someone earlier. But I didn't know anyone had gotten killed till my mom called hours later. And I didn't know he'd left paw prints till I saw you and you told me."

Edith Cunningham was the killer. She must have become so enraged with Cassandra during their discussion that she killed her in her own yard. I needed to get this last information to Sergeant Millay.

Half to myself, I muttered, "At least Edith's still at work."

Susan furrowed her brow. "No, she isn't. I saw her here. Wasn't she with you just a minute or two ago?"

"With me? No. Why?" My heart had already started racing.

"Because I saw her heading over to your property just a while ago." Susan pointed. "She was parked right on the street. Her car is gone now, so I guess she must have gone someplace."

Without another word, I rushed back over to my house to check on my dogs.

"Is everything all right?" she called back to me.

I didn't answer.

Deciding to forgo checking inside the house, I ran at top speed to the gate at the side of the house. It was wide open.

"Doppler, come!" I cried, listening in vain for the jingle of his collar tags.

Chapter 19

There was a sticky-pad note stabbed through the gate latch. This time yellow paper had been used, no doubt because the Haywoods now had the magenta pad. I snatched it off and read:

> Allida—If you want your dog to live, come get him. Make sure you come alone, or he dies. We're at the water tower.

"Oh, shit!" I screamed, battling tears. Only the killer herself could be so sick as to do something like this. And she'd be able to see for miles from that tower. There was no way the police could get there unseen. Regardless, if I notified them now, they'd gladly sacrifice a dog's life to capture a murderer. I had to follow her instructions and rescue Doppler myself.

Clutching the note, I ran inside, ignoring the other, frantically barking dogs, grabbed my keys, leapt into my Subaru, and sped down the driveway.

I hit the brakes. I had to leave a note. I didn't want to waste time going back to the house. I'd leave it on the mailbox.

My stomach was in knots and my thoughts raced. What was Edith doing with Doppler at the Berthoud water tower? What possible good could this do her?

My tires screeched as I hit the pavement at the bottom of the driveway. I scanned the Haywoods' property to see if Susan was there, thinking I should yell to Susan what was going on. She was nowhere in sight.

I grabbed a pen, added the words, "Edith's the killer!

Help!" to Edith's note, then threw open the car door, ran to our mailbox, and stuck the note on the door flap. Eventually, somebody would spot that and come help me. I could only hope that it wouldn't be too late.

I raced north through town in a state of such panic, I couldn't think straight. Why a tower, of all things? How had Edith known about my petrifying fear of heights? Mom must have mentioned it.

The huge, green-painted water tower soon loomed before me. It looked like some prop left over from *War of the Worlds*—an enormous Martian vehicle. I hated heights so much that I couldn't judge relative size, but the tower had to be at least a hundred feet tall.

I pulled into the dirt and gravel parking lot, kicking up a cloud of dust behind the wheels. Edith was there, an evil blemish on the tower, leaning over the railing. She had Doppler in her arms. He was just a lightish-colored speck from this distance.

Just looking up that high made my vision swim, but I was too frightened for Doppler's sake to take my eyes off Edith. She gave me a wave, mocking me. Satisfied that nobody was behind me, she set Doppler down on the walkway that circled the water tank.

I ran to the only ladder, a wrought-iron, spindly-looking thing. Just the sight of it and its never-ending steps made my mind reel.

"Come up," Edith shouted down. "The view is lovely."

I grabbed the railing. The metal was as cold as death. I climbed the first few steps, trying to focus only on the thought of saving Doppler, trying not to think about what I was doing.

Edith had such an advantage over me it was ludicrous. By the time I'd navigated the first ten steps, my vision was so distorted that it felt as though my eyes were crossed.

I kept going for as long as I could, then stopped. I told myself to go just five steps farther. Then five steps more. And so on. My progress was slow, each step agony.

My vertigo kicked in at full force. I wrapped my arms

around the handrails and leaned my body against the steps, eyes shut tight, battling nausea. My brain was sending my body false signals as if I were in a blender on full speed.

Edith's voice, still above me but louder now, called, "What's the matter? You can't possibly be more than ten stories above the ground. And the wind is hardly even making that ladder sway."

With rage seeping into me, I cried, "What do you hope to gain by this, Edith?"

"It's simple, really. You rescue your dog, or the dog dies. At least I'm giving you a chance to get your dog back. It's more than you gave me with Shogun. You climb up here, and you humiliate yourself as much as you humiliated me. I want you to suffer, the same way you made me suffer!"

I forced myself to look up, sweat running down my face, my hands now so wet that I was at risk of losing my grasp. I was perhaps halfway there, but the distance might as well have been a mile. "I can't do it, Edith. You win. I can't climb any farther."

"Then say good-bye to your dog."

Doppler yelped, and she held him over the railing so that he'd drop just beyond my reach.

"No! I'll come up."

Every step was more agonizing than the last. It felt as though I were crawling into a Tilt-A-Whirl at an amusement park. My hands were clammy, dripping with sweat, but I couldn't chance letting go with one hand long enough to wipe it. My stomach was so nauseated there was no way I could keep from vomiting, and Edith laughed with unabashed glee.

My anger gave me some strength to keep going. I now knew how horribly sick Edith really was, to take such venomous delight in humiliating me this way. "You killed Cassandra. Why? Was she going to report your labeling scam to the police?"

There was a pause. Then she let out a low, humorless laugh. "So you did figure that out, after all. That's what I was afraid of. And the real reason I dragged you up here. She recognized my sewing, insisted she could even tell that the labels were sewn on her former partner's machine."

Damn it! She wanted to push me off this tower!

Edith continued, "Cassie said that, out of friendship, she felt she had to tell me first, rather than go straight to the police. Then she refused my efforts to pay her off. She didn't believe me when I said I'd never do it again. I had to stop her. That store was all I had that was truly mine! We argued, and in a moment of rage, I hit her in the head with a rock."

"You didn't plan to kill her. You can stop this now. Turn yourself in to the police. Killing Cassandra in the heat of passion won't carry the same consequences as if you push me off this tower."

"You know what, Allie? We should come up here more often. I like it up here. It's peaceful. You can see for miles."

"Why are you doing this, Edith?" I asked again, stalling, hoping I could force myself to keep up a patter of conversation and keep from focusing on my climb. "You can't escape. It's too late. Besides, I left a note identifying you as the killer. You're going to be caught, no matter what."

She ignored me and said incongruously, "There was this foxlike black dog in my yard. I tried to chase him away, but he just barked at me." Edith's disembodied voice sounded dispassionate, as if she were almost in a trancelike state. "Shogun ran off instead. I had to get out of there before you saw me. As I was driving away, I realized that my note was still on the door, and that the police would know it was my handwriting, my fingerprints, so I doubled back and took the note. I figured the police might think you killed her. Then I went back to my boutique, washed up, and put on a new pair of white pants and jacket."

I was eye-level with the top rung, but I was now immobilized with fear. This was even more frightening to me than climbing the ladder. It felt as though I were climbing over the edge of a cliff.

Doppler was whining, trying to get to me, but I couldn't even look in his direction for fear of losing my precarious balance. I got my hands on the posts to either side of the ladder and climbed one more rung. These posts, like all of the others in the guardrail that circled the outer edge of the walk-way, were spaced some three or four feet apart. Not nearly close enough to provide me with any security.

Suddenly Edith loomed right in front of me, blocking me. "Good-bye, Allie. Your trip down won't take long at all."

She kicked me. I ducked as best I could, the blow landing flush on my forehead. I managed, somehow, to keep my grip.

Edith chuckled. "Come, now. Give up, Allida. How long do you think you can prolong the inevitable?" She walked back toward my dog. "If you don't go first, I'll just have to see to it that Doppler does."

"No!"

I made my way toward them. I had no choice except to crawl, but the flooring of the walkway was a thick grate. I could see through each rounded-diamond shape to the ground, a distant blur below.

Finally I risked a quick glance toward Edith to check on my dog. Doppler's leash was loosely tied to a post of the guardrail. He was still struggling against the leash to get to me. If he slipped off the edge in the process, he'd be strangled.

I retched. I had to shut my eyes and try to hold steady on all fours, though my brain was still telling me that I was spin-ning, moving toward the edge. My eyes still closed tight, I took a deep breath and let it out slowly. "You did all of this—killed Cassandra, framed me, stole my dog—just because you wanted to get away with sales fraud?"

She laughed at me. "Look at yourself. You look like a sick dog. You're pathetic. But to answer your question, yes, I did it to get out of going to jail. By the way, you stopped your list too early. You left out your own imminent free fall off this tower, my dear."

I looked at her. "As soon as the police get my note, they'll put all of this together."

She shrugged and faced me, but it felt as though she were staring past me, not really seeing me. "I'll take my chances. Explain that you set me up. I'm selling off my cheap merchandise at the store and replacing it with the real thing. That evidence will soon be gone. I just need to get rid of you to . . ."—she paused and smiled—"tie up the loose ends. I'll tell the police I ran up here to escape from you, Cassandra's killer, because I knew about your phobia. Only you were so determined, you followed me anyway. Tragically, though, you lost your balance."

"And what about Susan Nelson? Cassandra's former partner, who sold you that sewing machine. The woman who owns that little black dog who burrowed under your fence that day."

Edith shook her head. "She doesn't know anything."

I managed to stand up by pressing my shoulder against the wall of the water tank, as far from the edge as possible. "Yes, she does. And my mother also knows. I've been keeping her informed of everything. She knows about the label, too. She bought me the blouse. Are you going to kill both of them, too?"

"If I have to."

"And how will you explain that? Edith, for God's sake, think! It's over. Killing me or my dog will only make matters worse for you. You'll be facing murder-one charges and spend the rest of your life in jail."

She set her lips into a thin white line and shook her head. "The police won't believe a thing your mother tells them. They'll know she's just trying to protect you. And Cassie told me that Susan is a drug addict. No one's going to believe her, either. The only person with anything to worry about now is you, Allie. *You* have to worry about how you're going to feel when your body hits the ground."

She charged at me. I tried to run, but got only a few steps before she caught up to me.

Edith tackled me from behind, then grabbed my ankle and started pulling me toward the edge.

I clutched at the metal walkway, but couldn't get a grip. Only my fingertips were able to fit through the grating. Edith grabbed hold of my belt and, in one motion, pulled my entire body forward so that my legs dangled over the edge.

I managed to wrap one arm around both of her legs. If I was going to fall, she was going with me. At least then Doppler would survive. I nearly pulled her legs out from under her, but I also managed to get my free hand around one railing post.

"Let go!" she cried, trying to pry herself loose. I got a knee back onto the walkway. In spite of my vertigo, the instinct to survive had taken charge now.

I got my second knee up, and Edith lost her balance, falling harmlessly backward onto the walkway. She let out a groan with the impact. Her features were set in a horrid, wild-animal grimace. She kicked. I tried to move out of the way. Her foot caught me on the side of my face just below the temple.

Still on her back, from a crab-walk position, Edith braced herself, then released an enormous thrust of her legs and knocked me sideways. My leg bashed against one of the posts in the railing. I got hold of a second post with both hands.

Now Edith was pounding me mercilessly, kicking me in the side, trying to force my legs over the edge again. I fought to keep myself from curling up in pain, to keep my legs out straight so that she couldn't shove me between the posts.

The metallic taste of blood was in my mouth, and I realized my nose was bleeding. From the dim recesses of my mind, I could hear Doppler barking relentlessly. He was unable to help me now, nor I him. If I fell, what would happen to him?

"Allida! Hang on!" a male voice from below called.

At the sound of help arriving, Edith gasped and stopped kicking me. That she was running out of time only egged her on. She grabbed my ankle and started lifting it to force me to bend at the knee. I yanked it free and blindly kicked at her.

Edith let out a scream of fright. I tried to rise and scramble away from her, but looked back in time to see her topple over the railing.

I lunged in her direction, trying to grab her, but it was too late. She fell, her scream echoing against the metal tower.

I covered my ears and closed my eyes and lay on my

stomach on the walkway, retching helplessly. Though I'd lost all sense of time, eventually Russell was beside me. He pulled me onto his lap and held me while I cried.

"I found the note on your mailbox," he said when I was finally in control enough to listen. "It's all right. It's over now."

"Doppler," I muttered, struggling to find my voice despite my anguish.

"He's fine."

"Edith. Is she . . . ?"

"She's dead. She . . . landed near the ladder just as I was climbing up. We have to call the police."

I managed to force myself to sit up, but my vertigo was once again at full tilt and I felt myself spinning in agony. I wanted just to stop the motion. "Russell. Listen. Bring my dog down. Get me drugs. Anything to knock me out. I'll never get down otherwise."

"Yes, you can. We'll climb down together." He got up and grabbed my arm, trying to lift me to my feet. "Let's go."

"No!" I shook my head. "Doppler first."

Russell left and I stayed seated, knees to my chest, my back plastered against the water tank, waiting, too distraught even to try to get to Doppler to pet him. He was whining and struggling to get out of Russell's arms. Poor Russell was trying to keep his face as far away from the dog as possible.

"Doppler, no!" I said with as much authority as I could muster.

My dog obeyed well enough that Russell managed to carry him past me, under one arm and out of my view down the ladder. The thought of Russell's having to carry Doppler down that long ladder with only one free hand made me dizzy. I could only hope that they would make it safely to the ground.

An eternity later, Russell returned and all but dragged me to the edge of the ladder, making himself a human shield so that even in my half-crazed state, I could see that it would be impossible for me to fall. Still, the descent was torturous for me. Russell calmly talked me through it, coaxing me each step of the way.

We made it down together. My knees buckled the moment my feet hit the ground, but Russell held me in his arms. He shielded me from the sight of Edith's broken body as we made our way to his car. Doppler was inside, safe and sound, his front paws pressed to the glass, his black nose squeezed into the narrow window opening.

I realized then, finally, that it was truly over. A jumble of emotions surged through me. I hugged Russell and whispered, "Thank you," while Doppler's happy barks punctuated the air.

Did you enjoy
this Allie Babcock mystery
by Leslie O'Kane?
Then go back to the beginning . . .

PLAY DEAD

The first Allie Babcock mystery

by Leslie O'Kane

*Please turn the page
for an excerpt . . .*

PLAY DEAD

Beth was watching out the front window and opened the door for me before I could knock. "Sage is in the kitchen," she murmured. Her eyes were red-rimmed and her nose pink, as if she'd recently been crying. "I tried that trick you taught me . . . pretending to eat the dog food and offering it to him. He all but ran away from me."

I placed a reassuring hand on her forearm. "Let me see what I can do."

Beth took a halting breath and said, "You've got to do something to help me. I just don't know how much longer he can last."

I tried to project confidence as I nodded at her words, but I had no idea why Sage would starve himself here yet eat dog biscuits in my office. If there was one thing I knew for certain from my three decades of being in the company of dogs, it was that neither I nor anyone else could ever truly know what was going on in a dog's mind.

Sage was lying on his side in front of the refrigerator. Despite his lethargy, which was no doubt a result of his starvation and the walk to and from my office, his tail thumped on the grimy maroon linoleum when I entered the small, dark, and messy kitchen. I petted him, feeling heartsick at his skeletal body.

"Can I see his feeding supplies, please?"

Beth pulled out a nearly full forty-pound bag from beside the refrigerator. It was the same top-of-the-line brand that I fed my German shepherd. I grabbed a handful of the dry dog food, then dropped it back into the bag. My palm felt strangely sticky.

"This is the food you got from the animal shelter?" I asked.

"Uh-huh. Hannah's neighbor, Dennis, was taking care of Sage for a couple weeks after Hannah died. He donated Sage's food and dog treats to the shelter."

Underneath the window by the heater was a large red dog bowl, with the name SAGE in white letters. I grabbed a kibble from the bowl and squeezed it between my fingertip and thumb. I sniffed it. It smelled perfectly normal. The kibble had such a tacky surface, though, that it stuck to my index finger and I had to shake it off to drop it back into its bowl.

I touched my fingertip to my tongue. An acrid taste filled my mouth. "Can I see the dog biscuits, too, please?"

"Sure." Beth held out the box. "Why? Is there something wrong with the food?"

I grabbed a bone-shaped biscuit and scraped its surface with a fingernail. I touched that fingertip to my tongue. Again the taste was so bitter, my lips nearly puckered.

"The dog food's been tainted."

Beth's face paled. "You mean, someone poisoned it?"

"Not exactly. It's been treated with something, probably an odorless dog repellent, such as Bitter Apple. It's not poisonous, but it makes the food taste repulsive to dogs."

Beth's jaw dropped. "What do you mean? How could that be? I don't—"

"Could anyone have doctored Sage's dog food after you got it?"

She began to pace in tight circles, combing her fingers through her hair. At length, she shook her head. "No, that isn't possible. Somebody had to have done this to the food before I got it. Oh, God. This makes me so sick! Here I've been trying to get Sage to trust me, and I've been offering him only inedible food!" She punched her thigh. "Why didn't I think of that? But how could I have known? I mean, it's so . . . weird."

Beth sat down on the floor beside Sage and lifted his head onto her lap. She said under her breath, "I could kill whoever did this!"

Why would anyone want to hurt the dog? Was it possible somebody wanted him dead because of what he'd witnessed? Could he identify the killer of Hannah Jones?

PLAY DEAD
by Leslie O'Kane

Published by Fawcett Books.
Available in bookstores everywhere.